The Spy's Gamble

By Howard Kaplan

Also by Howard Kaplan

The Damascus Cover
Bullets of Palestine
The Chopin Express

ISBN-13: 978-1720606215
ISBN: 1720606218

FOR ASHER
Not only my son
but my friend

Author's Note

The truck ramming of Israeli cadets, the settler Bible Marathon closing Palestinian highways in the West Bank, the murder of an Israeli teen in her bed, an internecine Palestinian assassination, the accidental shooting of a Palestinian cancer patient, forest fires, and the Commanders of Israel newspaper ad depicted in the novel all occurred in 2016-2017.

CHAPTER 1

Khaled Fahmy sat at the far end of the bar in Washington, DC, listening to the two young men speaking Hebrew at the table behind him, wondering if they were soldiers. Though in civilian clothes they still looked military, maybe twenty, close-cropped hair, muscular beneath their short sleeved shirts despite the winter cold, two jackets casually tossed on an empty chair, one blonde, one dark haired. Fahmy had been born in 1992, the twenty-fifth year of the Israeli occupation of the West Bank, not long before these Israeli boys, he guessed. He had known nothing other than heartache under Israeli military rule, a vice on the neck of their daily life. Next spring, June 10, 2017 would mark fifty years of the Israeli occupation.

"My *Mashakit Tash* got me a pass to go see my mother before we left," the blonde Israeli said. "I'm completely crazy for her."

Khaled knew each military unit had their own *Mashakit tash*, a girl social worker their age from the unit who underwent a few months training for the post. Each solider was assigned to one.

"She's incredible," the blond continued. "Those legs, tall. In tight, white Navy pants they go on forever, and you know exactly

1

how they look when you pull off the pants."

They dove into talking about girls. Khaled thought about his sister, Sumaya, dead at sixteen years old. Seeking the glory of martyrdom, she had thrust one of their mother's old bent kitchen knives into a border guard at the Qalandia Checkpoint, a large crossing at the concrete and barbed wire topped Separation Wall between the West Bank and Jerusalem. Privately, Khaled thought she'd done it both for the cause and to escape the monotony and despair of the occupation.

Four hundred and forty miles long, the Separation Wall ran mostly along the Green Line, the 1949 Israeli-Jordanian armistice border, but some Palestinian towns were nearly encircled, cut off from the rest of the Palestinian Territories. Called the "security fence" by Israelis, the wall went up in 2003 in response to three years of consistent suicide bombings. Widely touted as an impenetrable success, the Separation Wall kept few out. At night, even a few meters from Qalandia, Palestinians hoisted ladders, snipped the barbed wire at the crown and shimmied down ropes dropped twenty-five feet into Israel. They found work with corrupt Israeli builders who let them sleep on worksites and paid below minimum wages, still far better than the pervasive unemployment in the West Bank. The Israeli military did not even bother to repair the barbed wire, knowing how easily it would be cut again. The Israeli Defense Forces (IDF) Chief of Staff Gadi Eisenkot estimated that fifty to sixty thousand West Bank Palestinians snuck into Israel each day. Fahmy believed the barrier was the long-persecuted Jews' way of erasing their domination of the Palestinians; out of sight, out of mind.

The dark-haired Israeli was smiling at two college girls seated at the next table, both in towering high heel boots. The blonde with curls smiled back.

"It's so free here," the Israeli said in Hebrew to his mate.

"Nobody checking bags at the door. Girls back home are so full of themselves, won't even let you buy them a drink cause they know what you want."

"It's wonderful," his friend said. "Same game but these American girls have fun playing it."

The dark-haired soldier stood abruptly and walked over to the coeds' table, his mate in tow. He stood over the curly blonde and spoke in heavily accented English. "Are you Jewish? Cause you is-raeli hot!"

She gave him half a smile. Across the table, her friend rolled her eyes. "I've heard about Israeli guys."

"What did you hear of us?"

"That I should never do business with an Israeli."

"Ah, maybe that is true but I promise you we are not in this bar for business." Without asking, both noisily pulled out chairs, startling the curly blonde as they sat at their table.

The second Israeli called to the bartender. "We are buying these girls another what they're drinking." He turned to the girls. "My people invented circumcision; you're welcome."

Despite herself the curly blonde laughed. Her friend lifted her half-full Scotch rocks and said, "Indeed, a very old procedure." She drained her glass. "Which means I can see the results easily anywhere."

Khaled squeezed his eyes and circled both hands around his small shot glass on the bar. To the victors, the spoils. He had grown up in between dirt alleys, cramped neighborhoods that housed thousands of refugees from Lod, Ramla, Beit Dajan and other Palestinian villages. In the soccer clubhouse near the Al-Am'ari Camp entrance, they had debated endlessly whether it would be possible to find some solution and live with dignity on their grandparents' land. He had at various times fiercely believed both sides of the argument, but had always known the alternative to their own state was *jihad*.

Meanwhile, their corrupt leaders lived in sumptuous palaces in the West Bank. What the Palestinian people sought seemed simple; divide this twice promised land into two states. Instead, teenagers continued to die on both sides. Sumaya. Guilt dropped through him like a weight, almost dragging him off the barstool and onto the floor. If he had been home instead of on this scholarship studying literature at Georgetown, he could have stopped her, would have held her to his chest and not let her go out. She had died a pointless *shahid*, a martyr, a tragic self-delusion.

As she approached the checkpoint, she pulled a knife from her sleeve and refused their calls to halt. When they fired in the air she ran faster. Then, as she was shot and started to fall, a cell phone video proved another twelve bullets shook her body. He had watched the video online repeatedly, counting the shots—two in the air, three as she ran, twelve as she started to fall—until it was flagged and removed from Facebook. The Israeli government loudly blamed the escalation of violence on online incitement. They weren't entirely wrong—each time he had watched that video he wanted to kill someone.

Khaled left his Scotch on the bar untouched because he wanted his faculties sharp. Anyway, this was his second. He paid with cash and then closed the small notebook at his side. He had not had much creative inspiration anyway. In Al-Am'ari, an UNRWA (United Nations Relief and Works Agency) teacher had connected him with an NGO called We Are Not Numbers, which paired him with a liberal Jewish American writer of suspense novels in Los Angeles, a believer in a two-state solution, who mentored him. They communicated on Facebook. At first Khaled had felt uncomfortable working with him, but the writer showed real interest in helping Khaled find more details in his depiction of daily disappointments and small joys in the camp. His short story published in the Kenyon

Review garnered the attention of Ramzy Awwad, the greatest Palestinian novelist of his father's generation. Awwad had honed Khaled's writings, also over Facebook, encouraging surrealistic dreamlike explorations, and forwarded his work to editors and friends. After two years, Khaled was published in four small literary journals, enough publications to attract the Admissions Committee at Georgetown. After two semesters in the MFA program Khaled had begun to doubt that anything happening in the workshops would ever affect the outside world. Literature was one thing, but tonight he would finally act.

Outside, a drizzle dampened the sidewalk and the car tires made soft sounds on the street. Khaled walked, increasingly angry. He blamed the Egyptians almost as much as the Israelis for the Israeli military rule over them. In 1967, the Egyptian president threatened to annihilate Israel with its great might, and then blockaded the Red Sea. Israel struck before dawn and destroyed the Egyptian Air Force on the ground. Egypt then claimed they had repulsed the airstrike so Syria and Jordan attacked. From living in America, Khaled saw that Arabs were swayed by ideas not facts. In the blink of an eye, Israel swarmed across the Golan Heights, the Sinai, Gaza and the West Bank. The Israelis called it the Six-Day War, the name a humiliating reminder to Khaled of how quickly the Arabs had lost.

Khaled turned into a deserted side street and hurriedly eyed neighborhood front yards. He soon found a faux rock river, looked around, then grabbed a large stone and dropped it in his jacket pocket. He approached a parked Lexus ES 350, looked up and down the street again and his heart not accelerating a beat, broke the window and was in the car. Once inside, he pulled down a panel under the steering wheel, used a small pocketknife to cut and rearrange a few wires, brushed the glass aside with his jacket and rolled the window down fully to hide the break. He'd known greater danger on a weekly basis when the Israeli soldiers entered Al-Am'ari and searched for weapons. On such nights, gun battles and bullets ricocheting off the cinderblock homes in the narrow alleyways were more common than not. A Lexus in DC was child's play. He drove around the corner and idled in a red zone, waiting, and let his head slump against the headrest. He was not sure what he would do if the girls came out with the Israelis.

Thirty minutes later, the Israelis emerged from the bar with the girls, though the brown-haired coed did not look happy. Khaled's face felt hot. He was jealous, but not so out of control that he wanted to hurt them too. He watched the curly blonde hug both men and then the two girls headed toward him on the sidewalk. Soon, through the open passenger window, he heard the narrow high heels of their boots clicking on the pavement. As they passed his car, he felt an impulse to call out to them but did not know what to say, so did not.

Khaled lifted his head to the two Israelis heading in the opposite direction and a small thrill rose in his throat. Ramzy Awwad had been, and likely still was, a Palestinian intelligence agent who championed their cause with the pen and the pistol. He had begun his fighting by killing some Israelis, a woman too, in the Israeli Embassy in Paraguay. Khalid felt useless loafing around in Georgetown on this full scholarship, editing mediocre undergraduate short stories while his family and friends remained squashed by Israel's military might in Al-Am'ari. He would not be going back to the dorms once he gathered the things there he needed.

The two Israelis moved steadily down the sidewalk, did not seem drunk. The rain had stopped and the street was empty. It was a weeknight and no other cars were out. Khaled eased the Lexus into the road and drove a little closer to them. In thirty seconds they would be beyond the parked cars and hopefully would cross the street in the direction of the nearby subway entrance. Cold air wafted in from the lowered passenger window. Khaled eased down on the pedal.

As the Israelis stepped off the sidewalk, Khaled accelerated, slowly at first so as not to warn them. At the intersection, he pushed the accelerator to the floor, swung the wheel to the right and hit them both, felt two solid thuds.

Bullets noisily burst through the rear Lexus windscreen and a tire blew, the car dropping now in the rear right. Khaled's eyes flashed to the rearview mirror at the same time he slammed down the accelerator, tugged the wheel and the car burst back onto the main road with the sound of metal against street. The shooter was running towards him, firing. The car bounced at high speed, screeching as he drove on the right rear rim. Another bullet whizzed past his right ear and through the front windscreen; the glass in front of him abruptly cracked everywhere. He lurched blindly around the next corner and the Lexus smashed into a row of parked cars. The airbag exploding from the steering wheel pushed into his face.

Stunned but not hurt, Khaled shoved it away, was out and ran down the empty street. He looked back, saw nobody was behind him, and the fear turned into pride. As he panted around the next corner, elation rose through him.

Eli Bardin walked into Montrose Park in Georgetown and grinned as he saw James Collins on a bench strumming his guitar. A stone's toss past fifty with wavy blonde hair, clean shaved with unfashionable tortoise shell glasses Eli thought of himself as the antithesis of the clichéd globetrotting Mossad agent. He was passionate about his wife and three children, his two siblings and their three children each, and his parents. As the oldest child, he felt pride at his fiercely close relationship with his father, who was talked about by a small group of Jerusalem intellectuals as a future candidate for prime minister. Eli felt he never quite stepped out of his father's tall shadow despite his being out of the country most of the time. Eli remembered his year at Tel Aviv law school as boring, had left and worked with his father in Jewish education, but had felt unsatisfied and often anxious working under him.

Eli kept the increasing toll of being away so much from his family deeply buried, even from himself. Often of late, anxiety he had not known since high school and his twenties ran through him like a quiet unease so familiar that at first he hardly noticed it. He was not sure if the current free-floating nervousness was worry about his country's future, a weariness from fighting a battle that these days seemed to carry his country further from peace, or a desire to do something different with his life.

A religious soul, Eli had stopped believing in God for reasons he refused to discuss. It had opened a small but painful rift with his religious father that Eli wanted to close but did not know how because his abandoning faith was a deeply personal and firm decision. When home, he followed tradition and studied Talmud, the vast compendium of ancient Jewish law, though he was an atheist. His attachment to the Jewish people ran through his every fiber, something gleaned from his father's life and work, which were uniquely inseparable. Eli disliked alcohol and cigarettes, though it didn't bother him to partake in either if his cover required it. What he loved was challenging himself, particularly parking in impossibly tight spaces and remembering long passages of a target's words verbatim. He sensed that he made little impression at parties until he started talking with his quiet erudition and natural warmth. He felt calm and comfortable when busy or with people, where he was often funny, absorbed too from his father. He was bothered that recently the anxiousness had begun creeping in when he was alone with his thoughts. Before heading from New York to Washington, he had their file on CIA agent James Collins emailed to him.

Ten years out from Oberlin College, Collins had imagined himself working in legal aid in public housing keeping with Oberlin's bona fides. A private liberal arts college, students regularly left Oberlin's small yet sprawling campus in the Ohio countryside for the Peace Corps and other service. CIA recruiters never made the trek to Oberlin, as they did to Yale, but Collins, who had Ivy SAT scores and state college grades but interviewed better than about everyone, was introduced to Langley by his banker father, a Yale alumnus, after Collins, who was inherently restless, tired of working as a legal aid assistant in New Orleans for $35,000 a year. Collins had a great time, however, playing guitar at small, dingy French Quarter clubs, where he made sure to enjoy the music and the women equally. Any Oberlin student could take classes in the renown Conservatory at the edge of the entrance grass quad. Students too could rent original Picasso, Chagall, Matisse and other such works for five dollars a semester from their art museum to grace dorm walls, a program begun in 1940, that had yet to have a work irrevocably beer soaked.

Collins smashed through life creating havoc he was eager to apologize profusely for, and then repeat, and had sidestepped the art rental program, afraid he'd be the one to destroy a painting in one of his fits of rage. Instead he found it wiser, when a freshman, to avail himself of jazz guitar lessons from a Conservatory female junior, for which they both received elective credit. Collins impatiently waited until three-quarters of the semester was over to sleep with her lest the lessons be impacted by his propensity to bolt post seduction. She was a greater virtuoso in the practice room than the bedroom, so he had been in a hurry to return to scouring the campus performance cafes.

"You got to Washington fast," Collins said, shifting into playing Elliot Smith's "Miss Misery."

"Very, because I was already here. Advance team for our

prime minister's christening ride aboard his new nuclear sub." Eli knew Israel had five German-built submarines, but this purchase was of a new class of American stealth submersibles.

"Bad timing that two of your crewmen were plowed through."

"Could have been worse, say much closer to the launch. And they're both going to be okay. We have replacements from Haifa arriving in the morning."

Eli was not sure yet whether his concern about the connection to the prime minister's arrival was prudent, or his sometimes ridiculous worrying about everything. He found he obsessed about small details, replaying them in his mind as if on a taped loop, but was clearheaded and decisive in a crisis. It always bothered him in movies when people hugged their bleeding loved ones rather than called for an ambulance.

"You get any prints off the stolen car?"

"Every finger and both thumbs. Khaled Fahmy, from the Al-Am'ari Camp in your backyard. Suitcase missing from his apartment, drawers open, clothes yanked out, cash withdrawn later that night from an ATM. Entirely amateurish, other than we can't find him."

"When I was about seven I played a chess expert by the beach in Tel Aviv. I had no idea what I was doing and moved everything wherever. It totally confounded him."

"You beat him?"

"No, but it took him forever to checkmate me, and with a lot of frustration along the way. His. I thought I was a genius."

"I'm already frustrated I can't find Fahmy."

With this government rapidly erecting more settlements in the West Bank, Eli knew in his bones that a new, terrible Palestinian uprising was inevitable. In this quagmire, which too many people accepted as normal, an attack of opportunity in Washington was hardly surprising. Positions on the sides of the Separation Wall reversed, Eli would strike wherever he could. However, only days before Prime Minister Uri Gutman climbed aboard his new submarine, accompanied by press photographers, an attack on two of the crew that would bring the sub home was suspicious.

"With the prime minister coming, we have a small army here. I'm going to hop home and look into Fahmy on that end," Eli said, looking forward to seeing his family. Collins could sniff for the trail here.

"Fab. By the way, your submariners okay?"

"They were just drunk enough they mostly bounced off the car. Who was the shooter that saved them?"

"Off-duty cop. Not his regular watering hole. His mother's in the hospital nearby. Send him a case of bourbon. He's a southerner. I'll get the address."

"What made him head outside just then?"

"God. He's a bit like you, Bible-thumper. Didn't hear God talking to him but did hear Hebrew. Thought he'd have a look-see. Detail oriented type. That part's a bit like you too." Collins began strumming again. "I, on the other hand, usually see the elephant but can miss the lines on her."

"Everybody can see the elephant."

A strong strum. "Therein lies my essential uselessness. Thrilled you're on this."

Eli smiled, not much used to modesty in his world, except from his mentor, Shai Shaham, but then again with Shai it could be tradecraft.

Eli caught the four p.m. United Airlines flight out of Newark nonstop to Tel Aviv. After dinner, he took a pill, preferring to store up sleep when he could. Once landed, a little after nine a.m., he made some calls and arranged a night incursion into Al-Am'ari. Excited, he headed for his father's, where his own eldest son, Yigal, was waiting.

From Ben Gurion International Airport, Eli drove the old Highway 1 at breakneck speed and soon began the ascent to Jerusalem. Ahead of him pines covered the steepening hills. He knew this highway like he knew the lines on his wife's face. For the next thirty miles the highway curved as it climbed through rocky forests. He passed the famous Burma Road, built by hand at night during the 1948 War of Independence to bypass the Arab blockade of Jerusalem. In 1947, the United Nations had partitioned the land into Jewish and Palestinian states, with Jerusalem and nearby Bethlehem one large International Zone. Four Arab armies invaded. Ten months later, Israel stood on sixty percent of the land promised to the Palestinians. Jordan took control of what was left, basically the West Bank and half of Jerusalem. Still, Israel had been paying a high price ever since that no Palestinian state was established.

At random intervals along the highway Eli spotted the nearly seventy-year-old rusted remains of military vehicles from the convoys that failed to break through. Eli wondered if all their focus on preserving memory, which was crucial, also blinded them to the kind of future they needed to build.

Past the Arab village of Abu Gosh, the road dropped then climbed again, offering breathtaking vistas off to the left of the terraced pines flowing up and down mountains and valleys. There was no place in the world that held his heart like Jerusalem. He loved this old highway and disliked the new shortcut with its checkpoints and high concrete walls where it skirted through an edge of the West Bank.

Soon, the road climbed the last ascent and flattened as he entered Jerusalem and he was home. Neighborhoods rose and dipped with the contours of the hills here on this mountain plateau. Neighborhood streets were narrow, the curbs jammed with small cars now that Prime Minister Gutman had removed the stiff vehicle import tax. The country was prospering, but in place of the old pioneering spirit something intangible seemed to have been lost. Eli could not quite put his finger on what it was, a selflessness perhaps, and then he thought he was being silly. A car accident on the highway, everybody still stopped to help.

Past Hebron Road, which led seven kilometers south to Bethlehem in the West Bank, Eli turned through a maze of one-way streets with pines in front of small, limestone apartment buildings, the flower boxes on their balconies red, pink and white with winter cyclamens.

When you lived here in the traffic, the shouting on buses and supermarket lines, it was easy to take the city's beauty, entirely constructed from limestone as required by local ordinance, for granted, Eli thought. Gone so much, he savored this moment and he consciously drove slower. He approached his father's building saw an easy parking space a block-and-a-half away. He peered ahead, looking for an even closer one. There was a small space half-a-block away. Eli veered into it head-on, quickly backed into place, jumped out, ran to his father's building and continued that gait up the inside stairwell.

Soon inside his father's study, Eli sat with his son Yigal and his dad, Meir Bardin. His father had emigrated from Australia at the age of sixteen, and alone among the three men wore a kippah. Eli knew that a half-century ago being religious and liberal was commonplace, though these days his father's blending of the two was increasingly unique. Yigal was in the graduate Sapir Film School in Sderot in the western Negev desert, less than two kilometers from the Gaza Strip, frighteningly controlled by Hamas fundamentalists who rained missiles into the city. Eli was proud of his son's artistic bent and did not care that advancing in film was like ascending a treacherous cliff. Yigal would find his path. The three generations were visibly excited to be together and Eli put a hand warmly on his father's shoulder. Again Eli longed to be home more.

Vibrant and voluble at seventy-four, with substantial dark hair and a short black and silver beard, several years ago Meir had been asked to lecture to the army. When he arrived, four people sat at a table, including a *Sgan Aluf—a* lieutenant colonel. Meir laughed and said he couldn't lecture to four people and began to sit for an informal discussion. The *Sgan Aluf* more than suggested he stand at the lectern and pretend he was talking to a group of five hundred. Meir spoke for an hour about how the Jews can be so different but still be one people, how it was possible through tolerance to be unified without being uniform. There could not be a single way to be Jewish, only multiple perspectives on the same truth. He talked about how this global, but part of a homeland, Jewish people must make their own particular contribution to perfecting the world. They hired him to speak to every officer in the Israeli Army. Soon attending one of his lectures became a requirement for graduating officer training school.

In Meir's book-crammed study, Eli looked at the photos of his father with various Israeli dignitaries. Only recently he had begun to realize that even taking his own path and mostly leaving the country had not made him feel entirely his own person. He cared a little too much about what his father needed from him which Eli felt emotionally though was not quite sure what he wanted. His father had changed the national discussion of how this returned nation should live in this land. Eli had saved lives but not etched his mark on anything tangible and he longed to do something of lasting importance.

Ten kilometers north of Jerusalem, Eli waited with a dozen Israeli soldiers on the dark highway just outside the Al-Am'ari refugee camp. Behind him rose the beautiful low limestone Arab architecture that blended into the hills of the West Bank. Satellite dishes and squat black water conservation tanks sat atop those homes, as Israel controlled water allotments. Ahead of the heavily armed, helmeted soldiers wearing Kevlar vests rose a stone arch maybe twenty feet high, the entrance to Al-Am'ari. Eli knew a key had been painted on the top back of the arch. Every Palestinian refugee camp entrance was similarly marked; the Aida refugee camp in Bethlehem had a huge metal replica of a key atop an entrance arch wide enough across for two cars to pass side by side. Old women in some of the camps still had the physical keys of the homes they had lived in prior to the 1948 War of Independence, which Palestinians understandably called the *Nakba*, the catastrophe.

Eli kicked at a dirt clod. There was so much foolishness on all sides here: the long disproven conceit that they could benignly occupy another people, this futile Palestinian fantasy of return to homes that no longer existed, that the Palestinian Authority (the PA) could represent their impoverished people by building two ornate governing palaces on top of hills that overlooked two refugee camps when none of those riches trickled down. One palace would not have been enough?

The Israeli captain for this area, at the front of their single file line, had met alone with the refugee camp head in his very small, makeshift office in the youth lounge with rows of soccer trophies behind glass—a conversation of mutual respect and equal honor. The refugees' ire at the corrupt PA was so intense that each of the nineteen refugee camps in the West Bank was governed independently by local leadership. They were neither looking for one of the Carlo gun factories they believed there nor making arrests, the captain promised. The homemade submachine gun was named after the World War II Swedish Carl Gustav M/45. The rudimentary automatic weapon, which often jammed, had been wielded the last six months in attacks on Israeli citizens and border patrol officers. Only basic welding shop machinery was needed to manufacture the weapon off blueprints from American designs now on the internet.

Though they were not here for the factory now, if the machinery was not dismantled they would be back, Eli had suggested the captain tell him. In exchange for the current leniency, the captain wanted the location of one family. Eli knew Khalid Fahmy would not be here, so there was no risk at alerting them. He was not looking for something specific, but for whatever might turn up, which was most often how he found the trailhead.

They moved single file under the arch on the dirt main entrance, not surprisingly eerily quiet as this patrol was expected. Eli watched the soldiers glance to rooftops where youthful snipers usually lay. Two-story cinderblock houses rose on each side of the alley, some with corrugated iron roofs. Eli passed a triangular limestone brick monument eight feet high, widest at the bottom, with maybe twenty-five small white rectangular plaques, each with the name of camp members killed over the years in clashes with soldiers. Then they passed another, smaller monument with half the number of names. He felt the pain of each of their losses. Placed in the center of the line, Eli wondered how many of these memorials there were here, how many names were young boys and girls hardly past puberty, seeing no future in the third generation in these dirt lanes, who lashed out at soldiers at an age when they should have be rebelling against parents. He hated and was frightened that his two sons served reserve duty in places like this, and in the quiet he noticed his nervousness.

Behind their line he heard loud thuds and then a crash. The soldiers spun around rifles ready. Someone had thrown a small refrigerator from a roof against the opposite wall, intending to miss them—a statement of defiance. A soldier shot a burst at the rooftop and the captain ran over and said loudly, "No firing." Near the rooftop a tangled mess of electrical wires, maybe a dozen lines wrapped around each other on a pole, sizzled where one of the soldier's bullets had struck. Eli understood the soldier's terror and lack of control but feared himself that bullets would explode at them now from every direction. The captain marched them forward at double-time down a lane to the left in the unholy quiet.

Stars shone throughout the moonless sky. Dirt paths branched everywhere and doors were painted blue to thwart the Evil Eye. Like the makeshift electricity line, houses abutted one another, shared walls, and rose randomly from any solid surface. The captain led them into a courtyard. Lights atop the soldiers' helmets danced through the dark. Ahead of them, a clothesline was strung between the cinderblock sides of two houses. A large black water container was covered with a sheet of rusting corrugated iron. Eli found his mind wandering to something he'd recently heard on the radio: in the Abu Dhabi heat the population stepped from air-conditioned homes into cooled cars and suffered from Vitamin D deficiencies from lack of exposure to sunlight. Eli caught himself; his lack of focus concerned him.

The captain dropped back to Eli, nodded, and Eli followed him towards a door. The captain went to open it and Eli stopped his hand and knocked. Soldiers fanned out to the windows and two hoisted themselves onto the roof. A male voice inside said in Arabic, "Enter."

The captain went in first and Eli followed. A man and woman sat on mattresses against the back wall, dressed and dignified, expecting them. Next to them on the wall was a very small picture of their dead daughter Samaya in a frame made of matches. A carpet woven of red, green, black and white, the colors of the Palestinian flag, filled the center of the room. The captain asked the parents to accompany him outside, and as they did Eli was alone in the two-room house. Their two teenage children and a younger girl had obviously been moved to friends. Eli knew the Palestinian population explosion would before too long make them the majority between the Mediterranean and the Jordan River.

He wondered how the prime minister, in his zeal to throw up two-story, immaculate, red tile roofed settlements across as many hills here as possible looking down on the Palestinian villages below, saw Israel's future? On that path Eli could only see Israel as a perpetually besieged fortress, its moral fiber deteriorating further to keep this burgeoning furious population subdued. And now the prime minister was off to America to grandstand again with the photo op ride on their new nuclear stealth submarine. When Menachem Begin, Israel's first prime minister from the right-wing Likud Party, was elected in 1977 he wanted to ride to his office on the bus. He was Eli's kind of a mensch and half a million across the political landscape flocked to his funeral. Gutman, head of the Likud Party and thus prime minister when they formed a government, never went anywhere in Israel without a ten-car motorcade, horns honking.

The room was sparse, a single dresser and a beautiful wood crafted bookshelf. Eli looked through the drawers and the women's undergarments with discomfort. He was back focused now.

On the bottom shelf he found several UNRWA school textbooks. In the aftermath of the War of Independence the UN established UNRWA to aid the Palestinian refugees, and it was the only organization Eli knew of that for so long had helped one group of refugees. Well, in the stalemate the people needed it. The electricity was not out here and he thumbed through a high school text and read: It is told by Abu Hurairah that the Prophet said: The End of Days will not take place until the Muslims fight the Jews, and the Muslims will kill them to a point that a Jew will hide behind a rock or a tree, and then the rock or the tree will say, 'O Muslin, O God's servant, there is a Jew behind me, so come and kill him.'

Eli opened another book and read a poem for Grade 5: Returning, returning. Borders shall not exist nor citadels and fortresses. Cry out those who have left: We are returning to the homes, to the valleys, to the mountains. Under the flag of glory, Jihad. For Grade 5. Eli squeezed his eyes. This was not the kind of help these people needed.

Then something on a higher shelf caught Eli's eye, an English copy of Ramzy Awwad's *Men in the Darkness,* which had never appeared in Hebrew. Little Palestinian literature did, and those translated did not sell well though Eli read a lot of it. He knew of this work. Eli opened the slim volume, which was autographed: *To Khaled Fahmy, I'm happy to call you a friend. Ramzy Awwad.* Khaled owning the book was not of particular note, except Awwad, one of the great Palestinian novelists, had long been a terrorist too and, in his time, a Palestine Liberation Organization (PLO) intelligence officer. He had to be in his late sixties or early seventies now, but Eli hadn't heard his name mentioned anywhere in two decades.

Eli slid the book back and decided not to ask the parents about it. If there was a connection between the two men that went beyond literary, Eli did not want Khaled tipped off. Eli subscribed to the absolute rule that there was no such thing as a coincidence, which meant a fair amount of the time he was wrong since the God he no longer believed in was playful, and He moved his players around the chess board of this planet with frequent happenstance.

Eli knew who in Israeli Intelligence to see about Ramzy Awwad—his mentor, and after his father, his closest friend, Shai.

CHAPTER 2

Shai Shaham left the TV on muted and, irritated, glanced at his watch—8:30 p.m. Gutman was due to announce the new head of the Mossad at 8:15, of course during primetime. The talking heads could do nothing but repeat what everybody already knew as the prime minister ratcheted up the suspense with delay. Gutman was leaving for the United States in the morning. The rest of the Israeli Navy's nuclear submarine flotilla of five had been manufactured by the German Howaldtswerke-Deutsche Werft shipbuilding company of Kiel, the last at an official price tag of two billion but generously discounted by Berlin as part of the 1953 Reparations Agreement. Still in force, contentiously in many Berlin government quarters Shai knew firsthand, the Agreement was in apology for exterminating the Continent's Jews. The submarines importantly allowed Israel to drop operatives on enemy coastlines, attack vessels undetected and served as a nuclear deterrent and second-strike threat to Pakistan, Iran and anybody else who might like them even less than most of the planet.

Shai was excited about Israel obtaining the new stealth class as it could operate undetected in the waters beneath Iran's soft southern flank. He'd have taken possession of it without fanfare but nothing anymore seemed to be done quietly. Shai looked at the stack of history and science journals on his end table. He liked obscure details, stayed up late at night reading here so as not to wake his wife Tami who he adored more than he could have ever imagined when alone for so long.

The science was way above his pay grade but he had wrestled with it. In St. Petersburg, the Krylov State Research Center had developed anti-solar coating using embedded active sensors to neutralize sonar search signals. Embedded electronics in the active coating could determine the radar frequency of the opponent's search and send back its own signal in the opposite phase, neutralizing the original probe. Global secrets no longer stayed at home in this electronic age, and the Chinese and Americans had not surprisingly developed variations of the stealth submersibles.

In the kitchen, Tami prepared tea and chatted with Tzipi Ben-Ami, a reluctant member of Prime Minister Gutman's cabinet, and Shai watched them. Tzipi looked great for fifty-one, a streak of unrepentant gray running along the top of her hair like a Mohawk. They had been friends for millennia. For twenty years, her hair then a gleaming chestnut, Tzipi had darted across the globe as a top Mossad operative and a good deal of that time he was her case officer.

Shai walked across the stone floor in his living room, his right hip hurting. Here he was thinking himself a young sixty-five, had jumped from a helicopter hovering just above the ground six months ago, and then he had injured his hip stupidly not bending his knees when Tami insisted he help her move the heavy bed so she could clean the space against the wall the housekeeper never reached. Tami also scrubbed the cracks in the bathroom tile with a toothbrush. Bless her heart. After Auschwitz, her mother arrived in Israel a germaphobe, but Shai found no fault in anything these survivors did.

Shai pressed his forehead against the cold glass window to try and relieve his throbbing temple. His Jerusalem suburb was increasingly populated by Anglo born Israelis, many religious themselves but fleeing the black-hatted, ultra-Orthodox who procreated like rabbits and were taking over suburbs like Ramat Eshkol on the way to Mount Scopus, where Shai had lived previously. He sighed. Never before in Israel's history had a prime minister publicly announced the appointment of the head of her espionage agency like this, with the nation holding its breath as if in final minutes of the Eurovision song finals, in which Israel participated.

The government had earlier revealed the three finalists, two by name and one by the protective initial N. Eleven men had risen to Mossad chief and bore the title *memune,* "first among equals," in line with the state's early socialist philosophy. Six had been plucked from inside the organization and five were former army generals. Shai suspected his new boss would be current National Security Adviser Ami Nir, a political puppy who sprawled at the feet of the Prime Minister. Nir had the sole responsibility of late for mending the rift with the US administration when the worst ever crisis between Israel and the United States blew up in their faces over the Iran nuclear agreement. Wisely, Nir had tried to dissuade the prime minister from speaking to Congress on the eve of the Israeli election, but who could tell Gutman anything, and to instead calm the rage in the Obama administration. At fifty-four, Nir had spent thirty years as a legendary agent runner while cultivating a full head of hair, dashing moustache, and a vast collection of ties that collectively won him the nickname of "the model." Well, the Mossad could make use of all types.

Shai was breathing hard. Ridiculously, he had managed to regain nearly all the fifty pounds that two decades ago he had over three years shed from his tall, portly frame. That he had kept the weight in check for so long he attributed to Asher's birth when Shai was forty-one. Tami's vigilant hovering over their household was not enough to curtail the large portions, sans vegetables, he had inhaled, but he had been resolute that he would not abandon his young son due to the suicidal sloth of ill health. But two years ago, Asher, following both his stint in the Israeli paratroopers and first degree in political science at the Hebrew University, had decamped to law school at Berkeley and stated that he was unlikely to return.

Shai lost the strength to control his eating. It had taken Asher exactly one deployment in the West Bank—where he argued with his fellow soldiers, who regularly held up Palestinian ambulances at a checkpoint for over an hour while they played shesh besh, Israeli backgammon, in their tent by the road—to ask his father's permission to study and maybe settle abroad. Asher had argued that he could serve better as a Jew and a light onto his fellow man elsewhere, as being here was grinding his insides, which were constantly and literally in turmoil. Shai had wanted to say that they had to fight both outside and inside the country's borders, which he believed entirely, but instead kissed his son's forehead and said, "Go." To his surprise it had not broken his heart. Asher was sensitive and emotional like his mother and Shai saw this was best for him. At his exodus, the light inside Shai dimmed but did not depart.

As he waited for the announcement, he felt a small fear at how fast the years had disappeared. He wondered how long remained ahead of him? His father, who was about as reflective as a stone, had worried little and remained mostly silent on their treks through the desert to meet his Bedouin friends. Shai supposed that he was half like his father and the other half had fled to the opposite possibilities of personality. As a child he had felt hungry for words, and ever since was garrulous, which seemed to flow naturally into his tradecraft.

Tzipi came over and rested an arm on his shoulder. "Look," she said. "The blowhard has to announce it before the nation falls asleep. He will not miss the opportunity to yet again regale us."

He smiled. She was absolutely fearless, spoke her mind, and was sought after everywhere from opposition parties to the private sector. Shai grasped her hand and then released it. She was tougher than any man he had ever known. She gave a small smile and they joined Tami at the couch.

Tami turned to Tzipi. "Have you ever thought about running for prime minister?" Tami had been the old Mossad head Meir Carmon's girl Friday when she and Shai met.

Tzipi laughed.

"Jump to Labor," Tami said, referring to the socialist Labor Party of Prime Ministers David Ben-Gurion, Golda Meir and Yitzhak Rabin.

Shai remained silent, curious what Tzipi would say.

"Labor are pussies. So afraid of the right they run on the apartment shortage these days." Tzipi sipped some tea.

"Some Scotch in it?" Shai asked.

"You have anything good?"

"I wouldn't know." He went to the cupboard and took out a bottle he'd bought in duty free at Schiphol Airport forever ago. He did not drink, as he knew that he could manage nothing in moderation. Five decades ago, after an American girlfriend returned home from her junior year in Jerusalem, he had spent the entire next year drunk on cheap cognac. When he had smoked, he lit up all the time. After he quit, for a year-and-a-half he carried a pack of cigarettes in his pocket just to prove to himself that he could abstain.

Tami would not be deterred and pointed an insipid sugar-free cookie at her. "Golda Meir did it. This is the time. Theresa May in England. Angela Merkel. It's a different world. Women can change everything."

"We're no longer a country that could elect Golda," Tzipi said. "The religious lunatics have gained too tight a foothold. Believe me, I have thought about it a lot."

"There can be a rebirth of the idealism of the kibbutz." Tami stood. "Working together, sharing, not all this materialism. You don't have to be left wing. The dream can develop again."

Shai finally spoke. "It's probably not the time. She wouldn't get anywhere at the top of the Labor list. Even if they let her ascend, Gutman would swat her all the way to Cyprus with fearmongering."

"We can't give up," Tami said loudly.

"I never give up," Tzipi said. "But I don't joust at windmills."

Just then, the prime minister ascended to the podium. Shai turned up the sound. Tami was right. Israel had moved from a bluntness where leaders talked less and what they said mattered, to the current prime minister's regular harangue, which Shai listened to yet again: the dangers of ISIS, Islamism, anti-Semitism.

"What shit," Tzipi said. "He's telling this to us?"

The prime minister continued about how he had met with many world leaders and how the Mossad will assist the government to develop relationships with these countries.

Shai looked down. The name please, was all he wanted. But he really did not need to hear it. There was really no choice, for the prime minister loved Nir's style, the way he dressed, the prestige and nobility he projected and his eloquent speech, all of which Shai found annoying.

Ami Nir headed to the podium. The prime minister, each hair meticulously combed over an obvious bald spot and sprayed in place, with a large grin that beamed certainty and an unwillingness ever to consider he might be wrong, threw an arm around Nir . Shai darkened the TV picture along with the sound. This was the new Israel—high-tech millionaires and Savile Row suits, an average house in Herzliya Pituach near the high-tech park cost four million dollars. And, ten miles to the east, military rule over the Palestinians. Maybe, Shai considered, after emancipation from the ghettos this was the inevitable destination, their hora dancing pioneers merely a stop on the train to modernity. Shai's stomach felt acidy.

At 11:40 p.m. the phone rang, waking Tami. Beside her, Shai was staring out the open window. Despite the cold, he loved the breeze over his body.

"Baha Nabata has been killed in Shuafat," the familiar voice of the night officer said.

Shai closed his eyes. "Us or them?" Israeli police no longer entered the Shuafat refugee camp and its nearby neighborhoods in East Jerusalem but the settlers did. A decade ago Israel had circled the 70,000 Palestinians in Shuafat with the high concrete separation barrier. Teeming and dangerous for Israelis, their ambulances and firefighters no longer entered Shuafat. So, twenty-nine-year-old Palestinian organizer Baha Nababta, a father of two and beloved by the Shuafat teens, who followed this Pied Piper, filled those vital services. Nabata helped residents pool funds and pave roads in front of their houses. He trained here as a firefighter and then taught others in Shuafat how to tackle blazes.

"Fifteen minutes ago. He was directing traffic. They were repaving the main road. The road is shit. Someone drove by on a motorcycle, ten shots, seven hit. Disappeared."

"So them," Shai said with no solace. When settlers rampaged they raced in armed caravans.

"Yes. Could be jealousy over his success and large following. He was getting help from Israeli community centers and civil rights activists. Or, the hard-liners want no cooperation with us."

"More likely it was that. How far they get on the repaving?"

"Thirty feet."

Shai knew there was not a single park or playground in

Shuafat, and few sidewalks as the streets were too narrow. He would make some calls in the morning, cajole, and get the rest of the road finished. He hung up, thought about how the immaculate, tall Jewish apartment buildings of Pisgat Ze'ev, the East Jerusalem settlement of fifty thousand, were visible over the barrier just across from Shuafat. He tasted the envy the Palestinians felt but wondered how one effectively shut their eyes when looking down at them.

Shai finally slept uneasily, and early in the morning darkness drove to the nearby Jerusalem Pool on Emek Refaim Street, one of the few public pools in the city. With large grass areas, it housed an indoor Olympic-size pool and a large outdoor swimming area for children. He purposely arrived a half hour before the 5:30 a.m. opening, rang the outside bell and the manager, a Russian émigré in her thirties, smiled when she saw him through the glass and unlocked the door.

"You have not been here in a very long time," Marina said with an edge.

"High on my list of things to do, always."

She laughed. "I'm sure. You look terrible. Doesn't matter, you are here."

"I've saved all my sizes of pants," Shai said with a smile. "How's your mother?"

"Better. Thank you for asking. After so long, you want me to remove the lane guards so you can swim the width?"

He sighed. "My legs have been hurting. I think I best start again at the beginning. Walk in a lane and try and swim a little when I can."

"Okay. But now that you've come, we have to be clear. I'm going to be calling and harassing you. You need to be here twice a week."

"Absolutely agree, more actually."

"Big talker. Go," she said, "before the lap swimmers show

up."

"I may need a small favor sometime soon."

"Too bad it will be with my clothes on. Young men are stupid."

Eli loved the Old City of Jerusalem and stopped at the entrance to Jaffa Gate, where a Palestinian stood beside a high flat cart piled with sesame bagels, oranges, and pomegranates, with a large plunger to squeeze the juice into small plastic cups. A nun in a beige habit and black cowl that fell a good way down her back walked past him. In a large niche just inside the limestone walls, a woman in an angelic white shirt and matching long skirt sat barefoot, legs crossed, on the wide stone perch, her harp leaned against the wall. Eli smiled as she texted on her phone.

From behind, a strong arm wrapped around Eli's shoulder.

"Hey, Shai," Eli said without turning.

"Bardin," Shai said loudly, and then enunciating and pausing between each word, "How are you?" Shai greeted Eli exactly this way every time they met.

Rather than share his increasing burdens and worries, which embarrassingly felt like mid-life angst, Eli said, "The family's great, everybody should have my problems."

"You have problems?" Shai said exaggeratedly, but he saw a burden in his agent's face, in the deepening lines around his eyes. "So how are you, really?"

Eli smiled. "Fine. Can't do the night flights like I used to, that's all. Let's see what's happening on the Temple Mount."

Shai decided to let this pass, for now. "Yes, let's."

It was Friday, and as they walked into the souq most of the shops in the covered marketplace had their metal grates pulled down for the Muslim day of prayer. Shai kept an eye out, as Fridays were when all the trouble started.

At the end of the souq, with the Jewish quarter off to the right that the Jordanians just had to destroy during their time here, Shai followed Eli single file through the airport-like x-ray scanner into the blinding sun, the light ricocheting off the huge stone plaza. Maybe thirty Israeli police vans were parked in astounding diagonal precision to the right of the outdoor walkway up to the Temple Mount, the Western Wall visible to their left. Above it, on the flat stone plaza where the Palestinians prayed and sometimes demonstrated, were the immense golden Dome of the Rock Mosque and the silver-domed Al-Aqsa Mosque.

The Jews had enough problems without provoking more, which they excelled at, Shai thought. After the Old City was captured in the Six-Day War, the rabbis forbade religious Jews to walk on the Temple Mount. The exact location of the Holy of Holies, the tabernacle where God dwelt, could be anywhere on the stone plaza since the Romans had completely razed the Second Temple. Recently, using Biblical text, some over-industrious right-wing rabbis calculated where the Holy of Holies had stood, and so where to avoid, and religious Jews flocked to the Temple Mount turning the area into a powder keg. Jewish prayer on the Temple Mount was forbidden, and of course the orthodox prayed there anyway.

In black T-shirts with their unit insignia and the word JERUSALEM embossed in white on their backs, the police were lifting flak jackets, machine guns and pistols from the backs of the vans—their normal Friday presence to prevent the prayer day from turning into stone or bottle throwing. At least all tourists and Jews were kept off the Temple Mount on Fridays.

Eli and Shai sat on a stone ledge. Shai's legs hurt from the long decline through the souq and he was grateful for the rest. It was quiet here as Jews crowded a short distance away at the Western Wall.

"You miss praying?" Shai asked.

"It's a bit like having a close friend who you decide is really a problem. So, no. But I do miss the comfort it brought me."

"It hard when you come home to fit back in?"

"No," Eli said truthfully. It was strange to Eli that Shai had become a father figure to him when he had such a wonderful father, and Eli felt guilty that he somehow needed too much when so many men were blessed with far less. He said, "It's becoming hard to leave."

"Not surprising," Shai said. "Even expected. You've been at this a long time."

"What do I do?"

"Change is difficult. When it's easier than continuing, come in. We'll find something for you."

"I don't think I can sit at a desk."

Shai smiled. "You won't really know until you try. Most of life is lived in between the certainty of what you should and shouldn't do."

"For you too?"

Shai was silent for a long time and then said, "Yes."

Directly across from them, police moved through the door opened in the wooden fence that blocked entrance to the ramp. Police hurried up the wood-roofed walkway. Shai remembered not so terribly long ago when there was no fence and the walkway always open.

"I feel like we're running out of time here," Shai said. "Though I can't see how it's all going to look when we do."

"Not our job."

Shai laughed. "Thankfully yes. Our lives are simple really in comparison. Protect."

"Ramzy Awwad," Eli said.

Shai watched a young Orthodox man, black jacket and pants, white shirt open at the collar, short beard that hardly covered his face, dart through the parked police vans towards the Dung Gate in the Old City walls. Shai felt a kinship with him.

"Haven't thought about him in a long time," Shai said. "At one point, I thought we were friends. He saved my life, then later betrayed it. I suppose I'd feel the loss of it, if I let myself. Too much else on my mind."

Eli knew the history. In the 1980s, they had pooled efforts to hunt for Abu Nidal, the extremist Palestinian terrorist in Europe who was killing Israelis, Jews and moderate Palestinian leaders positioning for a two-state solution. In Rome, they had Abu Nidal cornered when Shai was shot. Ramzy Awwad chose to save Shai rather than eliminate Abu Nidal. A few years later, Awwad had helped foment a plot to smuggle a nuclear weapon into Jerusalem to force Israeli withdrawal from the West Bank. The bomb had actually been assembled inside Jerusalem.

"Daniel Kahneman discovered people feel their pain far stronger than equivalent joy," Eli said. "More proof there's no God."

Shai had read the psychologist's book. There was a great section about the early days of the Israeli Army. Kahneman created an exercise where men had to cooperate to lift a log over a high barrier. They were looking at leaders for officer candidates. Eventually, Kahneman figured out there was no correlation, which Shai could have told him. Too clean an idea. Shai chuckled to himself. Still, the boneheaded beginning didn't slow Kahneman from winning the Nobel Prize in economics for his work in prospect theory.

Shai said, "Maybe we were created that way to goad us to find happiness. I need as much help getting there as I can get."

Eli laughed. "I don't believe a word of it. I think you're happiest when you're worrying." He then explained about Khaled Fahmy and the signed Awwad novel in Al-Am'ari.

"Interesting link," Shai said.

"I want to talk to Awwad. Can you find him?"

"With a little effort, I suppose so."

The wooden gate beyond the police vans was closed and soon the last of the officers made his way up the ramp and disappeared through the door at the top and onto the Temple Mount. A mixed cacophony rang out and Shai realized it was noon. A plaintive wail calling the faithful to prayer came through loudspeakers at the top of nearby minarets. Deep church bells rang from the Holy Sepulcher behind them to the left, continuing in symphonic cacophony for a long time.

Shai stood, thinking about his son's frustration and leaving for America, and sadness weighed on him. He loved this crazy city with every fiber of him, the exact way he loved his son. He would protect them both with everything in him.

Shai said, "Okay, let's go back. I'll make some calls. If I can find him at all, it will be quick."

Shlomo Avni grabbed a copy of the daily *Yediot Ahronot* off the newsstand on Ben Yehuda, the wide black stoned walk street. He was so angry, he continued several steps glaring at the headline before he remembered that he had not paid for it, and ran back.

Shlomo looked at the front-page photo of Prime Minister Gutman speaking to the press before boarding the plane to America. The headline blared for it seemed the thousandth time, **WHO ELSE BUT ME? WHO ELSE CAN DO THIS!** Gutman's claim that only he could manage and massage the Americans, the Saudi Peace Plan, the Iran nuclear threat, the disintegration of Syria next door, the cold peace with Egypt, Hamas rockets to the south, Hezbollah missiles to the north, and the intermittently restive Palestinians. The Iranian-backed Hezbollah terrorists had 100,000 missiles in Southern Lebanon pointed at them, the prime minister did not need to tell them. Shlomo believed this frequent repetition of *Who Else*

Can Do This? had subliminally entered the population.

The newspaper article at the bottom of the page explained Gutman's unassailable power. The Izz ad-Din al-Qassam Brigades, the military arm of the Palestinian Hamas organization, had said that one of their soldiers had been electrocuted while working in a Gaza "resistance" tunnel. Shlomo walked even faster. They used our cement sent in to rebuild Gaza to construct attack tunnels into Israel, sending us an invitation to turn those tunnels and too much else into dust.

In 2014, they had gone into Gaza again. That time, Hamas supporters murdered three Israeli teens in the West Bank. Israel retaliated with a targeted airstrike that killed seven Hamas leaders. Then Hamas launched barrages of missiles into Israel. The air and ground invasion lasted seven weeks, during which Hamas launched thousands of rockets into Israel. In that round, seventeen thousand homes were destroyed, a quarter million people displaced, and over two thousand Palestinians killed, including hundreds of children. The vastness of the devastation upset Shlomo. The army he had helped lead did not blow up civilian houses from the air and he didn't give a damn that Hamas placed their missiles there. They needed long-term strategic thinking not vicious reprisals. Hamas tunnel and rocket capability was already back to pre-2014 Gaza War levels.

Shlomo read as he walked. Local reports confirmed that rescuers had managed to pull out four of five bodies that had been buried in a tunnel. Surrounded by such neighbors, the population felt safe with Gutman. He spoke in unyielding certainties that assured them. Shlomo ducked into a café with pastries behind glass and mounted the narrow stairs to the second floor, which was empty save for his sixteen-year-old daughter Yael who had been visiting a friend. Since he had been in Jerusalem, he was eager to drive her the hour home, as about the only time she talked to him at length was when stuck in the car, which he thought pretty normal. She was nursing a cappuccino.

Shlomo was average height, with a full head of tussled brown hair, and thought of himself as a bit handsome. Despite great success in high tech, he had suffered major setbacks. Born on a secular kibbutz, after high school he had been selected to try out for the air force, the elite branch of Israeli service. Rejected, he had served instead in the Golani Infantry Brigade, where he met his wife. She did not want to live on kibbutz, so they rented a small apartment in Herzliya on the coast north of Tel Aviv. Soon he was asked to join the army permanently. During his training he was sent to the Hebrew University for his BA, and later to Columbia University for an MA in political science. He served three years as the military attaché at their embassy in Washington, and during that time his wife became a clinical psychologist. With three kids and a dog, as he rose to the army's top echelon he never strayed from the socialist values of the kibbutz. He had been a contender for Chief of Staff, but again, like with the air force, he was denied. He left the army, created a team of former army officers from the technology division, the kind of guys who improved on missiles for F-22 Raptor fighter jets, and soon made a fortune with a medical software app. But even moving into the elite enclave in Herzliya Pituach had not satisfied him. He longed to make a difference.

So at fifty-one, very quietly and unknown even to his wife, in cooperation with military intelligence he formed a new team using some of the former one. They dove into the hermeneutics of terrorism. In 2004, while watching the burnt-out hull of a Jerusalem bus from his car a block behind in traffic, the ambulances already there, the radio played the audio of the suicide video of the Hamas bomber from the Aida refugee camp in Bethlehem. It suddenly struck Shlomo that they could track the phrases used in these messages to head off attacks. They quickly discovered that Al-Qaeda called out, "God, count them, kill them, and don't leave any of them." Hamas favored, "Victory is with the patient." One of ISIS's top recruiters and bomb plotters, Abu Issa al-Amriki, and his circle sent instructions across the globe via encrypted internet messages on the app Telegraph that launched their bombers with, "Kill 1000000s of *kuffar*," the Arabic slander for infidel. Shlomo felt quiet pride that he had decoded the messages and found al-Amriki's location in Al Bab, Syria, where an American predator drone killed him.

They had developed algorithms that could beam light into the dark web and illuminate threats. Figuring he may as well make money while helping, his new company sold the technology to police, border, and intelligence services across the globe. His proprietary software, SuprView, now could speed through four million Twitter and Facebook posts in a day, and target where to look in the world's 2.3 billion social media accounts. Shlomo didn't care about the many millions more he had earned, anonymously gave half of it to charities around the globe, would figure out later how much to leave for his family, and would give away the rest. He was looking for another challenge.

"You have fun?" he asked Yael.

"Of course. There were boys at her house." She looked at the newspaper headline. "When your dream and everything you do is to stay in power nothing is legitimate, even if you accidentally follow the right dream," she said.

He laughed. "You're your mother's daughter."

"Obviously. Who else could I be?"

Just then a police loudspeaker blared, the tinny voice ordering everybody off the walk street and into the backs of the tourist shops and cafes. *Hafetz hashod*, suspicious object. The regular. There were no trash receptacles on the heavily trafficked downtown street for exactly this reason. Shlomo ignored the orders and went to the small second-story window and looked down. A female police officer, walking backward, was unrolling plastic blue barrier tape across the intersection to block all entrance. Police cars, sirens blaring, arrived from all directions and screeched to a halt as people scattered, some running, some walking quickly, others casually heading down towards the light rail on Jaffa Road.

Shlomo thought about the Sbarro restaurant just around the corner and the suicide bombing there more than a dozen years ago. Fifteen dead, including one pregnant and a bunch of kids, more than a hundred wounded by a guitar case packed with nails to maximize death. One of the dead boys had been his oldest son's close friend, and it was only by the fate of a dentist appointment his son wasn't there. He considered terrorists who targeted women and children cowards.

Shlomo looked at the last stragglers hurrying away in the street. He turned to his daughter and was glad his wife had persuaded him to talk to their kids early on like they were adults. "Those who think we can do this forever are fools. My God, there is another people. *Here*, among us."

"Daddy, you think this is the first time I've heard this from you?"

We don't think far enough ahead, Shlomo thought. The government reacts. Then Shlomo saw it. "There's a small backpack on the ground against the bank. Probably some American went to the bathroom."

Yael started casually across the room. "You want anything? Mom gave me money."

"Cinnamon roll."

Downstairs, the café was packed with those who had been sitting and walking outside and who were now, almost to a person, pushing and shouting out orders for coffee and cakes. Yael smiled and waited in the long line, loved all her people, even the ones she hated.

Back upstairs, balancing two plates with cakes and a coffee, she sat with her father.

"We're sleepwalking in this country," Shlomo said. "The country's prospering like never before. I want all you kids to see that everywhere a few kilometers away are millions of people broken by poverty, often without enough water, humiliated, with no way out. Who cares? They're not on TV, not in the papers—a whole population doesn't exist. We shut our eyes, until a bomb shakes them open. And then quickly we go back to normal."

"It's not normal and it's not Jewish," she said. "I care about everybody."

He loved her so much his heart beat faster. They heard the small thud of the exploding backpack that contained no explosives.

Shlomo said, "I don't know if we'll wake up in time."

CHAPTER 3

Eli sat on the lengthy El Al nonstop flight from Tel Aviv to Los Angeles reading Ramzy Awwad's *Men in the Darkness*, surprised how long ago it had originally been published, 1969. He had borrowed this slim English volume from Shai. It contained the title novella and seven stories. He had just finished the novella and was impressed with its depiction of the short comings of his own people who had expected the Arab states to battle for them.

The flight attendant rolled the drink cart near. Eli leaned back in his wide business class seat and suddenly felt the nervousness. He hated being out of control and was angry at himself for this stupidity. He had a job to do, he shouted silently at himself.

"Everything okay, sir? Can I get you something?" she asked.

"Red wine."

She smiled and placed two small bottles of cabernet on his open tray table and then a glass flute. He screwed the top off one and upended it in the flute. Like his father, he didn't drink, though for different reasons. He was aware that his father's larger-than-life excesses had made Eli quiet, soft-spoken and prone to moderation everywhere. He lacked his father's social graces, and when not on the job often left a gathering hurriedly without saying goodbye to the hosts. He supposed that was an immature reaction to his father's boisterous lingering. He felt all this moderation, this holding himself in check, was suffocating him. He downed half the glass and let the wine course through him. Since he was tired and had no built up tolerance, his face flushed and the wine seemed to flood away the anxiety. He finished the glass in one long pull.

Eli picked up the book and read a short story, about a boy in 1948 who had carried an orange from the tree in their Jaffa courtyard all the way in Lebanon, believing he could keep it with him and not eat it until he soon returned to that home for a fresh one. The story was autobiographical and Eli almost felt like he was prying, though he began to feel a kinship for this Palestinian he was about to meet.

He emptied the second small bottle into his glass but took only a few sips. The Israeli female attendant returned with her cart and swept up the empty bottles.

"Another?" she asked.

He shook his head no and she moved on. She was maybe twenty-four and blonde, a little older and the same coloring of his second born, Tamar, now in an army teachers' unit. That unit wonderfully allowed girls to join with friends, particularly helpful for religious girls. They taught soldiers who wanted to complete high school, as well as recruits from marginal areas, lots of Ethiopian émigrés, who needed help acclimating to the army. He didn't know of another military in the world as focused on its people. In the last year, he had missed every time Tamar came home on leave. He felt sadness tight in his throat and his mouth was dry. It had been fabulous to see Yigal, lucky that he was up from school.

He wondered again how long he could stay out here, how long was enough to give, and what he might do if he came home. Teach in the training school? Write a novel like Ramzy? Not that. He was too private to expose anything through fiction. What made him uneasy was he had decades ahead of him and not sure what he would do, if not this.

Fifteen and a half grueling hours to Los Angeles, but the flight had left mercifully at one a.m. to encourage sleeping, though Eli had not dozed off. He still had ten more hours in the air. He quickly drained the rest of the cabernet. Eli felt the tiredness reach every part of him with unusual warmth. He was feeling like himself again, and his last thought as he slipped asleep was that Ramzy was teaching a class at UCLA as guest lecturer and Eli intended to show up and listen before he approached him.

Irritated about being late for dinner in New York at the Harry Cipriani restaurant in the Sherry-Netherland Hotel on 5th Avenue, Tzipi Ben-Ami walked to a barricade on 59th Street manned by security and New York City attack dogs. The hotel was surrounded by a ring of both Israeli and New York police. Tzipi had to show her Israeli passport, and was infuriated when even after she passed through the metal detector a female officer patted her down, all to have dinner with Gutman, his wife, Hannah, and their New York consul. More than the pomp Gutman required, Tzipi hated his lack of a core. He breathed to hold on to power, and if the Labor party had mounted sufficient support for him to form a coalition with them, he'd have gladly galloped the country to a two-state solution with the Palestinians. Since the prevailing winds blew right, he leaned that way. Tzipi loved her revisionist right-wing family, all diehard believers in the Greater Land of Israel movement, and she still felt her heart there. But she had more respect for the assassinated Prime Minister Yitzhak Rabin, who had journeyed from a military hardline to peace with the Palestinians out of deep belief and not clutching at power. What a stupid tragedy that the religious right-wing idiot had murdered him at a peace rally of all places.

Tzipi moved through the glass front door of the restaurant,

which had its own entrance. The large dining room was crowded with small white cloth-covered tables of four with heavy wood chairs. She saw Gutman and Hannah mid dining room surrounded by Israeli security, who filled about a quarter of the full restaurant's seats. Few heads of state's wives accompanied them on every foreign outing, but Hannah always did. Though it was not generally known why, Tzipi did. No woman Gutman had or might bed was allowed in the cabinet. Tzipi had no romantic attraction to Gutman and Hannah knew it, so approved her, along with several others, ironically gorgeous women, who found better looking bedfellows. After Hannah caught him screwing around, she had his attorney draw up a contract between them, the attorney unbelievably, or maybe too believably, rewarded for keeping his lips sealed with the position of Attorney General.

A former airline stewardess, everybody knew Gutman had slept regularly with Hannah while married to wife number two. When originally running for Prime Minister, rumors rose that he had cheated on wives one and two. His poll numbers, especially among the crucial Orthodox, plummeted. With defeat apparently pounding in his ears, in a bold stroke he took the microphone and confessed to multiple adulteries, promising with utter passion and sincerity that he would never, now that he had married his Hannah, stray again. The audacity of it had surprised Tzipi though the brilliance did not. Overnight he became a national hero, but if he was caught again nobody would forgive him. Then Tzipi had heard Hannah trailed him to a liaison and squeezed her claws around him, literally and legally. She would destroy him before she was publicly humiliated, and their son was waiting in the wings, already a member of Knesset (the Israeli Parliament,) high up on the Likud Parliamentary list. The kid was already reaching for the stars.

Tzipi approached the table and Gutman and the consul, Avi, stood. Simultaneously, some twenty security officers rustled at their tables, silverware dropped on the tablecloths as they watched.

As she neared, she said, "Sorry, I was delayed outside."

Gutman came around to pull out her chair and a number of the security agents stood. With an outstretched wave and a smile, Gutman motioned them down and helped ease Tzipi nearer the table.

"Excuse me, all," he said. "Let me have a quick run to the men's room while I'm up."

As he walked slowly towards the restaurant exit to the hotel, all twenty men rose with a screech of wood against the large, square, white marble floor tiles.

Hannah lifted her white wine and laughed. "He always travels like this. Exhausting." She turned to Tzipi. "Any truth you're going to jump to Labor and run against him? Uri says you have bigger balls than anyone in the cabinet, except maybe Lieberman, and he has those Russian genes."

Tzipi actually liked and respected the Soviet-born Defense Minister. "None," Tzipi said. "My father would rise from his grave and come after me. Armed, I presume."

Hannah and Avi laughed.

"And I remind you I'm in your husband's cabinet."

Hannah lifted her wine glass in a toast. "Of course you are, dear."

Tzipi raised her glass. "To alliances that last forever, like Rome."

"To Rome." Hannah smiled, clinked her glass and swallowed a large mouthful of the light white wine. She actually liked that Tzipi didn't grovel like most of the others.

Tzipi turned and watched the entire retinue surround the Prime Minister as he walked. The other patrons stopped eating, watched and whispered.

"At least he's safe," Tzipi said with a smile.

Hannah laughed even louder this time, but said nothing more.

In the hotel lobby, three agents entered the bathroom and soon exited with a single bald man, late sixties. Then these three flanked Gutman and they entered together. One man stood outside the door and the rest stood in a line, arms up and linked, and formed a human wall so nobody could enter the men's room.

In the main dining room, Tzipi asked Hannah, "You going on the ceremonial ride on the new submarine tomorrow?"

"No, I'm going blonder. I have a fabulous stylist on the Upper East Side. Sometimes I get Uri to find an excuse to come to New York just to see her. If you'd like her name?"

"I'm actually enjoying the gray. Too much else in the world feels unreal."

"Who wants reality, my dear? You going with my dear Uri down into the deep?"

"*Hamilton*," she said. "My roommate from her junior year abroad at the Hebrew U got us tickets. Only reason I tagged along to this dreadfully overcrowded, and may I add, noisy city."

Tzipi prided herself that she had gotten along wonderfully with her younger, liberal, American dorm mate, despite all her partying and immaturity. Israelis served in the military immediately after high school, so by the time they entered university were serious, their playing around behind them.

Ramzy Awwad approached Moore Hall for the course he was teaching as a guest lecturer for the ten-week term. At seventy-four, he was physically fit, lean, his hair now silver, his moustache two-toned black and gray. His people were no better off than when he had begun the fight more than five decades earlier. He walked carefully, had tripped last year and torn a ligament in his ankle. As he climbed the outside steps, he felt the heaviness of someone who had failed more than succeeded, his greatest achievement his long marriage to Dalal.

Ramzy had not published anything in over two decades. All those years in the PLO he had formed his short stories in his head when on the run, then set them down in a fierce outpouring when he could steal the hours. For many years, now that he had the time he had always ached for to write, a small depression had overcome him. So, he had set down both his gun and his pen and taught with Dalal in the school in the Yarmouk Palestinian refugee camp in Damascus's southern suburbs.

Ramzy walked down the pristine Moore Hall corridor, perfect off-white stucco walls and ceiling, dark-brown doors, identical baseboards and wood stair railings to the upper floors. It was as if some deity descended at dawn each morning and blew the halls clean with an enormous breath. A lone Hispanic coed sat on the stone steps to the second floor, turquoise blue cap with UCLA in gold script, shorts, a tank top, long legs with no socks in black sneakers, brown skin everywhere. Ramzy loved the freedom the students felt here, had neither resentment nor envy at these kids' limitless lives in this unbelievable weather in mid-November.

As Ramzy entered the small amphitheater-like classroom, about fifty students waited. Today he would talk about a short story written by a woman in Gaza a few months ago.

As he approached the podium, students shuffled, set phones down on the desks before them, some opening notebooks, others positioning laptops. They were remarkably attentive. Ramzy had attended university in London and had a facility for languages. In the back of the room he saw an older man who had never been there before. Ramzy did not make eye contact, suspected who he was.

"Good afternoon, and thank you for being here rather than at the beach today."

A student called out, "They're almost all beach days."

Ramzy smiled. "It's not greatly known but Gaza has spectacular beaches. Just hard to get there now. You need permission from both Israel and Hamas to enter the Gaza Strip. Israel conquered Gaza during the 1967 War, which the Arabs call The June War. As part of a voluntary disengagement plan, Israel dismantled their twenty-one settlements there and withdrew in 2005. The following year, Hamas won a plurality in the Gaza Parliamentary elections. Israel continues to blockade the coast to keep missiles and other weapons out. The result is some of the humanitarian aid is also prevented from reaching the people."

Ramzy removed two carefully folded sheets from his pocket. "I've been working with Enas Fares Ghannam, a twenty-eight-year-old religious woman in Gaza, for about a year. She writes in English. She tells me she writes because it is easier for her than talking, which is something I feel myself. This is the We Are Not Numbers program I've talked to you about. She called the first draft 'The Curious Case of a Gazan Girl.' Later she changed it to 'Always on the Inside Looking Out.'"

A student in a black T-shirt with WE'RE THE BOMB and some logo Ramzy did not recognize said, "She change it or you?"

"In this case she was smarter than me. Second draft just showed up with this title. I'll show you one place where I suggested a change but otherwise I'll read her final draft. I did not do much work on it. General clarifications. As you might imagine, these stories are a combination of fiction and actual events."

A freckled redhead raised her hand. "So mostly memoir."

"Often entirely. The Gaza Strip is twenty-five miles long, seven miles wide."

He began to read.

I was surfing on Facebook when I saw a photo album of a friend who is not Palestinian. The cover picture

showed him sitting in a garden with a chair swing, green trees, and a round table in the corner covered by a red cloth and shaded by an umbrella.

"The original sentence said, 'In a garden that had a chair swing and green trees, with some comfortable decoration.'"

"Ah, cool change," the redhead said. "We can see the decoration now."

The class laughed and Ramzy smiled. He loved these young Americans.

It seemed like it was overlooking a sea or lake. It looked like such a charming place to be. I know my friend travels a lot, so I wondered where he was this time. I opened the album and started to look at the pictures. Suddenly, my eyes froze on the words "West Bank." I looked at the comment below: "Having a great time in the West Bank. Behind me is Lake Tiberias." I stopped smiling; instead, I started to look at one photo after another with envy.

"What is Lake Tiberias?" Ramzy asked.

Nobody knew.

"Where are my Christian Bible students?"

Two hands went up.

"Hebrew for the Sea of Galilee," Eli said from the back row with no discernible Israeli accent.

"Yes, thank you." Ramzy was surprised the Israeli spoke, but Israelis were like that.

"We prayed at Al-Aqsa Mosque," he posted. "The holy feeling when being in the Holy Land is indescribable."

He and his other friends were smiling and taking photos, with the Dome of the Rock Mosque behind them. There were also photos of Jerusalem, Nazareth, Ashkelon, Nablus and Jericho.

Suddenly my heart felt as if it wanted to leap out of my chest—to protest, explode and revolt. Hundreds of questions burst into my mind, but I couldn't focus on any of them as they were popping and disappearing at the same time. Only one question emerged clearly: "Why can't I go there? What or who gives him the right to go? I'm OK with not being able to visit any other country, but shouldn't I be able to visit my own at least? I couldn't help it. I cried.

"That's messed up," a curly haired boy said. "There's no, like, any way she can go?"

"Let me continue and the story will answer that."

I was twelve **years old, in the year 2000, when my father told us we would go to Jerusalem the next Friday. I felt very happy and excited; it would be my first time to leave Gaza. I told my friends, and they were jealous.**

I started to imagine how it would feel to travel, staying in the car for one whole day. I was daydreaming about different scenarios: Will we eat in the car? Maybe we will stop somewhere. I need to check that the camera is working. What will I ask Allah for when I pray at the Al-Aqsa Mosque? I need to prepare a list of all the things I need Him to do for me. I also need to prepare a list of things to do in Jerusalem. Will we stay there or will we go to other places? We have relatives in Nablus I have never seen before. Will I get to see the mountains of Nablus? I have never seen a real one. Will it be cold? Oh Allah, please make it snow; I would love to see it snowing. Oh, dear Friday, when will you come?

On Thursday, September 28, 2000, however, former Israeli Prime Minister Ariel Sharon strode into the Al-Aqsa Mosque and the Second Intifada started. I never left Gaza. I have never dared to dream again.

In the front row, tears ran down the cheeks of a small Asian woman.

Eman, my closest friend, had never left Gaza either. That somehow made the disappointment easier to handle, since misery likes company. Then she became sick and needed to go to Jerusalem for treatment. After months of working to get the Ministry of Health to certify that she needed help, and after the papers were delayed by the Israeli government for some time, she finally went.

"We are not alive," she told me when she arrived. She said that the moment you pass through the Erez Crossing you know that you are in a totally different, more luxurious country, with different people and a different way of life. She prayed in the Al-Aqsa Mosque and toured the malls of Jerusalem.

"You see all kinds of people there, Japanese, Americans, Asian, Europeans and whatever else comes to your mind." She was like my eyes. I listened raptly to her, feeling as if I was there, yet I wasn't. Should I become sick so I can go there too? I thought.

Ramzy looked up and saw that tears had dripped down the cheeks of his Israeli guest. He took note, not really surprised, as he cried for their dead children. The room was stone quiet.

When Eman and I went on a trip inside Gaza a month later, we boarded the bus and she said, "Oh that reminds me of the bus station in Israel." When she was there, she had waited on a bench for the bus to come to take her. "It doesn't wait for anyone," she explained. "It stops near a bench for three minutes, then it moves; it respects people's time."

I nodded and said "Aha. But…I felt betrayed. Before, when it seemed as if everyone else had traveled and seen "not Gaza" places, she, like me, had not. She had been with me, but now she was with "them." And now I feel alone.

The room remained still. A clean-cut young man said, "It was worse for her that her friend went. How terrible. I bet in time she'll be glad at least her friend got to go."

"I think you're right," the redhead said and looked up at Ramzy. "What's her future?"

"She knows one day she will see Jerusalem. She doesn't yet know what the future holds for her—wife, teacher, mother, maybe a student in another country. She believes everything is possible."

"That's great, it's actually amazing. But fuck," the redhead said. "Twenty-five miles long, that's maybe not out of Los Angeles."

"More like to Long Beach," someone piped up.

"Okay," the redhead said. "But still. Fuck."

"I'd like to explain one term she used," Ramzy said. "*Intifada*. In Arabic it means tremor or shuddering, the way an animal shakes off water. It's the name for the Palestinian uprisings, as the people attempt to 'shake off' the occupation of the West Bank. There have been two intifadas thus far. The first, in 1987, was characterized by civil disobedience and general strikes. The Second Intifada of 2000 continued for five years. Many suicide bombings and very tough Israeli retaliation. Several thousand died, three-quarters of them Palestinians. As Enas indicated in her story, Prime Minister Sharon and some right-wing politicians, surrounded by hundreds of Israeli riot police, marched across the Temple Mount, though he did not actually enter the Al-Aqsa Mosque."

"How did the first one start?" someone asked.

"A military vehicle accidentally ran over several Palestinians in a refugee camp."

Later, after the last student had filed out, Eli approached and Ramzy said, "Walk with me to the botanical garden."

Eli nodded.

"It's quiet there. Nobody in the city seems to know it exists."

"Around here, likely their backyards are as nice," Eli said.

Ramzy laughed.

As they walked, Ramzy saw his interlocutor was equally on comfortable terms with silence. Eventually they came to a wide-open double chain-link gate. A similar fence surrounded the large gardens. A sign on the gate read: UCLA IS A TOBACCO FREE CAMPUS. What a luxury to be concerned with such matters, Ramzy thought.

"When I first left all the destruction in Syria, I could not bear beautiful places," Ramzy said. "Didn't feel it was right to surround myself with beauty." Ramzy put a cigarette in his mouth but did not light it and then let it hang quietly between two fingers. "Terrible cliché. Turns out, this kind of more wild natural beauty, say as differentiated from a perfect rose garden, soothes me in the way that writing stories once did. Shai said he was sending one of his best.

But then, all his people are the best, aren't they."

"He just thinks that because we're devoted to him."

Ramzy allowed a small smile to form. They headed down a narrow granite entranceway that immediately gave way to a dirt path with smooth, round stones forming a wall to the right as the path descended.

"Shai admits his mistakes. Certain people like to be around that. It inspires confidence in him."

"Doesn't mean he won't keep his best in the dark if it suits him."

This time Eli laughed. "Yes, there's that."

Tall pine trees with narrow trunks rose ahead of them. To their left, in a small open area with grass fighting for sun and life, a lone woman student sat meditating next to a vast tree that was mostly bark, gnarly low branches winding and spreading in all directions. In blue jeans and a gray T-shirt, she sat ramrod straight in the dirt just below a thick, twisted, horizontal branch. Eli felt a longing for more carefree times.

"Australian willow myrtle," Ramzy said.

The chirping of birds mixed with the sounds of heavy traffic on nearby Hilgard Avenue. They passed a male student in a niche on the stone wall, large headphones on, eating noodles out of a Styrofoam cup. Ramzy motioned to two outdoor oak chairs in a grove of broad and redolent Eucalyptus trees. Nobody was in earshot and they sat.

Eli said, "Khaled Fahmy. From the Al-Am'ari Camp. We found *Men In The Darkness* personally autographed by you there."

Ramzy nodded. His first effort had set the Palestinian streets aflame. "Different world when I wrote it, though for my people the same problems. I was young and angry. Saw the world from the refugee camp in Lebanon where my father took us. If I was young today, I'd be even angrier than I was then but I'm no longer young."

"I read 'The Land of Shriveled Oranges' on the plane. The young boy, you, it must have been terrible."

"My father believed everything he read in the Arab newspapers about Tel Aviv burning. I believed I'd soon be going home. It taught me to be cautious."

"Fahmy ran over two Israeli servicemen in DC last week. The authorities have left his name out of the papers."

"I read the accounts. Did not know it was Khaled. Not surprising. He's emotional. Your soldiers used his sister for target practice. So you're surprised he did this?"

"No, we should be stopping these kids without killing them. We're surprised how someone untrained disappears so thoroughly."

Ramzy looked at his cigarette, longing to smoke it. "How's Shai? I heard he'd lost that impressive stomach of his."

Eli smiled. "Lost and regained."

Ramzy tugged on the unlit cigarette. "Life often circles back. So what exactly can I do for you, about Khaled?"

"Shai's asking for one last favor for an old friend. Put an ear to the Palestinian ground. See if you hear his footsteps. The army blew up the parents' house. We've quietly moved them to an Arab village in the Galilee, gotten the father a job. They'll remain there whether you help or not. Blowing up houses is theater to make it look like we're taking action. Never deterred anyone."

"The opposite."

"Obviously."

Ramzy stood. "I'll leave you here. Tell Shai I'll see what I can find out." As he began to walk back up the dirt path, without turning back Ramzy said, "Tell him he now owes me." Eli watched him move up the incline, carefully it seemed. Eli had an urge to tail Ramzy, was not sure why. Eli wondered if he was drawn more to Ramzy the man or Ramzy the foe, the eons-ago retired intelligence agent, and was unwilling so soon to relinquish the chance to know more about him. He particularly wondered why Ramzy had stopped writing. At the very least, Eli would read the rest of the short stories he had.

Ramzy exited the Botanical Gardens across from the three-story, red-brick School of Dentistry. Beautiful perfect building, he thought. One of his strengths was his ability to compartmentalize, to shut off thoughts running at him from every direction. He had developed this facility as a child in the Lebanon camp, when all memories of the reality he had both left and now faced were unbearable, so he survived by taking long walks and living in his imagination. He thought about the novel he had finally begun several weeks ago, after all these arid years. He was a little scared that he could not do it, could not create characters and a voyage for them that said anything that transcended outrage and self-pity. He was hoping he had one last disciplined *cri de coeur* in him before he acquiesced into the hopelessness that his people would be occupied for as far as the youngest among them could see, and beyond.

He exited the campus past the new David Geffen School of Medicine. Westwood Village was quiet, too far for the students from North Campus, and besides, they had a Wolfgang Puck Express in the Student Union that served wine and beer and far better fare than the quick restaurants here. The smartest among them realized all this was a gift and not entitlement. He walked slowly and peacefully. Writing again buoyed him and he actually typed now into his small laptop, unable to remember every word that he formed elsewhere in his head like he once had, but his words thus far did not carry into a strength that remained with him. He knew once he crossed that barrier, when he began to believe what he was writing was worth doing, a well-being would lift the rest of his day. It was very much like being in love.

He passed the Geffen Playhouse across the street from campus, which displayed a large poster: ANDY GARCIA AND THE

CINESON ALL STARS. Classic Cuban jazz and mambo. Ramzy wondered what it was like to have so much money that you could spend part of your day, maybe every day, determining who to help and that you could fund even projects that were not the most dear to you. He could not imagine it.

Ramzy entered the Chick-fil-A at the edge of Westwood Boulevard and was immediately struck by the cold air conditioning mixing with the smell of deep frying grease. The two together, that the cheapest food would be served in a perfect temperature controlled environment, struck him as perfectly American, the façade paramount. The small, cheap tables were crowded, primarily with ethnic workers from the chain restaurants and coffee houses and miscellaneous small shops in the Village. He sensed a seething underbelly in America that eventually would explode after the experiment with the right exhausted itself in ineptitude. The Palestinians too would not remain indefinitely enchained. For a moment, Ramzy let his rage fill his body and then he shut it away in a box inside him. He ordered to carry away and then he made a call.

The seven-unit, two-story building around the corner on Weyburn Avenue housed short-term faculty. Each unit had its own entrance, and people coming and going were not much noticed. The building was like many areas of Los Angeles he'd observed—in his free time he rode the bus wherever it went—older Spanish-style architecture, red terracotta roof tiles, large terra cotta pots with brilliant yellow and green succulents lining the dozen steps to the front apartment. A strengthening fusion of cultures the Israelis could learn from. Ramzy proceeded into a wide driveway with seven perfectly painted olive-green garage doors, and at the back climbed the few steps to the other units. He stepped into a courtyard of magenta bougainvillea, birds of paradise with orange flowers and blue beaks, small succulents in a brown wood-chipped bed lined with bricks, a small pink table and two pink wood chairs. In his mind's eye, he saw the devastated Yarmouk Camp, overrun by ISIS and then the Syrians dropped shrapnel-filled barrel bombs killing more refugees than ISIS insurgents. At the moment, he was not truly certain which was more surreal, this or there?

Ramzy slipped his key into the lock, entered and set the already greasy bag onto the white kitchen table. He heard a rustling upstairs.

"I have the extra hot sauce this time," Ramzy called up. "My short-term memory is terrible." Often he went into a room and then could not remember what he'd intended to do there, or an hour after breakfast was unsure whether he'd taken his blood pressure pills after he ate. Though not frightened, it led to an urgency that the time to accomplish what he must was short.

Khaled Fahmy came down from one of the two upstairs bedrooms. "Thank you."

Ramzy began to unpack the food. "We're going to have to move you. It will take a little while to arrange. But there's unexpected very good news about your parents."

Outside, just around the corner, Eli sat parked in a white Toyota Camry watching the entrance to the faculty housing where Ramzy was staying. On his lap, he read one of the short stories from *Men in the Darkness*. He wondered again if he was more drawn to the personality or monitoring an actual threat. He had a small fear that he was slipping, unfocused, beset by too many questions, longings both personal and for the country. He tossed the Awwad volume into the back seat. If he didn't snap out of it, he could end up looking the wrong way, and maybe even when a bullet was headed at him.

CHAPTER 4

Meir Bardin looked out from the army vehicle carrying him the half-hour drive from his home to Hebron for his lecture to officers on the base there. He enjoyed and hated traveling to Hebron. He always had in mind that in the 1920s and 1930s Jews had been massacred in the Jewish quarter and that no Jews remained there after Jordan took the West Bank. Now, eight hundred settlers had moved into Old Hebron, surrounded by 200,000 Palestinians and ridiculously protected by an entire Israeli brigade. Jews had come back because of the Cave of the Patriarchs there, the burial place of Abraham, Isaac, and Jacob. After Meir had visited the cave inside a stone building that protected it, he had stood outside and watched the military checkpoint a few feet away at a side branch of the Hebron souq. All Palestinians who emerged had to go through a floor-to-ceiling metal turnstile to prevent anyone from running out, and then stop at the checkpoint.

White earbuds dangled into the iPhone in Meir's pocket and *La Boheme* sounded loudly in his head. At home, he conducted the air with his arms to a slew of operas. As they approached Hebron, Meir pulled the earbuds out and silenced the sounds. He wanted to absorb the Arab life as they entered the teaming city. In the car, the radio news announced that Prime Minister Gutman had boarded their new submarine in America for a celebratory deep-sea dive and had spoken to the press from the deck before descending into the submarine. Typical Gutman. Meir asked the driver to turn off the radio.

He saw the glimmering Kiryat Arba, eight thousand settlers on a series of peaks, looking down on the hills of Palestinian homes and minarets. They drove past the central square, the shops shut here for years by the Israeli military, so people had moved their wares onto tables on the sidewalks and streets causing traffic mania. Constant honking blared. Anger rose in Meir each time he saw this.

The soldiers lifted a long, wooden arm barrier and they passed into the settler enclave in the heart of the city. Israeli snipers stood in small, newly constructed, square rooftop rooms at various locales, each with a single door on one end and on the other an open area to fire from a wood wall that lifted on hinges. Just beyond the compound, past another sawhorse barrier, was a two-block long street, eerily quiet, every shop shuttered by metal grates. Soldiers with Uzis casually in their arms stood guard just past the sawhorse.

Meir said, "I thought the military commander said the Arabs could reopen these shops."

"They opened them," the army driver said. "Even put in a small market. The settlers came at night, armed, and told them to shut them or they'd come back and do the shutting for them."

Meir was furious. "Who the hell is in control here?"

The driver shrugged. Before them was a fenced-in Jewish full basketball court, its floor painted green, and beyond it a large three-story Yeshiva with immaculate limestone facades. Behind the Yeshiva, Arab houses completely covered a series of hills, the light-blue sky huge above them. They continued into the barrier-surrounded military base.

Inside the main classroom, some sixty people waited, mostly officers, but Meir saw a smattering of area settlers not in uniform. He recognized Mordecai Gilboa, leader of the Kiryat Arba Council. His parents lived in Rehavia in Jerusalem, and Gilboa had grown up in Bnei Akiva, the religious youth movement, with some of Meir's oldest. They had bumped into each other last year and had coffee. Gilboa had lost his only brother, with whom he was very close, on the Golan Heights in the 1973 Yom Kippur War. Meir felt Gilboa's loss like it was his own, but Meir also felt that maybe it had all horribly been necessary. The initial Egyptian and Syrian victories and the high Israeli death toll had returned pride to Egypt and allowed the Egyptians to sign the 1977 peace treaty that had held to this day.

Meir nodded to Gilboa. Before the conquest of the West Bank, their worldviews would not have been that different. Gilboa was a straight arrow, a warm and friendly man, and utterly honest, opposed to any kind of corruption. However, Gilboa's chief goal in life was to insure that not one inch of land was given up. His response to his brother's death was to have nine children.

At coffee Meir had asked him, "What about the Palestinians?"

Gilboa had answered matter-of-factly. "If God brought us back to the Land of Israel, it's because He decided to forgive his people for sinning," he said, referring to the sins of competition and infighting that resulted in the Romans destroying the Second Temple. "The Palestinians are His problem and He should solve it. Ask me personally, Jordan is the land of the Palestinians. And don't tell me about demography—God will solve that too. This is our land."

Meir completed this argument for him. Referencing the great eleventh-century Biblical commentator, he said, "Rashi asks, why does the Torah, a book of laws, begin with Creation? To tell us the world is God's and he can do with it what he likes."

"Exactly," Gilboa said. "You argue for a two-state solution, you undermine our historical claim to the land."

In the base classroom, Meir went to the podium. He was always comfortable lecturing and took pride that his highly organized presentations, with unplanned digressions, seemed extemporaneous.

"Hebron is very important to me," he said loudly. "It is central to the Jewish people. But since Hebron is always in my heart, I do not have to be here!"

There was some rustled disapproval from the settlers, while the officers remained silent.

"I have the dream of Hebron and I'll continue to have that dream, but fulfillment is not dependent on me moving here. I expect the Palestinians to continue to have a dream about Jaffa. I'm sovereign there but I don't expect the Palestinians to give up their dream."

He enjoyed making these remarks, and then he began his regular talk.

"Who are the Jews? What are they? Why are they so different? How can they all be one, and yet so different? We were never uniform about how to Jew, but until the Emancipation we were always uniform about what it meant to be a Jew. That does not exist today. And I'm bothered by the question: is it possible to be unified without being uniform? I have searched for a way to contend with that question. I'd like to share with you what I've developed..."

After the talk, amidst loud applause and even louder talking, an older, uniformed officer approached Meir at the podium. "You should run for prime minister," the soldier said. "You're what the country needs. Someone who remembers that we came here to do more than survive."

Meir smiled. He'd been approached before on this subject,

but long ago his wife had told him that if he did she'd leave him. She was an intensely private woman and could not bear all the scrutiny. He knew she meant it.

From the back of the hall, Mordecai Gilboa approached and then said, "Except for that Hebron part at the beginning, excellent. But you need to understand we're here to push back on bullies." He said calmly, "In Hebron, we're victims of a juggernaut of Jihadists."

As they headed outside together, Meir controlled himself at the lumping of an entire city into terrorists. When they reached the sawhorse, they stopped. Just beyond ran the street of shuttered shops and he looked at the folding metal grates, some blue, others yellow.

Meir turned to Gilboa. "Who the fuck do you think you are telling them to close their shops? There is military rule and the army said they can open them. If it was up to me, I'd get the army to kick the shit out all these settlers anytime you do this."

"You forget the Middle East is about respect and being strong."

"A bully is never strong. You're getting a hard-on from showing these shopkeepers that you have power over them. To hell with you. I live in Hebron as much as you do but I recognize there are people living here."

"Hebron is thriving," Gilboa countered. "Produces a third of the Palestinian economy in Judea and Samaria. We're only two percent of the population."

Inject two percent poison into your body and see what happens, he didn't say. Just then another man approached Meir. Almost his age, similar paunch, though without Meir's short black beard streaked with gray. He was not in uniform. Meir had seen him sitting off to the side near the exit and assumed he was a settler. Gilboa headed towards his pickup truck.

The man took Meir's arm. "May I walk with you for a

moment before you return to Jerusalem? I'm a friend of Eli's."

"Sure."

A solider lifted the horizontal pole barrier and they proceeded along the shuttered shops. Shai turned and headed into the Arab marketplace. Meir knew it was illegal for Jews to be here, but accompanied by a high-ranking officer he was interested in seeing this souq. He noticed that shops here, so close to the settlers' enclave, were shuttered too.

Shai said, "I've wanted to meet you for a long time. Have heard an absurd amount about you from many you've lectured to. And rather unfair to the rest of us struggling fathers to have a son who loves you so deeply."

Meir was a little surprised he spoke so openly about being Mossad, but Meir supposed he was senior enough to do what wanted. "My grandkids say my work and home life is the same, building family."

"Sounds like great work."

They came to the barrier between the Arab souq and the settlers' apartment buildings. A wide, spiked, iron wall closed off any passage to the dwellings, barbed wire wrapped chaotically around it from top to bottom. Plastic bags snagged on the barbs. A Palestinian had placed a colorful scarf around a low strand of the spiked wire. To block some of the blight or as a sign of peace, Meir wondered. On the settler side of the barrier the entire stone walkway, with two-story homes rising on each side, was covered with trash two feet high tossed down from the settlers windows at the Palestinians. On the souq side of the gate, a worn sofa sat against the walls, a faded painting of the Palestinian flag above it. Here, the Arabs had hung netting above the souq, in which a number of plastic and glass bottles were caught and prevented from crashing in the marketplace.

Meir had stopped and was staring at the trash. "Why the hell are you allowing the settlers to behave this way? They're not behaving like human beings."

"I've heard settlers justify this by saying they have to give back twice what they get."

They continued to walk.

"Nonsense. I learned two things about the Holocaust," Meir said. "First, what can happen to a people with no power. Power is vital. On the other hand, I learned what can happen when a people with no power gets power. As happened to the Germans. The Jews have to balance between the two—the struggle to have power and the fear you'll behave inhumanely with that power."

"You don't hear much about people afraid of having power," Shai said.

"They're throwing trash to dehumanize these Palestinians. That's the reason."

They walked.

Meir asked, "Did you want me to see this?"

"I thought I might get you away from the crowd and have you to myself, and it is the most interesting way to walk."

"I'm glad you did. I'm giving a talk tomorrow to an American youth group. Now I have the subject of the lecture. This speaks to young people in particular."

The souq began to come alive with open shops and locals. Ropes stretched horizontally across the facades and immaculately folded shawls and colorful hand-embroidered black cloth purses on plastic hangers hung from them.

Meir heard the sounds of their guards' boots nearing, loud on the gray flagstones. "The assassination of Rabin killed a dream," Meir said.

"Even I never expected it could happen here."

Meir considered Rabin's death one of the most effective assassinations of all time, as the peace process ended and the right wing rose. "I came here to follow a dream. We did some terrible things to create the state. Maybe the worst was marching out the entire Arab population of Lod. But we couldn't have a Jewish state with such a hostile mass in the middle of it. The greatness of the dream legitimizes it. I'd do it again but this, all this, because our forefathers are buried here, is about power not survival."

Shai could see Eli in him, and where Eli had fled from him to be quiet and bury his passions. The souq was teeming now, shops open on both sides, large tables in the suddenly broad lane filled with combs, household supplies, shoes. Shai loved and often walked these marketplaces, had brought the guards for Meir.

"You ever lose your sense of humor?" Shai asked.

"If you lose your sense of humor, what's the point of living?" Meir turned and looked back the way they'd come. "Though sometimes I get goddamn depressed. Then I really tell jokes."

Eli had switched cars at the rental agency and sat in a Mercedes SUV on Tiverton Avenue. He'd concluded after watching the cars in Westwood Village that the high-end van would be less conspicuous than the Camry. This was a limited stakeout, as they had nothing concrete on Awwad. Eli's thoughts turned to his wife. He had met Noa when some high school friends brought her to sleep out on the beach near the Crusader Fortress at Atlit. After the campfire died down, the religious kids stretched out their sleeping bags, but not right next to each other. He said to Noa, "When everybody's asleep, why don't you come in my bag." She had laughed. He didn't actually mean it, was showing off. Later, she had gotten out of her bag, and with most of the kids asleep, walked towards him. His heart raced. She bent and said, "I'll get you a rock from the fire to keep you warm." She did, and at that moment he knew he would marry her. Eli was shy with women and happy to have the anxiety of dating towards marriage finalized early, and Noa was beyond wonderful.

His thoughts turned to the prime minister, who had boarded

the submarine this morning without incident. Made sense. Their two boys had plenty of time to replace the injured. Coming here was a waste of time.

Eli had observed that sometimes Ramzy trekked the fifteen minutes to Bella Pita that served Middle Eastern dishes and sometimes to the nearer Chick-fil-A, but never ate there, choosing to carry the food home. Eli wondered if, as an outsider, Ramzy felt uncomfortable eating among the Americans, or if he preferred the solitary environs of the spacious faculty housing. Eli didn't know why, but he imagined Ramzy could be writing again. Shai had heard nothing thus far from Ramzy and had ordered Eli to spend a few days in surveillance. "Just as well, while you're already there," Shai had put it.

Eli watched as a blue Saab sedan driven by an American woman with blonde hair in a small ponytail, early forties, pulled into the faculty housing parking area at the front of the building.

Inside the apartment, Ramzy picked up the ringing burner cell phone, listened, and then hung up.

"She's outside."

Ramzy felt Khaled would create no undue attention. He was dressed in sweatpants, a button-down plaid shirt, and carried a sweatshirt over his arm. He had no luggage.

"How long will I be on the freighter?"

"A long time. You'll be busy, working as a cook."

"I'll have time to write at night."

Ramzy smiled. "When I can, I will come see you in Lebanon."

"After Sumaya was killed, I wanted to do something more than sit in America. I did not believe I ever would. Thank you for approaching me."

"Helping other people is mostly what life is. It's ultimately what marriage is too."

"I hope to find out. I was becoming too Western. Maybe

someone will find a bride for me in Beirut, someone from the camps."

"God willing."

"Can you tell me why all this?"

"Come, Anne is waiting. We have many American friends, often Christians, involved in NGOs."

Khaled did not seem to understand.

"Non-government organizations. They make no profit. They exist only to help."

As Ramzy headed to the front door, Khaled pulled on his sweatshirt and followed him into the courtyard. It was warm, with soft blue skies and higher, gray-white clouds. Khaled was too hot, stopped, and lifted off the sweatshirt.

Eli watched the Saab, memorized the license plate, mostly out of boredom. The woman was obviously waiting for someone, but there were six units in the back and Ramzy, he felt certain, did not have affairs. Eli had had an American woman from their consulate take a walk around.

Eli watched as Khaled Fahmy walked down the steps from the courtyard, strode across the driveway and got into the unlocked passenger door. Just like that. Eli's palms remained dry as he turned the ignition, and then a small smile raised his lips. Damn if this was not unexpected and fascinating. Ramzy Awwad was less retired than he appeared.

Eli drove behind at a discreet distance through Westwood Village. Many shops were empty, windows with FOR LEASE signs on them. The community, both in the heart of so much wealth and a short trek from the self-sufficient campus, seemed betwixt and between, and soulless.

South of the skyscrapers on Wilshire Boulevard, Farsi script crowned multiple restaurants and shops primarily owned by Persian Jews. The consulate was less than a mile west on Wilshire. Though he was confident he wouldn't lose the Saab, which was making no efforts to avoid a tail, Eli lifted his phone to marshal quick backup.

Except the phone rang in his hand. He recognized the number of the emergency line in New York. After two sentences, Eli's heartbeat pounded against his chest. He had forty minutes to catch a flight to Washington, DC. Jimmy Collins would try and hold it with some national security excuse if Eli was delayed. He was just about to dial for someone to follow the Saab when a black station wagon, a Volvo XC70 he saw too late, swerved from the lane to his left, smashed into the corner of his car and sent him spinning onto the right sidewalk. He braked gently, the airbag didn't deploy, and he stopped.

Both the Volvo and the Saab were gone.

Eli spun the wheel and bounced back onto the street. He took off down Westwood Boulevard, eyes peeled, and burst through a red light. He gave the man on the line the Saab plate. He could not oblige with the Volvo plate because it had been smeared over with mud. Eli drove with the sound of his left front tire scraping against the metal of the bent fender. He saw neither the Saab nor Volvo. Balancing the steering wheel with his left hand, he called Shai's private encrypted phone in Jerusalem and filled him in.

"You sure it was Fahmy?" Shai said.

"Of course."

"I'll phone Ramzy now," Shai said. "Goddamn him. What the hell's he up to?"

"You tell me, why don't you," Eli said.

An hour later, as Eli sat on the plane, and several minutes after the flight attendant had ordered phones off, Shai rang.

"He's gone," Shai said. "Cleared out. Cell left on the kitchen counter without the SIM card. May as well have been a greeting card left for me."

"What was it saying?" Eli asked.

"From Ramzy, probably 'I'm sorry.'"

As the flight attendant strode intently towards him, Eli said, "I'll call when I land," and turned off his phone. As he leaned back in the seat, his neck hurt from the impact.

He had been right to watch Ramzy. The submarine with Prime Minister Gutman aboard had not returned to port and was missing.

Mordecai Gilboa sat in their bedroom and looked at his wife, Tali. The younger four of their nine children were in various stages of awake before school. Tali was short, with thick, frizzy red hair covered by a scarf, from which wild hair protruded. Coming to Israel had both fulfilled a Zionist dream and liberated her from the American insecurity about her lack of traditional beauty. Instead, she sought to be good and believed she had been sent to this land to temper Mordecai's excesses. It was just possible it was true, and he adored her. Born Nancy in Brooklyn, she had taken the name Tali, derived from the word "dew," as she loved dew on the leaves in the early morning, her favorite time of day. Israel truly was a land where one could come and reinvent themselves. She was the principal of the Kiryat Arba elementary school, a position of honor here. With this job, she would have been looked down upon in her parents' Upper East Side circles.

Seated on the edge of the bed, his laptop open, Mordecai said, "Come look."

He showed her a video on a Palestinian Facebook page of a Palestinian in a keffiyeh headdress sharpening his knife, sparks flying, then a very jumpy montage of quick shots: Ariel Sharon next to a dead baby at the Sabra and Shatila refugee camps in Lebanon, Palestinian stone throwers, someone carrying a coffin at an Israeli funeral, Palestinians in prayer at the Temple Mount, Israeli soldiers running on the Temple Mount, Hassidic Jews being stabbed in the

Old City, Israelis carrying victims to an ambulance after a bombing, and on and on, no shot more than a few seconds and no sound.

"Most everything else on this page has been taken down," Mordecai said. "This one wasn't removed because there's no incitement. And it doesn't meet Facebook's definition of graphic violence."

"It seems graphic to me," she whispered.

He showed her another photo from the same website: a Palestinian, keffiyeh around his neck, grabbing an orthodox Jew from behind, knife raised to his throat. And another: a Palestinian in a green keffiyeh, cleaver raised, sitting on the chest of a bearded Israeli, a Star of David on his hat. The cleaver dripped blood, as did the Jew's neck.

"They're almost all with knives," Mordecai said angrily. "You think it's a coincidence? These videos incite these kids to stab us. And the Palestinian Authority makes payments to the families of anybody killed attacking us, far higher than their normal welfare payments."

"Please. It scares me," she said softly, stood and walked away from the iPad.

"When they roll burning tires, it takes all the humanity of our soldiers not to shoot to kill. I understand if sometimes they are so frightened they do. God forgives them. They are eighteen-year-old boys."

"But why do we have to outlaw the mosques using loudspeakers? It's calling them to prayer, Mordecai. Why a new law now, if it just makes them angrier? I'm really frightened for all the children after Hallel Ariel. Really frightened. I keep telling you."

Mordecai was enraged that a few months ago a seventeen-year-old Palestinian had entered thirteen-year-old Hallel Ariel's bedroom through a window a few blocks from here. While she was sleeping with her sisters, he stabbed her to death.

Mordecai crossed the room and held his wife. "Shush, darling. It won't happen again. We've tripled the perimeter night watch." He stroked her head. "The government has deemed the loudspeakers noise pollution."

She looked up at him, her eyes wet. From the minarets in the valley and lower hills below them, she heard the call to prayer five times a day. "I'm used to it. They've been doing it this way forever. Mordecai, I actually like the sound. They're beckoning people to come to God, the way I come to Him."

"Do they need loudspeakers? Let them call from the mosques with the human voice as they did in the time of Mohammad."

"These laws will just cause more attacks."

"Laws don't cause attacks. Settlements don't cause attacks. They've always hated us. When you're weak, you end up in the gas chambers."

Just then, Gideon, sixteen, and Rafi, two years younger, burst into their bedroom.

"I want to make pancakes," Rafi said. "Gideon says I always mess up."

"He does," Gideon said. "And he spills and I have to clean up."

Tali went to Rafi. "How about if Gideon teaches you and I supervise?"

"Yay," Rafi said.

"Okay," Gideon said, "but he has to listen."

"I will. Promise. I want to learn to do it good."

Shlomo Avni stood in his upstairs bedroom by the large plate glass windows and looked out at his swimming pool and beyond at the large houses of Herzliya Pituach. Winds whistled through the trees and ashes covered both the lawn and the rippling surface of the pool.

In the distance, he could see the black smoke of the over two hundred fires that were licking the dry forests, mostly in the north, but throughout the country for two days now. The weather was cold, even for November, but what was shocking was the humidity, plummeting to 7% from typically 60%, and the northern winds howled at forty kilometers an hour, four times normal gusts. There had not been a drop of rain all season. The nearby sea looked beautiful with wind-whipped whitecaps.

Shlomo listened to the radio through the house sound system. The Israeli police commissioner claimed that fifty percent of the fires had been set by terrorists. A rather broad term of late, Shlomo thought, that included eight-year-old stone throwers—Israeli helplessness run amok. Yona Yahav, the mayor of Haifa, the largest northern metropolis with whole neighborhoods burned to a crisp, reported there wasn't a single Arab town in the country that hadn't contacted him to offer help. One of the settler leaders from Alon Moreh said the fires were divine punishment for the government's plans to uproot settlements. Sixty thousand people had been evacuated from Haifa. Arab residents, who comprised ten percent of Haifa, were opening their homes to the evacuees and university students. Twelve people had been arrested so far, though in the last major fires of 2010, during similar weather, the announcer said after investigation most of the blazes had been attributed to Israeli negligence, particularly tossed cigarette butts.

Government officials were saying that every fire that was caused by arson, or incitement to arson, is terrorism and will be treated as such. Shlomo squeezed his eyes. The only known fact was that the country was desperate for rain. The reporter continued that the United States' Evergreen Supertanker, the world's largest firefighting plane, would arrive in twenty-eight hours. Eight additional countries had offered assistance. The Palestinian Authority too was sending their fire trucks to the Haifa front. The country was in need of rescue from these crazy special interests. Israel had twenty thousand full-time kosher food supervisors, but only twelve hundred fifty firefighters.

Six years ago, almost to the day, during the Carmel fires Gutman had leased the Boeing 747-400 flying tanker that was again headed their way. It had released tons of fire retardant before Gutman arrived for a photo op. The day's mission was completed. At a ridiculous expense, Gutman had the supertanker reloaded and its contents wasted in an unnecessary drop while he was photographed looking out at the scene, linking himself to generations of heroes who had protected this land. It was strange, Shlomo thought, that Gutman in America had thus far made no public comments on the fires—arson, incitement and alleged terrorism were his specialties.

Shlomo watched the wind bending the trees, listened to the howl, which he found comforting. It was a reminder to remain vigilant, that danger often came from the unexpected. It reminded him of the government's arrogance in 1973, when full of themselves, they dismissed intelligence reports that Syria and Egypt were preparing to attack—had the Arabs not learned their lesson six years earlier in the Six-Day War? And bringing up the reserves was costly. Cost was a consideration! The Arabs striking on Yom Kippur was an overly clever miscalculation, everybody in synagogue rather than scattered so mobilization swift. Still, twenty-six hundred of his boys had died. Politicians basked in the trap of past glory. Military men looked ahead.

The assault on the Palestinians for the fires was being led by Minister of Culture, Ayelet Stern, though Shlomo was hard-pressed to see where this fit in her portfolio. The women members of Gutman's innermost circle were particularly virulent: Stern, Miri Shaked, the Deputy Minister of Foreign Affairs, and Batya Berg, the Minister of Justice, who had called on Facebook for the destruction of the Palestinian people, "including its elderly and its women, its cities and its villages, its property and its infrastructure." How could these people lead them anywhere but over a cliff? It was as if women, so long subjugated, had stepped into politics with generations of pent-up rage. They were physically gorgeous women, and Shlomo suspected some or all had been made to suffer for it somewhere along the way. Now he listened to the voice of Defense Minister Avigdor Lieberman claiming that at least seventeen of the hundred and ten wildfires were the result of arson. "The best response is to expand settlements," he thundered.

Shlomo laughed out loud, wondering where he got his figures. Education Minister Naftali Bennett called the arsonists, who Shlomo noted had yet to be unearthed, fire terrorists whose only goal was to murder Jews. Shlomo wondered what fires the government ministers were actually fanning. He shut off the speaker.

For every incitement on social media calling on the Palestinians to attack Israel by fire, a thousand Palestinians, maybe ten thousand, had risen and risked themselves to help. In Haifa, people came home expecting a burnt-out house and found Arab workers from the West Bank, who they were employing, on the roofs with hoses. This generosity was true of all the peoples of this land and why Shlomo loved this place.

Shlomo calculated that six years after the devastating Carmel forest fires, failing to plan for its repetition or these even worse fires, or taking into account the dangers of climate change, the government turned to chasing scapegoats—sadly, painfully, infuriatingly and frightening, since Jews had so often been cast in that role. He had witnessed nothing like this growing up on kibbutz, where people abhorred blame and prized collective achievement. He did not believe this leadership bombast was what the majority of his people wanted. He wondered if Israel could go back and learn from its past, and who might lead them there.

CHAPTER 5

Tzipi Ben-Ami sat waiting on a bench in Central Park thinking about the past, as she often did during quiet moments, uncomfortably aware she lived too often there. She and Moshe had been best friends since fifth grade and lovers since her sixteenth birthday. He was the most sensitive, most intuitive human being she had ever known. By early 1982, the PLO under that scraggy terrorist of theirs, Yasser Arafat, continually snuck across the border to shoot up schools and buses, and fire missiles from Lebanon. On June 6, the date important to her, Israeli forces entered Lebanon to end this and drive the PLO from the country. At the time, emotional, Tzipi supported the invasion, which turned out to be folly. Seven hundred dead to force the PLO to flee to Tunisia—Israel's greatest military failure. The Iranians filled the vacuum in Southern Lebanon with their surrogates, the Shiite Hezbollah.

Then the wily Arafat hoodwinked everybody. In 1994, Arafat began flirting with the peace process. She had let herself hope, as much as she hated him politically and for her own loss, as Israel allowed him to move to Gaza and travel through the West Bank, and ultimately even to set up the headquarters of the Palestinian

Authority in Ramallah as its president and prime minister. This fighting had to end. A half-dozen years later, Prime Minister Barak offered Arafat seventy-four percent of the West Bank and Gaza for a Palestinian state, which would jump to ninety percent in twenty years. Arafat went to the Camp David Summit. She could see the photos of him with that wide grin when he should have humbly accepted the great gift they offered him. The Palestinians would have controlled the Temple Mount, all Islamic and Christian holy sites and three-quarters of the Old City, leaving us the Jewish Quarter. Arafat wanted everything, likely had always been a fraud. He told President Clinton that the Arab leader who would surrender Jerusalem was not yet born. Idiocy. She abhorred absolutism.

Then, this time, she went to thoughts she had avoided for a long while. On June 5, the day before they charged into Lebanon, Moshe was killed in a training exercise at the northern border. She could still feel that grief, which had entered her body as physical torment. For an entire year she was literally curved in sorrow and could not straighten her back. It was impossible for people outside of Israel to understand how, for all of Israel's existence, the killings of their soldiers and civilians was like a ceaseless scream in the night.

Cold, though the sky was clear, Tzipi tightened the red scarf around her neck. Living so long in the field, Tzipi was content to never have married or assembled the material possessions of upwardly mobile Tel Avivians she thought of as traps. Her longest love affair had actually been with the Syrian Ambassador to Paris and then to Great Britain, where she moved with him, him believing she was a Parisian painter. After university, she had spent several years painting seriously in Paris and selling a lot of her work, until Shai showed up there and recruited her, saying they could use her facility with languages. She had said, "Not my legs?" He responded that he could be persuaded to find use for them too.

She had actually loved the Syrian and his highly physical lovemaking on any almost flat surface, indoors or out, and while she was photographing the contents of briefcases, recording phone conversations, and absorbing conversation at embassy parties, she felt most wives ultimately betray their husbands in deed or word; this way she was free from guilt about it. Fiercely loyal, she slept with no other men during those years. In the years following Moshe's death, she bedded a lot of men and indulged in a sexfest— ten different men on consecutive Paris nights, the last a Russian whose large handprints on her thighs were visible for a week and about which her new, older lover who had cheated on all his wives said, "Oh." She loathed Russians everywhere, and especially in the bedroom, but at the end of a binge thought, what the hell. Or maybe she knew being with him would finish the run, which had been great fun but which could soon go the other way. Virtually nobody other than Shai knew that when not on a mission, either in the espionage game, painting or playing jeu de boules, she slept all night and day for days, sometimes waking in the morning and then shutting her eyes and disappearing for another eight hours.

She saw the two men she was waiting for approach.

As Eli Bardin walked with James Collins beside him, he saw her on the bench wearing the identifying red scarf and long black coat. As he strode faster, he tried to forge the link between Awwad, Fahmy, the attack on their two submariners and the prime minister's disappearance, which thus far wisely they had kept from the press. It was impossible that Fahmy had simply run the sailors down and gone to his mentor for help without there being something larger there. Frustrated with himself, he felt in his lack of focus he had missed something but could not see what he had.

He approached Tzipi, excited to finally meet her. Over the years, Shai had shared some of her exploits. While living with the Syrian Ambassador in London, she had recruited East End Jewish cab drivers to queue at Arab Embassies. Eli was amused Shai had thought of this. The large black cabs had their luggage space in the front and the drivers rifled the briefcases as they steered with one hand.

"I'm Eli," he said in English. "This is James Collins."

"*Enchante*," she said without rising.

"Shai asked that you be briefed since you were already in New York and are in the cabinet."

"Shai has no use for cabinet ministers." She patted the bench, which was wide enough for both men. "I've been out for more than forever."

"A clear head then," Collins said with a smile.

"Horseshit. So until you get to what you really want, how much goddamn trouble are we in?" Tzipi asked.

"Up to our necks," Eli said. "And rising. To begin with, the test ride with Gutman aboard went perfectly."

"Other than the submarine forgot to come back to port," Collins chimed in. "And the communication's off."

Tzipi asked, "An explosion, pieces floating to the surface? Nuclear radiation? Any signs he's dead? I can hope, right?"

Eli believed she was joking.

"All this quiet *has* to be foul play," Collins said.

"Nobody taking responsibility. No chatter on social media. Right now the circle of those who know is tight."

For a moment, Tzipi wondered if she really wanted him found or not. Maybe better if he wasn't. Then she caught hold of herself; he had to be rescued. "It won't take long to widen," she said, waiting for what they wanted.

Eli said, "Until we have more to work with, we're putting out a press release that Gutman and Hannah are escaping somewhere for a holiday. I thought you might convince her."

That was it. "She'll make a lot of noise but I'll make her do it.

I'll talk to her as soon as I leave here. We're in the same hotel. But you know that."

Eli said nothing to the obvious.

"Unfortunately it's a stealth sub and they're running silent, so at the moment we have no idea where they are," Collins said. "Traditional sonar dropped in the water from helicopters won't work. So we're a victim here of our own technological brilliance."

"The crew?"

"Fifty-one," Eli said. "Mostly our people, a handful of theirs."

Tzipi looked at Collins with a wry smile. "Your people behind it? From your perch, he's been the major obstacle to peace for millennia."

"Sure we could be," Collins said. "We topple governments all the time, or used to. I think we're coming around, not to any moral sense but to a practical one. Never works. But if we were getting rid of him, it would be decided on floors high above my pay grade. I'm charged with helping you folks find him. Then up to you what you do with him. I gather he's not much liked in a whole lot of places, including intelligence quarters here, who don't take kindly to his interfering with our Iran nuclear deal."

"*Il es tres charmant,* which has its uses and accounts for a lot of his success. I'm just not afraid of him because I don't give a fuck how high I climb or how low I fall."

Tzipi was thinking about Hannah, who watched Gutman like a hawk, which means in addition to not trusting him she likely didn't much love him. For a fleeting moment, Tzipi entertained the notion Hannah would not mind at all to have her son, already elevated in the Likud leadership, vault to its head on the emotional tide of terrorists killing his father. Then she silenced those meandering thoughts. Hannah was known for collecting bottles after government meetings, selling them back and pocketing the change. Waving a cape in front of a submarine and making it vanish was a much different effort. Of course, unless she had help.

Eli turned to her. "From your inside view, who might want him... let's start with unavailable."

"Almost half the country, led by all points left. Then there's everybody on the off the charts right who see him as too moderate. His lock on power is virtually absolute. So anyone in any crowd who wants to walk in his shoes..." She smiled. "I might have done it, if I'd thought of it."

"Then there's the moderate Palestinians," Collins interjected. "The Palestinian Authority and all their cheerleaders in the European Union."

"Highly risky for them, if there's any proof," Tzipi said. "You kill the prime minister the first reaction is a sledgehammer. The second is something much worse."

Eli said, "But they haven't killed him. That would have been far easier. Nobody's immune to a sniper despite the bathroom brigade. Even you unusually competent Americans, as your long list of assassinations shows." Eli was embarrassed that the accompaniment at the Sherry-Netherland Hotel had popped into a lot of newspapers. "Let's say the sub or its parts never turns up. Easy for those on the left to trumpet accident at sea. Showboating. Should never have been aboard in the first place out of a foreign port. Might even steal from the Right's playbook—act of God." Eli had an appreciation for how far believing in God drove men.

"What leads do you have that you've overlooking sharing?" Tzipi said.

Eli removed his heavy glasses, set them on his lap. His chest hurt from where he had slammed against the seat belt, but he massaged his eyebrows with one hand. "One or two, basically two sides of the same incident."

Eli trusted her and ran through the Khaled Fahmy-Ramzy Awwad connection.

"Of course it wasn't random," Tzipi said. "Who replaced the two submariners?"

"Our people from Haifa."

"Shai's looking into them." Tzipi was not asking a question.

Eli nodded then turned to Collins. "I wouldn't be surprised if there was someone on the inside. Either your people or mine."

"Yup."

Tzipi asked, "Where's Awwad?"

"We're going back to LA to try and find out," Eli said. "James is trying to track down the Volvo that hit me."

"What do I tell Hannah? How long do you wait to release news?"

Eli said, "I gather the appropriate higher-ups in Israel are being briefed as we speak. I don't know who makes the decision with him missing."

Tzipi stood. "I better get to Hannah before she opens her big mouth to the press. I'll get her moved and stay with her. I made a lot of mistakes by ignoring unlikely possibilities too quickly. Khaled may simply have hit the submariners because of his sister and then gone to Awwad to hide him. Nobody better to help him."

"Yes, it could have gone that way," Eli said, thinking about how the Talmudic rabbis always had parsed all sides of a question even if the answer first looked obvious. "However, I'm asking myself." He lifted his hands and shifted one higher, as if weight was pushing down on one side of a scale. "Palestinians are a talented people. Doctors, engineers, lots of PhDs. But even Ramzy Awwad could not have pulled this off on his own. So who helped him? One of the two replacement submariners was born in Moscow and came to Israel as a child with his family, the father formerly a very prominent translator for the Soviets."

"The Soviets would have a big hard-on to get their hands on an American stealth submarine," she said.

Eli nodded. "I'm considering that taking Gutman has nothing to do with this, that he's the misdirection."

"Wow." Tzipi almost smiled. "And Awwad gets him as a reward for arranging that misdirection for them."

"They may have made sure we were led to Fahmy. I'm considering the cop who fired at Fahmy was no accident. Shot out some windows, but no bullets hit the driver. His car crashes and we have Fahmy's fingerprints instead of his getting clean away."

"You question the cop?"

"Yup, I did," Collins said. "He's sticking to his story and we can't link him anywhere, not even to this particular bar."

They all stood. Eli turned to her. "I'm asking myself why the fuck Fahmy is still with Awwad when Shai's told him I'm coming."

Collins was silent, had literally never heard Eli swear before. Enjoyed it, but something about Eli's mood worried him. "Unlikely Ramzy would think you'd be watching him given that you went to him for help. Could have taken time to arrange where Fahmy was going."

"Glad this is your problem and not mine," Tzipi said. She hugged Eli. As Shai's boy, she considered him family.

Collins hurried in late to the ballroom at the Willard Hotel in Washington, DC. He'd never been here and marveled at the numerous chandeliers hung from the ballroom ceiling, where the guests sat at rows of long narrow tables with tall cushioned chairs. The walls were engraved wood. Though he loved the '60s and felt he had missed something great being born too late, this place wasn't bad at all, for a visit. Wouldn't want to live his life in these claustrophobic halls. He saw standing on the Saban Forum dais the Israeli American philanthropist Haim Saban, famous for the kids' show *Power Rangers*. Well, people made fortunes all kinds of ways, his father rather boringly in banking. Collins had googled the event on the hop down from New York. Beside Saban were Martin Indyk, former US Ambassador to Israel under Bill Clinton, and outgoing Secretary of State John F. Kerry. The Democrats had lost the election, and it seemed to Collins that Kerry had a month left in office to notch his mark on Middle East history. The subject of the forum was the future possibilities for peace in the Middle East.

Saban was reading from notecards, his native language Arabic, born a Jew in Egypt, so he was clutching the cards for dear life as he stood near a small table with the large silver plaque Kerry was to receive.

Saban finished, "...for his unflagging pursuit of peace based on a strong relationship between the United States and Israel, with deep appreciation, Cheryl and Haim Saban and the Brookings Institution want to say thank you."

Secretary Kerry said, "Thank you, my friend."

As applause rose, Collins sat at an end seat that had been waiting for him next to CIA Assistant Director of Operations Paul McEnnerney.

Indyk then introduced journalist Jeffrey Goldberg from *The Atlantic*, and he and Kerry sat in two chairs.

Goldberg opened his notes and began. "Is it too late for the two-state solution?"

Collins tried some of the coffee in a cup before him, and though cold, he drank it anyway and thought, nothing like getting right to Graham Green's heart of the matter.

Kerry began in the diplomat's thanking of all present. Collings moved the cup back and forth on the white tablecloth. He hated decorum. Part of why he loved the '60s—just say it like it is, man.

Kerry spoke extemporaneously about how the solution need not be as perplexing as people thought. He praised the beautiful thing called the State of Israel, a place where the Jewish people had their identity that was defined by their history. He likened it to the movie, *The Greatest Story Ever Told*, but emphasized that the story was not finished. The end had not yet been written. Kerry self-interrupted sentences mid-stream as new thoughts occurred to him. He spoke forthrightly that there was no status quo and the situation was deteriorating.

Collins wondered why McEnnerney had summoned him to hear Kerry, whether the point was the speech or something McEnnerney would impart afterwards. However, to his surprise, Collins was becoming caught up in Kerry's feelings. There was a love and sadness, a weariness, and frustration in his tone.

Kerry felt there was a real opportunity now to redefine the region and meet both Israel's security needs and the security requirements of her neighbors. He ran through his love for Israel and his record: had talked to Uri Gutman more than three hundred-seventy-five times in this term, had made over forty trips to Israel. He knew Uri back when he was—they had coffee in Cambridge at The Charles Hotel, when Gutman was at Harvard. They had dreamed together. He recalled how Uri had said that if they were both ever in a position of responsibility the two of them could really accomplish something important. Kerry had really looked forward to that.

Collins glanced at McEnnerney, in a casual, dark linen suit, trying to read his face. McE, as the people he was close to called him—and, unusual for a man of secrecy, or maybe because of it, he was close to everybody—gave nothing away in his expression. Collins could not read him, never could.

Kerry's voice toughened. The Obama Administration gave Israel twenty-three billion in military aide, more than half of what they gave the world went to Israel. They had just signed a new agreement for thirty-eight billion over the next decade. But Kerry who came as friend, was concerned about the long-term ability of

Israel to continue to exist as the state he believed the Israeli people wanted it to be. There was a fundamental choice in creating a solution based on two states.

McEnnerney turned to Collins and whispered, but his soft voice was like a roar. "Who benefits from this thirty-eight billion largesse? Us, of course. It comes right back in military contracts. Bit of a shell game. Not just the Israelis. We've sold the Saudis so much in exchange for oil they have enough arms to equip all the armies of Europe and have a good bit left over to more than bother their neighbors."

There was an increasing air of despondency about Kerry now, but not of defeat, like a fighter who was used to picking himself off the mat. He quoted the Right in Israel's belief that the settlements were not a barrier to peace. But in fact, they wanted the land, because they believed it belonged to them. They wanted to block the peace because they wanted all those places to belong to Israel. He then challenged with what this vision of one state between the Mediterranean and the Jordan River would be. Checkpoints everywhere? Roads that lead to island settlements? No vote for the Palestinians? This is not a choice that had been put to the Israeli people and it needed to be. Could the Arab Street come to accept this one state? He did not think so.

Kerry's voice rose again. He was convinced from endless meetings in the Arab world that they were ready to move to accommodate Israel's security needs. They had come around. The United Stated maintained its long standing position, two states drawn along the pre 1967 lines with land swaps..."

McEnnerney leaned to Collins. "They'll trade some uninhabited Jewish territory near the border to the Palies and draw the big, just across the border settlements over to the Jews."

McEnnerney motioned with his head that they should head out the back way. As they cleared the room, Kerry's calm voice reverberating behind them, Collins said, "I was moved by the young Kerry and young Gutman talking in Cambridge. They dreamed a big *what if* and amazingly here they are. Had the sense Gutman meant it then."

"Agree. Something happened to him along the way. Kerry almost can't believe it did. Kind of thing I actually expect. Who holds on to youthful idealism? People are more interested in holding on to their house, if not building another story."

"Nobody knows yet that Gutman's missing?"

"I'd say the jig will be up tonight. Some of the Israeli *machers* put out a story that Gutman decided to sail up to New York and dock there in about two hours, to a big media splash."

"And nobody doubted it was true?"

McEnnerney's lips curved into a small smile. "Nobody." McEnnerney pulled a cigar from his coat pocket. He unwrapped it but made no move to light it. Instead savored the taste in his mouth. "I'm about two puffs from lung cancer." He laughed. "It's empowering knowing I can choose when to start up again and leave this sorry little planet. The Palestinians could use Gutman as a bargaining chip."

"If we were helping them would you tell me?"

McEnnerney was genuinely enjoying the taste of the cigar. "Why would I do that?"

"Help them or tell me?"

"Either."

Collins was enjoying himself—the puzzle, the joust with the senior officer who seemed in no danger of falling off his steed no matter how hard he was struck. "It's astounding that Gutman takes the money and then thumbs his nose at us."

McEnnerney laughed. "That's Kerry's mess. We don't give a damn about that. We need their intel, especially on Iran and Russia in their backyard. They're ridiculously adept about both. And we're

very fond of their modifications to our little toys, love having that."
McEnnerney glared at the cigar as if it were an adversary. "You have
a match, young James?"

"No."

"Pity. I'm about ready to light up and blow myself to
kingdom come before the incompetents in this next administration
do it for us. Don't have one of those little lighters all the pot
imbibers carry?"

"Sorry, no. I merely sing like a hippie."

McEnnerney laughed. "Don't believe it for a moment." He
tossed the cigar in a trash receptacle outside the hotel. "Then let's
call it fate and I'll stick around for a bit to see exactly what these
true believers do to us. I suppose from an advanced age, one can
look at it as entertainment."

Collins pulled out his phone and checked the time. "I should
have left already."

"I could hold the plane for you. Still think I'm able to do that
kind of magic. And by the by, Ramzy Awwad was back in Syria not
too awfully long ago. Now that he's somehow linked to this, the
computers hummed through the tapes. Picked up an intercept of
him meeting with Al-Nusra near the Turkish border. Apparently was
in Europe and went in by land through Turkey."

Al-Nusra, the al-Qaeda affiliate in Syria, held the northwest
of the country. They were the fiercest of the fierce.

"He detour south to see the Russians? Or they come up from
Latakia to join the festivities?" The Russians' Khmeimim air base
was south of Latakia, on the Syrian coast.

"No idea. Something I wouldn't at all mind knowing."

"Any indication why al-Nusra? Beyond the obvious that
they'd love to have Gutman's head in a canvas bag, quite literally."

"The why, young James, is for you and your Israeli heroes to
unearth for us. As for Kerry, brought you down as a schoolmarm to

impart a lesson. As grizzled, cynical and bigmouthed as we can be in the upper echelons of our work, we consider hope one of the sacraments. As a reminder, even in the roughest patches, never to abandon it, John Kerry is a gift from the gods."

CHAPTER 6

Shai sat at his desk in the offices near the Knesset building in Jerusalem, looked up as the young recruit, Arik Navon, across from him, fidgeted with a pile of printouts. Shai felt Arik was too eager for field assignment and wanted him in research, hoping that he might wear down his sharp impatience just enough so that he would not get mowed down in the first dark passageway he rushed through. Shai liked the tall, handsome Israeli, with his curly dark hair, irrepressible smile, and overall quickness of mind and body.

"So, of the two submariner replacements," Arik said, "one is somewhat of a malcontent, and the other the best of the best. As we discussed, the latter, our Russian, came here at nine years old with his parents from Moscow during the big wave of immigration in the '90s. Which one do you want to hear the details about first?"

"Which one do you want to tell me about?"

"Is this a test?"

"What isn't?" Shai said.

"Good. I'd focus first on the Boy Scout. He might not want to stand out. Could be cover."

"In this country behaving makes you stand out."

Arik went a little pale. "Yohanan Orlov," he said quickly. "Spent a lot of his childhood in Vnukovo in the Moscow countryside, family dacha. Father's older, seventy-three. Lives alone in Tel Aviv, wife died earlier this year, dementia. So the father might not have a lot to lose. Wife had spent some time in the Gulag and it came back to her when her mind unraveled. She was ravenous all the time, talked about Siberia without food. Gained fifty pounds in a year. She choked on the last large bite of a tuna sandwich before the caregiver could stop her wolfing it down. The family lived in some luxury under the Soviets, as I indicated."

Shai sat up in his chair, intent now, and gave a small nod that Arik should continue.

"The grandfather was a well-known author, one of the founders of the Soviet Writers Union, killed at Stalingrad in early 1943. Yohanan's father, Mikhail, began taking courses in naval engineering but switched to this elite school that Stalin personally started."

Shai noticed Arik was reciting from memory.

"The Referent Faculty of the Moscow Institute of Foreign Languages, created to produce real experts in foreign languages and culture. He had an extraordinary talent for English and became the top translator in the Soviet Union from Russian *into* English."

"The point being that linguists always translate from their learned language into their mother tongue, where they have greater facility."

Arik smiled. "He translated Dostoevsky and Alexander Herzen into English, books and papers on philosophy, hard science in maybe sixty fields. They gave him a country house in Vnukovo, where Andrei Gromyko and several Politburo members had second homes. Then and now he has a penchant for eating fresh raspberries on a bed of crushed ice."

"Yet he came here instead of London or New York. He much

of a Jew?"

"About the same as most Tel Avivians."

"So nothing. What's he doing now?"

"Mostly he plays chess on the beach. He still writes magazine articles and blog posts warning of the weakness of the West in the face of the stronger totalitarianism in China. He has some insistent thoughts on the Chinese using nanotechnology to develop weapons and wants Israeli high tech to work on a defense."

"I'm guessing he has only theoretical evidence and hasn't generated much support."

"About none."

"Resentful?"

"Of course. He believes. There's one other thing. Did some digging on Ramzy Awwad. He was in Moscow for a week in 2015. Special screening of the old Arabic-language version of *Men in the Darkness* at the 37th Moscow International Film Festival. Roughly translated under the title *The Victims*."

"Didn't know that. Good opportunity to see old friends or make some new ones. How long was Ramzy there?"

"No way of knowing. Festival runs for a week."

Shai leaned his large body back in the chair, which squealed in protest. "You look a little pale. Maybe some beach air would be beneficial. Tail the father for a while. I'll arrange something for our other family. Chance for you to get out in the field." Shai smiled.

"That'd be great!" Arik said. "Anything to get out of here." Then he checked himself. "I know I have a lot to learn, a lot. But..."

"Go." With a paw, Shai waved him out the door.

When he was gone, Shai smiled at the boy's eagerness, thinking Eli had been like that in the beginning.

Collins walked into Ford's Filling Station, a gastropub in the Delta Terminal at LAX, where Eli was already waiting for him, having flown directly from New York. Collins knew it was owned by Ben Ford, actor Harrison Ford's son, whose mother had been a cook and illustrator. Ben had grown up in the 1970s Hollywood Hills, full of hippies and artists. Collins completely envied that upbringing, though his father being so famous would have been a pain, people stopping them all the time. After his long-standing restaurant in Culver City failed, Ben Ford was bringing high-end fare to those trapped in the continually refurbished but still somehow dilapidated airport. Collins liked turning messes in opportunities.

Collins sat and asked, "You faced with a lot of sleepers among the Russian immigrants?"

Eli had thought about this often. Since the 1970s, a million Russian Jews had come to their shores, an awful lot of people to worry about. "Early on the KGB recruited hundreds of them to spy once there in exchange for granting their families exit visas. Most refused after they arrived but a small number rose through military ranks, run by case officers in Russian Orthodox churches. Russian Foreign Intelligence liked to seed the field with agents who remained inactive while they groomed their children."

Eli was eating the Simple Green Salad with comte cheese. He tried to avoid meat to keep kosher when he could. Collins looked at the menu, was going to have the Ford's Bacon Burger, but decided what the hell, he may as well go chichi given he was here, waved a waitress over and ordered the Duck Carnitas with green chili salsa.

"What do you have on the Saab?" Eli asked.

"Anne Thompson, her own car. Active in Gaza fundraising for an organization called Make the Circus Real. Since there are no movie theaters, skating rinks, fucking *nothing* in Gaza, some older kids started a circus. The past five years they've been putting on shows in schools, hospitals, for the elderly, but they have no regular place to practice, costumes or whatever circus equipment is. She fundraises. Her Facebook page is full of posts like 'One More

Manifestation of Big Brother,' 'The Fascist Israelis.' The regular."

"It's hard to express outrage and helplessness together. It's a very difficult feeling, so people yell. Fabulous they created a circus."

"A Belgian circus visited five years ago, offered the kids some classes after their shows, and there you go."

"Not worth following her," Eli said. "With Ramzy, and her own car, this would be a one-off."

"Yup," Collins said as his Duck Carnitas came. "Use someone we could easily trace because the trace goes nowhere. Public person actually doing good work, and when asked can drive someone to the airport, or to Canada, no questions asked." Collins took one bite of the carnitas and frowned. "Should have gone with the burger. I actually hate this stuff, don't know why I ordered it."

"You seem pretty good at not caring what others think. Maybe you're trying to impress yourself?"

"Maybe." Collins laughed. "Thanks. I'll keep that in mind."

Less than an hour later, with Collins behind the wheel, they pulled into the parking lot of Rancho Park on Pico Boulevard and Eli looked at 20th Century Fox Studios across the street, which seemed commonplace here. It had rained the night before, washing the Los Angeles sky; billowy white clouds sat still in clear, light-blue skies. The parking lot was near empty and the vast park quiet. However, standing at the backstop Eli saw the tall, bald Yuri Alexandrovich Popov wearing an Armani suit and gleaming loafers Eli assumed were not usually dampened by park grass.

Collins had called in a favor from a member of the Russian Embassy in Washington, a balalaika enthusiast with whom Collins played duets in a small Georgetown club in the spirit of détente—a back channel to higher-ups. Collins had indicated that most nights were spent downing copious quantities of vodka that had little to do with détente.

As they reached him, Collins said, "Thanks for meeting us so quickly."

The Russian released a wide grin that Collins suspected was reserved for such almost friendly encounters. "Cultural attaché in a city of so little history or culture." He shrugged and let his smile collapse. "I have much free time."

Eli said, "You'd be very busy in Jerusalem."

The Russian's smile returned. "I wouldn't mind to see the churches. My mother is a solemn believer. Photographs of me in them would make her happy and I like to make her happy."

Collins said, "Two days ago, my friend here was driving. Westwood Boulevard. A Volvo happened to knock his car onto the sidewalk. Somehow forgot to stop and exchange information. XC70, new or thereabouts. License plate number unavailable. Covered with mud. Odd, given how clean the rest of the car was."

"Was it black?"

Eli nodded.

"Right front fender smashed?"

"You hit me?" Eli asked.

"Ah, if it were so simple, I might even say so." The Russian lifted both hands, palms up, in a signal of friendship, faux or not. "Just that morning it was stolen. I made the police report myself. They found it the following afternoon parked with an array of citations. Belongs to the consul himself." He looked at Eli. "Fortunately, it appears you were not hurt."

"Only my pride that I didn't see it coming," Eli said. "Do you know Ramzy Awwad?"

"No, in what capacity might we have been acquainted?"

"His books. He was teaching a course at UCLA on the Palestinian novel and short story."

"I'm not acquainted with any Palestinian writers," Popov said. "Can you point me to something I might read where I could enjoy without much knowledge of the subject? Americans cannot read Bulgakov, don't have the context. *Master and Margarita* is a dark cave for them. All Russians love this book and feel Stalin's Russia, no matter when they were born. Context is everything, don't you think?"

"I actually think truth is truth." The Volvo had not been stolen but the Russians had reported a theft. Popov was in on this up to his bald head and Eli felt the rush of the chase. *"Men in the Darkness.* Palestinian themes are straightforward, as is their suffering."

"I shall have a look at it. We Russians bury pain deep in our hearts and sometimes act on it much later. Maybe it is the same with the Palestinians?"

"Actually, that's everybody I ever met," Collins said.

Popov smiled. "Anything else I can help you with?"

"Not right now," Collins said.

"Good. Then I will take my leave."

After a round of shaking hands, Eli watched him walk with a confident, unhurried stride.

"So," Collins said. "He's hardly hiding that he's lying."

Eli tugged on his chin. "So maybe we have the Russians and Awwad working together to run over some submariners in Virginia, which then leads to the kidnapping or killing of the Israeli Prime Minister and a missing submarine everybody, especially our Russian friends, would like to get their hands on."

"We're missing some pieces," Collins said.

"Oh, I think we have the pieces, just not the picture after they fit together. Awwad's gone. I'm going to London to see an old friend, have an idea how I can find him."

Fear hard in his throat and damp under his arms, Meir drove fast towards Sderot. The news was everywhere that the submarine carrying the Prime Minister had disappeared, but he couldn't even think about that now. Gaza was celebrating and Hamas lit the sky with Qassam rockets aimed at Sderot. In bad periods several of the errant homemade projectiles screamed towards Sderot a day. Meir had been there when the sirens rhythmically repeated *Tseva Adom* (Red Color), but with Gaza so near people only had fifteen seconds to reach one of the shelters. It pained Meir that a great deal of the people, especially children, suffered from PTSD, anxiety and sleeplessness. As he neared the city, Meir unlatched his seat belt. Seat belt use was forbidden in Sderot, the seconds lost too valuable if sirens sounded.

Israeli fighter jets streaked overhead breaking the sound barrier. Meir looked through his windscreen at the white trails in the sky. Our children suffered and now their children will. Full of fear, he could not grapple with anything beyond worry about Yigal, who had been grievously hurt. If he died, Meir worried Eli would become unhinged.

Across from the hospital, Meir ran past a playground, the bomb shelters there two long, thick concrete caterpillars with yellow faces, blue eyes, an orange frown and orange antennas. The concrete noses were black, the bodies yellow and black with orange circles running down their sides. Smartly, each had an entrance near the huge head wide enough for several children to burst into simultaneously. Inside, the children would sit on benches built into the curved walls and read or color on the round interiors. Strength, Meir suddenly thought, had to be more than persevering.

Meir puffed hard as he ran into the hospital. He was almost alone among his friends in that he had lost no children or grandchildren to the conflict. Meir asked for his grandson's room and after a quick scan of the computer was given the number on the third floor. This was Israel; anybody wanting to see someone in a hospital was immediately helped.

He ran into Yigal's room panting and stopped so short he

slid. Bloodied gauze wrapped around his grandson's head and his eyes were shut. One leg was elevated in a sling-like contraption and covered with a plaster cast. Meir half gasped, half screamed and Yigal lifted his eyelids.

"I'm okay, Grandpa," he whispered.

Meir started to cry silently, made almost no sound as the tears of relief dripped down his cheeks and into his beard. "*Baruch Hashem*," Blessed be His name, he thanked God.

"I had headphones on. Soundtrack. Until I saw running. Didn't hear."

Meir sat on the edge of the bed and gently kissed his cheek. "How are you, really?"

"My head is so terrible I can't even feel my leg."

"Your leg looks bloody awful. Once your head heals a bit you'll really know it." Meir pulled a chair over from the wall and sat against the bed.

"Grandpa, before the... I read about Gutman. Missing. Really?" He grimaced from the pain. His eyes looked to a plastic cup with a straw on the tray to his side.

Meir was up, grabbed it with both hands to steady himself, and lifted it to Yigal's mouth. As he sipped, Meir explained the news. Yigal leaned back and Meir set the cup on the tray.

"Is he... dead?"

"I don't know. So many things that happen seem like they could not and then they do."

Yigal closed his eyes again, the pain running through his skull like waves pounding a seawall. He spoke without opening them. "Where's Dad?"

"I don't know. Maybe on this."

His eyes remained closed. "Don't tell him."

"Okay. You want me to call your mother now?"

"No."

"I'll talk to her from the car when I leave."

Yigal nodded but the motion stabbed pain through his head. He did not move but his eyelids opened. "My friends. Find out. Who's hurt?"

"I'll ask and come back."

Yigal shut his eyes again. A snore parted his lips.

Outside, Meir watched more jets streak overhead and the explosions in nearby Gaza felt like they were inside Sderot they were so loud. Dark smoke rose in separate plumes, then slowly joined. Meir felt a small amount of guilt that he had always been in an education unit and never fought, but he was useless in any battle where he could not use his mouth. Meir trudged for the film school, his steps heavy. *Mowing the grass*, Israel too casually called the periodic ground invasions into Gaza to cut down Hamas. What a toll, all this fighting. He felt as a personal loss the recent wave of Israelis emigrating to Berlin: artists, writers, directors, technology entrepreneurs. A left-leaning intelligentsia of over twenty thousand fleeing the politics, the high cost of apartments and the occupation for bohemian freedom. Jews were going back to Germany because Israel failed them.

He approached the circular grass quad before the white concrete Academy Building of Sapir College, surrounded by transplanted palm trees, the defiant students already back on the grass, though more talking than studying. He looked out at the dozen reinforced concrete buildings, lush trees and greenery everywhere, the desert in the near distance. Turning the sands into a center of learning—this was why they came here. Now that he knew Yigal would be fine, he allowed the thoughts that had been pushed down by the worry to slowly rise.

Every effort and more needed to be expended to find the prime minister. The disappearance was an assault against the nation. However, if by chance Gutman was not found, a crowded field would rush in to fill the opportunity. Without Gutman, he would have a real chance if he ran. He wondered if the grandchildren en masse, all fifteen of them, could win his wife over to the idea.

Arik Navon had to slow his pace to follow the old Russian as he walked from his apartment on Zamenhof Street towards the Mediterranean. It was a half-dozen blocks to the sea and Arik saw that despite his years, Mikhail Sergeiovich Orlov had the strong stride of someone accustomed to movement, probably both mental and physical from what Arik had gleaned from Orlov's writings. Arik was concerned about longevity and read articles on the benefits to brain health of physical exercise; one could never start too young. He rolled up his long sleeves, the weather nice and warm for winter now that the winds had disappeared, with none of the humidity of a Tel Aviv summer.

Past some great artistic graffiti on the side of a small apartment block, Arik crossed the street to appear less conspicuous, but the old man probably made this walk daily. He moved neither with concern nor curiosity. They reached Dizengoff Square, a wheel spoke of streets heading into it. The traffic crossed beneath a plaza with the Agam kinetic fountain, big, stacked wheels of colored geometric shapes that produced different images every few steps around it. Arik liked to sit here and read, as at random times it shot both water and fire into the air.

At the seaside strand, Orlov moved deliberately toward the chess tables. Arik decided to get a protein shake. He knew Orlov would stay put for a good while. Arik literally breathed easier in Tel Aviv, which like a rocket easing free of gravity, had separated itself from Jerusalem's repressive religiosity. He felt more carefree the second he arrived here. By the late 1990s, drugs had come to the seaside. Not hashish, which had been around forever, but LSD and MDMA, the joy through chemistry dance club drug ecstasy—"Molly" the Brits called it, the Americans, "Mandy." On ecstasy, you went through your normal day but happier, everything heightened; when making love you felt every touch. His friends made fun of him but he was a wide tent guy about love. When he fell in love with a girl he'd seen on the bus for twenty minutes that was true love because the feeling was pure. Love was simpler than the poets cried, and Arik wanted to be in love as much as possible. He was thinking about moving back to Tel Aviv, rising early and driving to Jerusalem for work.

Protein drink in hand, he enjoyed the sun from his perch on a wall overlooking the chess match, long legs dangling. Both old and new hotels lined the edge of the wide sand beach. Arik thought about how Tel Aviv had become a world center of House music. From Paris to London to New York, they talked about the underground club scene here. They were no longer some provincial outpost. His generation of Israelis, unchained from the terror of war against an Arab Army, demanded freedom from worrying, deserved happiness, and near worshipped fun. He pulsed with love of life.

After a while, Arik saw Orlov look at his wrist, stand and start to walk back in the direction of his home. Except after a block, instead of continuing straight he turned left on HaYarkon Street. Where was he going? There wasn't much up that way but beach. Maybe he was taking himself to a late lunch at Molly Bloom's, the Irish pub. Arik followed him. Orlov headed past Molly Bloom's, then past the busy Frishman Street, lined with ugly, old, brown stucco apartment buildings with shops on the lower levels, where he could continue to a million places, except he kept due north.

As Orlov passed Mapu Street, Arik's breathing quickened. It couldn't be. The first day tailing him. It made no sense. The last likely place for Orlov to stop past Mapu was the Patio Bar, with its great outdoor bar, tall stools, fantastic sandwiches and live piano player. But Orlov didn't stop.

"It just can't be," Arik said out loud. Beyond the Radisson Hotel, Orlov approached a new six-story stone building with a flag flying next to tall communications antennae on the roof, the flag a tricolor horizontal—white, blue, red. A tall metal fence surrounded the building and a portion slid left as a car entered. He watched Orlov checked his watch again, go to the intercom outside the Russian Embassy, buzz, and after a few minutes he walked in.

Arik quickly called Shai.

Shlomo Avni walked along the southern Jerusalem promenade wondering if one or more of the prime minister's opponents had engineered his disappearance. From these heights he looked down at the blinding white City of David and the hills and valley below filled with limestone buildings. The gold dome of the mosque glistened above the Old City walls, which looked toy-like from here.

It's a stunt, Shlomo said to himself, Gutman was up to something. He walked, thinking about all their boys who had died here in the wars defending this ridge. All of the marvel of Jerusalem lay open and vulnerable below. On the far horizon, the Hebrew University campus spread across the ridge, its tower jutting into the sky. Down to the right was the Mount of Olives, the ancient olive trees mostly gone, replaced by East Jerusalem apartments. A three-thousand-year-old cemetery, more than a hundred thousand Jewish graves, covered the lower slopes. Their ties to this land were old and deep.

As Shlomo came out to the car park, he saw young soldiers had descended from a bus at the curb and stood in two lines, about twenty of them with epaulettes of officers in training. Youth groups and soldiers were often brought here for the view and the important history. Near the promenade entrance, another thirty or so uniformed eighteen to twenty year olds with backpacks stood facing each other in two lines, M-16 rifles casually pointing down from shoulder straps.

A heavy white Mercedes truck with a big front cab and long, empty flatbed suddenly veered out of traffic and sped at the soldiers lined up at the bus, so fast nobody reacted. Shlomo ran towards the kids, watched in horror as the truck jumped the curb, rose like a whale from the sea, slammed back on the sidewalk and plowed through the line of people at the bus as if they were light mannequins. Cries rose near them but the young soldiers were frozen. Shlomo ran harder, could be an accident. The shocked young soldiers still didn't move.

Then the huge truck spun with the noise of tires scraping street, and in reverse raced back at the soldiers. More screams. The tour guide, not in uniform, ran around the side of the truck gripping his pistol. Young officers shouted for the cadets to take cover behind the low stone wall surrounding the parking area. Some sprawled flat behind it as others scattered into the thin trees. The tour guide fired calmly through the passenger window. Glass shattered and the heavy truck slowed but kept rolling towards the dead and injured on the ground. Recruits raced around to the front of the truck. Loud bullets peppered the windshield and the truck slowed further. Shlomo was terrified as it rolled towards those on the ground who could not move. Somehow it stopped just short of them.

Shlomo's heart pounded as he reached the bodies. He pulled off his jacket and pressed it against a bleeding boy's head. "It will be okay," he told the boy, who was shaking. Shlomo turned his head. At least four dead he saw, three of them girls, and more of than a dozen injured kids. The sound of sirens rose in the distance, growing louder. The pain inside Shlomo was so great he almost screamed out loud, but held the sound down. He did not want to frighten these kids further.

He held his jacket hard against the boy's head. Color began to come back into the bleeding soldier's face. The frightened boy whispered, "Thank you."

"The paramedics are here. You'll be okay." Men wearing orange vests ran towards them carrying stretchers.

"I have him," a medic said to Shlomo as he bent to the boy.

Shlomo rose, took a step back, looked at the blood in the dirt like streams from a hose, pooled in places, and his tears came freely. This was the deadliest attack in the last year of stabbings and vehicle rammings. The perpetrator would certainly be found to be from East Jerusalem, likely Shuafat or Jabal al-Mukabbir, as the truck had yellow license plates of the united Jerusalem and all Israeli and settler vehicles, rather than the green or white Palestinian West Bank plates. Soon the security services would enter his home, bring his parents, his many brothers and sisters into the Russian Compound police headquarters, confiscate their computers and cell phones, search for documents, links, conspiracy. They would withhold his body, the funerals became angry anti-Israel demonstrations, and then blow up the family home—all of which they had done umpteen times. Doing something created the illusion they were actually doing something, but they were powerless to prevent individual attacks when there was no cell to disrupt. Later they would allow a night burial attended by only immediate family members.

Two hours later Shlomo arrived home, and rather than punch the navigation to slide open the driveway gate in the wood fence that circled his property, he turned off the engine and sat. He pictured his childhood on the kibbutz, where everybody left their doors unlocked and ate in the communal dining room. He had been drawn to a career in the army, where he found the same camaraderie. He had an irrational desire to take an ax and chop down this stupid fence, there when he bought the property. His whole body started to shake and he gripped the steering wheel tight with both hands trying to stop it. He'd walked through far greater carnage on the battlefield, but something about mowing down defenseless recruits broke his heart. The country terribly called the conflict *hamatzav* (the situation), and in dumbing down the tragedy to such a manageable description became accustomed to it and lost the characteristic Israeli will to think big and resolve it. Well, he had not.

As Shlomo came through the front door Yael rushed at him. There was no visible blood on him, as he had thrown his jacket away and put on a soft sweatshirt he always kept in the trunk of his Audi as the winter weather changed quickly, especially on the climb to Jerusalem.

As she hugged her father, Yael, who had been crying, spoke hoarsely. "Three girls and a boy, dead daddy. *Dead.*"

"I heard it on the news in the car." He did not share that he was there, as it would frighten her.

"I looked at their Facebook profiles. I always do."

He brushed her long, thin, brown hair to the side and kissed her neck. "I know."

"I wasn't friends with any of them. But lots of my friends were. It always happens."

"It's a small country."

"I'm not afraid. I'll go anywhere. Nobody's going to stop me. But it hurts *so* much."

He allowed himself a small smile. "Don't tell Mom you'll go anywhere, just go."

Her tears turned into laughter. "Okay. Good."

"Want to go for a swim now?" He wanted to pound his tension out in the water.

She pulled her head back and looked at him. "With you? No. I have things to do, homework too." She headed towards the stairs and then turned abruptly, hair flying. "But if you want to come to the pool right before dinner, swimming would be fun."

He loved her messing with him. "Great."

"Don't be late." Then her face drooped and she ran up the stairs.

CHAPTER 7

Eli had gotten off the tube near the Thames, and needing to stretch his legs, walked through Hammersmith. He approached the entrance to the Mission of Palestine in the three-story, dirty brick building with the Palestine flag, green, white and black stripes with red triangle, jutting from a pole on the second floor. It would be great, no amazing, not to be a nation alone in the Middle East. These were the pan-Arab colors of the 1916 Arab Revolt against the Ottoman Empire. The Kingdom of Jordan added to the same flag a seven-pointed white star on the red triangle to symbolize the unity of the Arab people. Well, that was often more in word than deed. Israel was becoming a shrinking island. In his childhood, his father had taken them to shop in the West Bank, his friends' parents drank in Bethlehem bars, he had snorkeled in Dahab in the Sinai's unbelievably blue waters, his youth group often hiked in Wadi Qelt (a dry ravine except in the rainy season) along the stream that descended from Jerusalem to Jericho, lined with spectacular desert flowers. It was no longer safe to do any of that. Eli felt isolated and somewhat bereft in the field, in some parallel to the country's increasing isolation from the rest of the world, and with the occupation, from many young American Jews. There was a sense too that many of her supporters were not true friends of the Jews but championed Israel as part of their political agenda. Or maybe he just missed lying next to his wife and having neighbors stop over?

Inside, his old friend Dr. Ismail Hadawi, the Palestinian Ambassador to the UK, welcomed him with a warm smile and it heartened Eli to see his old Arabic language teacher. Hadawi was typical of many Palestinians—an MA in Foreign Relations from SUNY Binghamton, a PhD in Comparative Politics from New York University. He had lectured across the globe as a visiting Middle East scholar—Georgetown, the University at Reims, University College Dublin. For two decades, Hadawi had taught and been Dean of Students at Birzeit University near Ramallah, the largest Palestinian university in the West Bank. Eli had periodically had coffee with him before he left to become Head of Mission here.

"Tea or would you prefer coffee?" Hadawi asked as Eli dropped tiredly into the seat opposite his desk.

"Tea with *nana* would be perfect," Eli said, using Arabic for spearmint.

"You were of enormous help to us," Hadawi said. "Even if I was not in your debt, I would be happy to assist you."

Eli had spoken to the military commander during one of the biggest closures of Birzeit, the spearhead for protest against the occupation among the West Bank universities. The Israeli Army had often closed the university for days to months, usually for violent clashes when the army entered to make arrests. After this particular melee, the military placed most of the students and faculty under house or town arrest. Eli had not anticipated what set the students off, which often seemed the case dealing with people. They had rioted against Israel placing a civilian in charge of the West Bank, claiming it moved the occupation towards permanency. Eli had managed to get most of the faculty members released.

Hadawi picked up a phone and asked that tea be brought, then he turned to Eli. "I have the information you seek, but I will need certain assurances."

"I would expect no less," Eli said.

"If you want to talk to Ramzy Awwad, I can arrange such a meeting. But I will need your word that this is all that will transpire, a conversation."

"Of course."

A woman entered bearing a tray of tea with mint and butter biscuits, which she set on Dr. Hadawi's desk. She left soundlessly, her steps a graceful, slow gait.

"You don't look yourself," Hadawi said.

Eli had no desire to lie to this older man he respected. "I'm not. But I'm okay." He reached for a cup. "Tea will help."

"I doubt that."

Eli smiled.

"So what has happened to your prime minister? Not that I'm in mourning."

"Shall I tell you the truth?" Eli said.

"If you wish to."

"I'm surprised how little we know."

Hadawi did not react, despite the mythology knew the Israelis were mere humans and Eli had always said what he pleased. Hadawi lifted his glass of tea, drank slowly and then placed it down. "Your eldest is now in film school, I believe."

"He's just great."

"Artists, writers, filmmakers are usually ahead of the politicians in pointing the way."

Eli smiled. "He may want to go to Hollywood and make blockbusters."

"Then he will make important ones."

Eli sipped the sweet Arab tea and the mint flooded him with

a familiarity of home that boosted his spirits. "Ramzy?"

"With his wife. He has nothing to hide. I understand he helped a friend who came to him for assistance. As you once did for me. He's in Germany, at the Wurzburg camp for Syrian refugees. He is doing what he always does. Helping. You see, you two have much in common."

Arik drove Shai on the shortcut from Jerusalem to Tel Aviv, was glad Shai preferred the wide four-lane Route 443 that ran straight along the mountain crest without the tedious hairpin curves, drops and climbs, of the old road. As the highway headed into the West Bank, Arik glanced at the high concrete walls that rose now on both sides. To the left, a Jewish settlement spread over a hill. To the right stood the large, walled detention center for Palestinians. This was Israel, love it or leave it. For forever, the Palestinians had used this unimproved highway to reach Ramallah and other West Bank cities. They keep trying to kill us, so now they were allowed only on the stretch between Maccabim and the turnoff to the Israeli settlement Pisgat Ze'ev in East Jerusalem. Israeli military checkpoints stood at both ends, where you left the West Bank stretch and returned to Israel. Arik moved his eyes back and forth between everything in his view. There had been attacks here—one eighteen-year-old IDF soldier stabbed to death at a 443 petrol station, civilians hit with flaming bottles.

"You ever worry traveling this way?" Arik asked.

"Worry about what? Being shot or that we've closed off Palestinian access to the West Bank from here?"

"Shot, stabbed, firebombed, rammed."

"Ah, that. No. With the way I abuse myself, God must be watching over me. A little faster please." Shai never wore his seat belt.

Arik pushed the accelerator. "Sir, do you think the prime

minister is dead?"

Shai said nothing, his not answering legendary in the service. He heard the question, but his thoughts on more important matters he didn't bother to respond.

"Sir, what happens if he is?"

Shai turned to the young agent. "Let's see if we can find out exactly what happened and hope that's not what did. Make a call. I want to know exactly where Orlov is now."

Forty-five minutes later, Shai headed along the Tel Aviv strand with heavy steps, his breathing slightly labored from the walk. He noticed that Arik had slowed his gait to not surpass him, and then saw Orlov at a game. Orlov turned, looked at them standing near watching him, and returned to the board. Shai approached, saw this match was in the early stages. Orlov had aggressively opened with the Sicilian defense, taking control of the center and denying the opponent's black pawns e4 and d4.

"Mikhail Sergeiovich, may I trouble you to interrupt your game? My apologies, especially with this masterful start. White to ie4?"

Orlov smiled with a grin wide enough to expose one gold tooth on the right side. "Apparatchiki are the same everywhere. I enjoy the game of that talk too." He made his apologies to his opponent and stood.

Shai was impressed at Orlov's opening with him too. As the three of them walked, Shai waited for Orlov to speak first.

"My son is on the missing submarine," Orlov said. He did not pose it as a question.

"Yes," Shai said.

"But you are not navy officers."

"Yes to that too. When did you last speak to him?"

"Several days ago, not sure exactly when. He phoned to say he would not be coming to see me on Saturday."

"He came every Saturday?" Arik asked.

"When he could."

"How did he sound?" Shai asked. The beach was mostly empty this early on a winter day, but a kite soared high over the small waves.

"Like always. He said, 'Nana, I cannot come on Shabbat.' I asked no questions. He is an officer. He would not answer them." Orlov stopped and looked at Shai. "Is he dead?"

"Not that we know. I give you my word, which is good when I do. The submarine has disappeared but there is no wreckage, so until we know more we consider everyone on it alive."

Orlov showed no facial response, put both hands behind his back, one hand holding the other wrist, and continued walking. Shai saw a slight shaking of one hand, which could be Parkinson's, but he guessed was relief exiting his body.

"Any contact from those responsible?" Orlov asked.

"No."

"Would you tell me if there was?"

"I would tell you if I knew he was alive," Shai said. "May I ask what you were doing at the Russian Embassy yesterday?"

"Nothing," Orlov said. "I am an avid stamp collector. I received a phone call from the ambassador's secretary inviting me to come to the embassy and discuss stamps with him. She said he was a collector and also followed my writings on the China threat."

"Certainly the Russians are more concerned about the China threat than about anyone," Shai said. "Given their proximity."

"The ambassador is in fact not a stamp collector, however he was highly familiar with my work. He invited me for tea and we talked about my writings."

"Had you ever met him before?" Arik asked.

"No."

"What else did he ask about?" Shai asked. "Perhaps your

son?"

"No. He asked if I missed Moscow."

"What did you say?" Arik asked.

"Of course I miss Moscow. But that does not mean I long to live there." He spat. "Putin's a Cossack with a closet full of suits. Brave people still disappear."

Shai stopped. "Well, I've taken you away from your game for long enough. Please excuse the interruption."

Orlov stopped and moved close to him. "How will I know about my son? If I don't hear from him."

"When we know something for certain, this young man here will either show up or phone you. He will use the name Tsvi. I genuinely hope your son is okay."

Orlov stared at Shai, one apparatchik to another. "Thank you."

Shai and Arik headed inland and left Orlov.

"Of course, he's lying," Arik said.

Shai said nothing for a number of steps, and then said, "Yes, he is. Puzzling too why he came here rather than to America."

"Do you think he's a Russian sleeper?"

Shai worried that their innovations in satellite communications, remote controlled warfare, and data encryption were gold the Russians sought to mine.

"I don't know yet," Shai said.

Tzipi was refreshed as she sat in Meir Bardin's study, had slept the whole way on the flight from New York. "As I mentioned on the phone, Sue Berger suggested I come see you. Took twenty of us to see *Hamilton* on Broadway. Not that she can't afford it, but I hear it's impossible to get two seats."

"What a generous human being. I've lectured at her synagogue in the Berkshires several times. How do you know her?"

"We were roommates on her junior year abroad."

"Ah, I recall now she told me." Berger was a fifty-year-old heiress, both parents dead, a sixty-thousand square foot home in Connecticut, had been a big Bernie Sanders backer, and was as down-to-earth as anyone he'd ever met. "She tells me she'd like to move to Tel Aviv, even if the boyfriend here doesn't work out."

"She and I sit on opposite ends of the spectrum," Tzipi said.

Meir laughed. "Clearly."

"She mentioned that she had dinner with you several months ago here with some of her Tel Aviv friends, tried to persuade you to run for prime minister."

"It was flattering. They knew I couldn't win against Gutman. Their idea was for me to run as a Bernie Sanders type candidate, and though I'd lose, I could effect changes in the Likud's platform."

"As Sanders did on Hillary Clinton's."

Meir nodded. "Though we didn't imagine Hillary would lose, but the model still worked."

"But with Gutman gone, if he is gone, and let's keep this conversation to ourselves, you might win if you had some solid backing from the Right too."

Excitement spilled through Meir and he became emotional, which he sensed in part was related to his grandson's near death. Everyone knew Tzipi had risen from the right-wing Betar youth movement and was deeply respected for her Mossad service. Her tentacles spread deep in the Israeli body politic. "Can you tell me anything more about Gutman's disappearance?"

"Nobody seems to know anything. It's a mystery across the board. It's a hell of a daring maneuver by somebody, or a tragic accident, but for our purposes it may not matter which."

Meir was troubled, felt his interest was indecent. Israel had already lost one head of state to assassination and that was one too many. "We must find him."

"Yes, but what if he isn't. Sue tells me you have a monthly poker game with some people of stature. You take a third of every pot and give it to charity."

Meir grinned. "In the last ten years we've donated over three hundred thousand shekels. Each week the host chooses the charity."

"And you discuss what changes you'd make to our political terrain. May I hear what you've come up with?"

Meir was a little nervous, as suddenly this seemed a possibility. "We need a separation of powers," he began. "The Knesset should control the government but the government controls the Knesset. It's ridiculous that more than half of you Likud members are in the cabinet."

Tzipi laughed. Likud held thirty seats in the one hundred twenty-member Knesset. The next largest party, the Zionist Union in the opposition, had twenty-four. She knew how different the country would be if the largest bloc wasn't always forced to form a coalition with the religious parties, a mere ten percent of the vote, who basically got whatever they wanted for their participation.

She said, "I know, it's a disaster. There's regularly not enough committee members to get anything done. So you want a new law. No one other than the prime minister can serve in the cabinet and Knesset. You empower the Knesset so it can supervise the government."

The quickness of her mind impressed him. "Exactly. You become a cabinet minister, you resign your seat and the next person down on the Likud list joins the Knesset. Then I'd get rid of the Chief Rabbinate, only serves the Orthodox." Meir instinctively touched the kippah on his head. "You want a Chief Orthodox Rabbi, fine, let the Conservative and Reform movements have their own head rabbis. People don't know that the Chief Rabbinate as a branch of government is a holdover from the Turkish Law of the Status Quo. No more status quo. This way Reform Jews could marry anybody in Israel." It was shameful that reform Jews, so vast a part of his Jewish people, could not be married by a reform rabbi here without an Orthodox rabbi present to sign the documents.

"I'm guessing you'd limit the size of government?"

He smiled. She either had traveled this road in her own thoughts or Sue had briefed her. Currently there were thirty-six cabinet ministers, cabinet seats doled out to small parties to join his coalition.

"Eighteen cabinet ministers. It's a very Jewish number. No more buying favors with cabinet seats." He loved that the number eighteen in Hebrew represented life.

"I understand you'd run on health, welfare and education."

"I'd assign a percentage of the budget for those three."

"To determine the priorities in government," she said, seeing where this went. "It would reduce the huge amount spent on the settlements."

"Yes. Say the minister of defense needs an additional hundred million. The security budget is the biggest invitation to corruption." He shrugged. "You can always convince people we need it. But this way, it automatically triggers increases in the budget of the other three."

"Proportionally?"

"Yes," he said. "And the prime minister can serve only as prime minister, no additional cabinet posts."

"Wow." Tzipi laughed. "We are a little fiefdom here." She hated that Gutman served additionally as the foreign minister and the minister of communications in order to control the granting of all licenses for television, radio and print journalism, to deny those who might attack him.

"The next idea I've stolen from America—put certain issues to the general public. In America they have states' rights, but since we have no states and we're only three million voters, I'd hold plebiscites for the entire country. Things that Gutman's millionaire friends won't let come before the government, like a flat tax, could be put to the people. As the first countrywide proposition, I'd mandate that some percentage, I don't know, fifteen percent, of all housing has to go for rentals. Controlled rents." Everybody forced to buy an apartment was too great a burden for young couples, was killing the country and forcing some of their best to leave. The absence of rentals caused terrible inflation in apartment prices, a seventeen percent rise in the last year alone.

He looked at her, impressed she left the gray streak in her hair. "You're a national hero. You should run not me."

"I want to. I should. I don't think our little maniacally religious country today will elect a woman prime minister."

Tzipi's cell phone rang. She removed it from her large purse and looked at the number, then at Meir. "I'm going to have to call this person back. You're something this country needs more of, a liberal Orthodox Jew. Should be a natural fit, if you're going to be religious, belief in God and belief in liberties and caring for all human beings. Not sure how orthodoxy turned so insular. I'm going to call on you again, if I may?"

"It would be a privilege."

He walked her across the stone squares of the floor, ubiquitous in Israel as the sands blown in were easily cleaned.

"Your grandson, is there anything you need?"

He had not spoken to her of Yigal and Sue did not know. "Yes," Meir said. "His father, my son, he's traveling on government business you might say. Likely about this disappearance. I can't reach him. If someone could ask him to call me. He doesn't know about his son."

"Of course," Tzipi said. "It's done."

Ramzy walked through a cold, slanted rain and hoped it

didn't turn to snow and further restrict movement at the Balthasar-Neumann military base in Wurzburg. It was hard to fathom that eleven million refugees had fled Syria in the five years of civil war. In the last year alone, a million had turned up here in Germany, a tsunami of hope that Ramzy worried could overwhelm the goodwill of the incredible German people.

He entered their empty room in the refugee camp, a converted barracks in a corner of this operating army base. Concrete walls, and divided from the next room by a tarpaulin. It was smart, rather than close off people behind barbed wire. Dalal was teaching a hundred kids in a classroom, many standing in the back and against the walls. It was exactly how he had taught a lifetime ago when fresh from earning his teaching degree at Manchester University. First, he made the emotional Hajj to Mecca, the holy pilgrimage that all Muslims must complete once in their lifetime, and then in the Damascus refugee camp he was confronted with 1200 Palestinian students and only one other teacher. With a strength he could hardly imagine now, they split the mass into classes of one hundred, and each taught a group for two hours from seven in the morning until seven at night every day but Friday. Many nights, he walked alone through the oasis orchards, stopping to grab an apricot, plum, peach and a handful of walnuts, and as he ate, he continued into the desert full of faith that soon his Arab brethren, and maybe even the world, would rise up and rescue his people. To be back in identical circumstances over half a century later made it feel like his feet were sinking into those sands.

To push away his fear, in the deep quiet late into those nights he began to write his first stories. He was rewarded for his faith and five additional teachers arrived, one of them Dalal. Late in 1967, not long after the Israelis shocked him by defeating the Arab armies so quickly, PLO officers arrived at the school to recruit the older children. He and Dalal had married by then and they had watched the children, excited with unexpected hope as the jeeps screeched to a halt inside the courtyard and the men jumped out, Kalashnikovs raised. He was surprised that he agreed to the establishment of a base there, and even more surprised that soon he himself was training.

He remembered truly as if it was yesterday, how he had lain beside Dalal in the freezing concrete hut at exactly this time of the year, and not wanting to ask but knowing he must, she agreed that he leave her for unknown stretches of time. They spent the next two weeks together and he imbibed her like a camel at water about to leave for a vast unknown journey. They parted simply, with little said, and he made his way to the Karameh Camp in Jordan, where the PLO had their main base. In the times of his return, she had been unable to conceive a child, which he tried to tell himself was for the best since he was mostly away. But it was not for either of them, especially her.

He heard noises outside of a group returning from some class. The refugees were anxious, desperate to find lost family members and upset by the long wait for transfer into better housing. Despite all that Ramzy had witnessed for so long, he was unable to become accustomed to suffering. Some had been settled into permanent housing after six months, while others had languished here for five years. The refugees' biggest employer thus far was Deutsche Post, who had hired only sixty. Thirty thousand had been placed in low paying service jobs and several hundred in training internships. The Daimler CEO had proclaimed the refugee labor would drive a new economic miracle, however they had taken only a handful, as the refugees lacked the skills and the language facility to learn them. Language deficiency exasperated the refugees at every turn. They spoke Arabic, Kurdish and Farsi, but despite intensive classes they found German hard to mouth. So Dalal was teaching the children and he spent his days translating from English and German to Arabic and vice versa.

"Ramzy," a voice called in English from the other side of the partition. "May I come in?"

Ramzy would have recognized the voice even if he had not been expecting him. "Eli, please do," he said, lifting the tarpaulin to the next room, empty at the moment.

"Interesting place to hide," Eli said as he entered, "on an army base."

"It would be if I was hiding," Ramzy said. "I'm working."

Eli decided not to bring up Khaled Fahmy, as all Ramzy could be charged with was aiding the escape of someone who had fled the scene of an accident. The Germans would hardly bother to extradite him.

"I'm sure it's hard here," Eli said.

Ramzy was quiet, and then said, "They're lucky, they're alive, and their lives will slowly get better."

"Let me ask you something. If you had to guess, will Gutman be found alive?"

"Has there been any attempt at ransom?" Ramzy asked.

"None."

"You mean knowing nothing about what has happened to him," Ramzy said. "Just from what I see on the news?"

"Your instinct," Eli said.

Eli saw that the small partitioned room had virtually no possessions. Some clothes sat in a plywood cupboard. Several airport plastic duty free bags leaned against a corner wall, unopened, beside a single suitcase. Eli assumed he and Dalal had come from Syria with very little. Eli realized that Ramzy had not used his contacts with the Russians to secure privileged passage and had arrived with the refugees. He wondered if it was cover or a refusal to use his influence.

"A little too elaborate for ransom. Could still get a fortune with someone a lot easier to grab."

"You think he's still alive."

"If you haven't found a submarine scattered at the bottom of the ocean, why not? If you were going to kill him right away, why not leave him dead on a raft for the birds to feast on?"

"And if you wanted to kill him at some later date?"

"He's not a very likeable fellow. No moral center, stands for nothing. His friends are more interested in what he can do for them. He can do more for them in power than missing, so I doubt they're behind this."

"How much time do we have to find him?"

"He's what, sixty-six, sixty-seven? Seems in okay shape. So you can look for, say, another twenty, twenty-five years before reasonably sure he's dead."

"And the Russians, what might they want with him?" Eli asked.

"What do the Russians ever want? They're no different than your American friends. To be considered exceptional. To be admired. Women, wealth. The Russians want influence in the region. Their involvement in Syria has put them back on the Middle East map. I doubt the Russians would have any need for Gutman. Why would they care if he's dead or alive? Russia bombs ISIS to clear a path so Assad can murder without breaking a sweat. You're on opposite sides. Israel aids ISIS in Syria, you foolishly dance with the devil to thwart Iran. That's what you've become in all your arrogant power, an ally of ISIS."

Eli refused to react. Only solving the Palestinian conflict and bringing the world to Israel's impressive shores would win his people real security. He would not divulge they knew about the al-Nusra link, didn't want to reveal too much.

"But to snatch him right under the Americans noses," Eli said.

"What would be a better display of Soviet strength? To steal your great new submarine technology in the Americans' backyard, before you got to use it. Russia and Iran are probably laughing and toasting each other. Who cares about Israel? You are just a place with a lot of Jews nobody else wanted. Everybody would be interested in the stealth the Americans developed."

"What happened between you and Shai?" Eli asked. "You were friends." Eli wanted to know who Ramzy had been then.

Ramzy sat slowly on the edge of the narrow bed he shared with his wife. "You don't mind if I sit?"

Eli smiled to indicate that it was both his room and he was already seated.

"I saved his life in Rome," Ramzy said matter-of-factly. "That part you know. If not for my writings and their acclaim, there are many who would have killed me for doing so."

"Why did you?"

"It was more than thirty years ago. I believed then. It was supposed to be a temporary occupation, this thing you have done to us. Today, if it saved one Palestinian life from Abu Nidal, who was killing my friends, I would have let him bleed until his life dripped onto the floor of the car and then shoved him into the street."

Eli looked at Ramzy for a long moment, tried to read his calm expression but could not tell if it was resignation or determination, or hatred. "Maybe it's not too late for you to feel like you once did towards him and us. Thank you for talking to me."

"Tell Shai if it's not too late, it soon will be. Then more of you will die than you can imagine."

"I'll tell him."

Outside, as Eli walked across the military base in the hard rain, he saw a woman with two small kids hurrying, her children in yellow slickers but the mother in a thin sweater that absorbed the water. He approached them, took off his thick, lined, waterproof jacket, handed it to her and silently walked away, the icy rain quickly soaking his shirt. He felt no better, and in fact a little worse, as in this large landscape of loss it accomplished so little.

Arik walked into Shai's office laden with an iPad and a stack of physical files. Before he sat, he started talking. "Petr Orlov arrived with his family at age nine, which you know. In high school, he changed his given name to Yohanan but kept his surname."

"Nothing nefarious there, kids want to fit in. He certainly wasn't going back to Moscow. As far as we know. Yet, anyway."

His hands full, Arik dropped hard into the wood chair opposite Shai's comforting desk strewn with papers, chewing gum, a dripping old ink fountain, pens, but no electronics.

"Straight into the joint program at the combined Naval Command School and Haifa University," Arik continued. "Graduated in 2013 with a BA in political science and military strategy, rank of Lieutenant Junior Grade."

The Naval Command School was nearly as prestigious and demanding as the Israeli Air Force Flight Academy, the suffering of little sleep and freezing waters impressed Arik, though he far preferred Air Force Intelligence, where he'd landed.

"Expect as much," Shai said, "with his genes. Political leanings?"

"That's what's interesting. I was just getting there."

Shai waited with no patience whatsoever.

"Father is not easily pegged, thinks the Left and Right are equal fools. The son skews way left, sympathetic to Breaking the Silence."

Breaking the Silence was a controversial group of former IDF officers the government ridiculously tried to outlaw for talking about what service is like in the territories, both for them and the Palestinians, and the silence about it when they return. The government thinks anybody sane likes patrolling refugee camps.

"In addition to his coursework, he took extracurricular classes in Hebrew literature from none other than A.B. Yehoshua at the University of Haifa."

Shai leaned forward in his chair. Yehoshua was one of Israel's two greatest living novelists, along with Amos Oz, both Peace Movement leaders. Highly unusual for Russian Jews who stormed en masse into the Israeli Right, fleeing as far from Communism as their Slavic legs could carry them.

"So he's a lefty," Shai said. "Believer in justice, humanity, Israel as an actual democracy—everything we might not expect from his provenance."

"So the father comes here, when by all logic he should go to America. But he doesn't. Because what, America's too decadent?"

"I don't see him making pilgrimages to the Western Wall."

"And the son," Arik continued, "is exactly who he shouldn't be. He should be dancing with the settlers like the rest of them. Could make this legend the perfect cover for a Soviet sleeper recruited by his father. They're truly close, that comes up everywhere. I mean everywhere."

Shai smiled, not at the prospect Arik was right, but at the young agent looking at this from the wide view. He expected Arik would get his posting to the field before much longer, though he doubted the boy would find it glamorous--more watching from an apartment window than sidling up to beautiful women in a hotel bar--and might end up happier home in research. Better chance from there to find the love he sought.

"Or he could be even more of who he appears to be," Arik said, "and working with the Palestinians, the Soviets, or to stretch a bit, even American Intelligence in removing our democratically elected prime minister."

"Yes," Shai said. "An unusually long list of suspects."

"What do we do?"

"Dig deeper into Yohanan Orlov and let me know what you find. I think he has the key to this lock."

As Arik left, Tzipi Ben-Ami was sitting alone in the entrance foyer. Arik recognized her, smiled but said nothing, as she did not introduce herself.

"What aren't you telling me?" Tzipi demanded as she walked into Shai's office.

"What aren't I telling you? That I'm embarrassed I stopped swimming and my legs hurt even on short walks."

"So get in the pool. Idiot."

"We have leads but no solid trail," Shai said. "It's as if he's Jonah and a giant whale swallowed that sub whole."

"The goddamn Americans must have had something up their sleeve. The new president hates his own intelligence services and I bet they'd play behind his back."

"We're hearing no. Resolutely. They say everything is where it should be. I may fly over and shake that tree myself."

She sat. "I had tea with Meir Bardin in his study. Very charming, charismatic. He says exactly what's on his mind. He'd have to learn that doesn't work in government. I think he's imagined about running for prime minister for a long time. Though not seriously."

"And now?"

"He wants Gutman found. If he's not he'd consider it. He's sweet. I'm afraid the ugliness of the process will really upset him. Is he tough enough to get through it? Maybe."

"I met him recently for the first time. He reminded me a little of me, boisterous but silent when it suited him. I liked him."

"Who doesn't like looking in the mirror?"

"And you, Tzipi?"

"Run you mean?"

Shai nodded.

"I think Gutman will turn up. He has more lives than any dozen cats."

"A sub is too big to hide for too long. I believe we'll find him. But if we don't?"

"The loss of the prime minister would be terrible for the nation. Maybe," she said. "Or maybe I'd run with Meir Bardin as his number two and babysit his behind. He's going to need someone to do it."

"Would you be disappointed?"

"No," she said. "I accept things as they are. Nothing happens for a reason. There's no reason behind Auschwitz, the Syrian dead, or the way men treat women. I don't have to do anything yet. I'll wait and see what develops."

"You going to see Bardin again?"

"What do I have better to do? He's refreshingly smart, and I don't think he wants anything for himself. We never see that. He's actually why I'm here. Eli's son was hurt in the Sderot attack."

"I didn't know. How bad?"

"The kid's okay, or better put, he's banged up pretty badly but will be okay. I checked out Meir before we met and heard about it. I think he doesn't want his dad to know, but Meir would like to speak to Eli. So take care of it."

"That's about the easiest thing I've been ask to do all day."

"He on the disappearance?"

Shai nodded. "Everybody is."

"That leaves us vulnerable elsewhere. Any movement by Iranian forces? Hezbollah? Al-Nusra? They're right at our feet. The bastards keep threatening to turn around and march up the Golan."

"All quiet. We're watching." Shai was silent forever, uncharacteristically long even for him.

To show her displeasure, Tzipi yawned.

Finally Shai said, "We see an al-Nusra tie to the prime minister's disappearance. Not sure yet how it fits, if it's the bull's-eye. But they could be taking Gutman to them."

CHAPTER 8

Eli sat in a safe house in the heart of Wurzburg Old Town, an Airbnb found for him by the Berlin Embassy, a one-bedroom apartment all blinding white: walls, leather furniture, cabinets, the stands beneath glass tables, with blonde wood slat floors. Sixty-four dollars a night. He looked around. His environs did not affect him, and as long as the bed was reasonably solid he did not much notice the rest. Eli picked up the Nikon he had bought and practiced with the setting, had told the rental agent he was photographing the refugees for an Australian magazine.

Eli set the camera down and stretched out on the sofa, in the quiet ran over everything that had happened since the ramming of their sailors. He looked at the ceiling. He'd driven down that road innumerable times now and was parked on the side of it. A message had come from Berlin instructing him to call his father. His father had never before sought him when in the field. Scared, Eli sat, picked up his burner phone and dialed his father's cell phone. Meir answered on the first ring.

"It's me," Eli said. "How are you, Dad?"

"I'm fine. Listen, Yigal's okay, but he was hurt. A missile hit school. He was grazed by fragments. His head, but no long-term damage. One leg is broken in a few places."

Eli squeezed his eyes and sank deeper into the couch, could hear his heart sounding in his ears. "Where is he?"

"The hospital in Sderot. Eli, I drove down. I saw him. He'll be fine. It went right through the window. We're lucky. Really lucky. He doesn't want you to know. Can you call Noa?"

"Yes," Eli whispered. "How is she?"

"Your wife's tougher than both of us."

Eli laughed because it was true, and the reflexive response released some tension. He thought about the word his father used: luck. He was lucky to so love his parents and to have his children so love him and Noa. Meir's expressive warmth, physical affection and almost obsessive attentiveness had created a model for all of them that Eli consciously emulated with his kids.

"I'm not going to tell him I spoke to you," Meir said.

Eli felt a little dazed. "Okay."

"I don't know when I'll talk to you again," Meir said. "Before you run, can I tell you something?"

"Okay."

"People are suggesting if Gutman isn't found that I run for prime minister. I really don't want to think about it."

Eli did not answer for a long moment. He felt some of his own burden lift but did not understand why. The press hounding and scavenging through all their lives would be relentless, past deeds dredged up and magnified as either heroic or incompetent.

"That would be great, Dad. Terrible for you. Catastrophic for Mom, but really wonderful for the other three million Israelis."

Yigal would be fine, Eli told himself; wounds that healed and wounds that did not were a world apart, both in body and in one's heart. Close friends had died on the battlefield and he felt their absence and the desire to talk to them often.

"How's it going out there?" Meir asked, knowing he was crossing a boundary. He would not have called to ask, but since they were already talking.

"It could be better."

"That's probably often the case."

"It always is."

Eli suddenly realized when they rescued the prime minister it would end his father's chance of election and all the good he would do.

"Don't think about me," Meir said, as if he was reading Eli's mind. "You have a job to do, so you do it."

"Of course, Dad. Kiss mom for me. I have to go."

"Eli, none of his friends were hurt. His spirits are good."

"Thanks. Bye."

As soon as he ended the call, Eli pictured his son in the hospital and felt like he was sinking below the surface of the sea. He slipped down the leather sofa and sat on the floor. Eli saw that night when he was fifteen and had attempted to run across the wide Eshkol Boulevard. He had darted between the parked cars, and in the dark, had not seen that one was a truck with a pipe sticking out of the rear bed at an angle. His forehead and then the soft skin beneath his eye collided with the sharp metal end. Blood streamed down his face as he was slashed to his skull. He had lain in the emergency room bed at Hadassah Hospital, his father at his side as they waited for the plastic surgeon. He had felt stupid and very scared and he remembered the exact words he said to his father: "I'm glad you're here." Now, he was not there for his son. His entire body felt heavy, like it was metal, and he could not rise.

Eli exhaled and then picked himself off the floor. Enough. Whatever he was feeling, he would face later. In half an hour he was meeting Sami Abadi, who he had infiltrated into the camp as a recent refugee from Syria.

Eli went into the gleaming white bathroom, and for the first time noticed the shower tiles were lime green. He splashed water on his face. Abadi was an amazing recruit, had been among the last of the 75,000 Syrian Jews to get out of the country. Most had escaped or been smuggled to Israel after the creation of the state, but by the late 1970s Hafez al-Assad, the current leader's equally belligerent father, tightened his grip on the 5,000 Jews still in Damascus. For literally decades, the relentless Jewish community in Toronto raised funds, and using networks created by those who had escaped, one by one secretly bought the release of these Jews. Sami had been ransomed at the age of fourteen, an orphan, and was groomed while in high school to find a family in the Mossad. It was a find for them to have someone young with the right Arabic accent, who could pass easily in Damascus as a follower of Bashar al-Assad.

Eli walked to the Marktplatz not far from the Main River. The weather had cleared and a bright sun shone in the cold sky. The plaza was filled with umbrella-covered tables where the hearty Germans drank coffee. Across the plaza, he saw Café Michel sat on the ground floor of a four-story building with three floors of apartments above.

Inside, Eli found Sami at a corner red-vinyl booth in the large café, with pastries behind glass against the far wall and a semi-circular table jutting into the middle of the room laden with more delicacies under glass, the top shelf whole cakes and pies and the larger lower area filled with slices, cupcakes, waffles and chocolate candies. In the last decade, Israel emulated a lot of this café society.

Eli slid in across from him and spoke in quiet Arabic, which would arouse much attention but little suspicion in a Germany awash with refugees. Sami was short, mid-thirties, with a receding hairline of jet-black hair, thick dark eyebrows, light-brown eyes and a quick smile that everybody in the Mossad knew charmed the ladies on both sides of the Golan Heights.

"It was easy," Sami said. "I have a half a dozen people on him around the clock. Nobody knows who he is. He's not telling them. Either modesty, security or both." Sami motioned for a waiter to approach. The makeshift rooms on the army base were freezing and he wanted a double espresso. "These people are desperate for money. For what I'm paying them nobody will say anything."

"They ask any questions?"

"Nothing. They've been through too much to care about where Euros come from."

"They'll find you if he makes any move to leave?"

"Immediately," Sami said. "Why the obvious questions?"

"Sorry," Eli said. "Lot of things. Sorry."

"A lot of the kids talk about his wife, Dalal."

"I bet they adore her."

"They all say the same thing, 'She's really nice.'"

Though Eli expected this, for some unknown reason hearing it irritated him. They should all be here having dessert, he realized he was feeling, instead of blasting each other's children into ambulances and hospital beds.

The waitress arrived wearing a starched white shirt beneath a long red apron. Eli ordered ice coffee because it came exactly as it did in Israel, with ice cream in the tall glass instead of ice cubes. The drink arrived with a small, blue, paper umbrella planted in thick whipped cream, decadence that annoyed Eli. He longed to hug Yigal, thought about how far away they were from finding the prime minister, and he took the small umbrella and threw it on the table. Where the hell was the goddamn submarine?

At sixty-one, Paul McEnnerney believed himself testament that people changed little. He still favored the comfortable linen pants and shirts he had in his youth when he first became a CIA field operative, though more color now rather than all white. He gazed at the staid yet stylish brown, round Persol shades on his desk, though he sometimes missed the flashy Vuarnet wraparounds. He was proud that he came from old money, but felt no disdain for the high-tech millionaires descending on Washington as their next playground. He did enjoy that they were discovering that this city venerated team sports and lone hotshots were most often treated like pesky flies and swatted against the glass.

As he waited to impart the big news to Collins, he gazed at the photos on his windowsill of his daughter, Jessica, riding horses and several of his wife in their vast flower garden, her favorite spot on the planet. His globe-hopping days were gladly behind him and he thoroughly enjoyed soaring with the winds in the Langley stratosphere. He had married late and Jessica was in her sophomore year of high school at the prestigious Sidwell Friends, a Quaker establishment founded in the rather fanciful belief there is God in everyone. After decades in the world's cesspools, McEnnerney was entirely certain God could not be dug up anywhere, but his wife was a less lapsed Catholic and what mattered to her, and eventually to him too, was the school's academic excellence and reputation for being, as the beatniks would have said, "square." The school prided itself in inspiring active care of the environment, global citizenship, and service, all of which McEnnerney valued, as deep down, despite his veneer, he was fairly square himself, which is how he landed in the CIA to start with. He wanted to serve, albeit with a good deal of excitement. Sidwell fostered reflection and shared silence, with the goal of students finding deeper truths about themselves, "to let their lives speak"—none of which McEnnerney was any good at, and thought was mostly hogwash, but he wanted his daughter to lead a richer existence than his.

He looked up at a knock on his office door and Collins entered without waiting to be invited. "You found the sub!"

"I think it would be more accurate to say it found us."

McEnnerney slid several satellite photos across his immaculate shiny desk and Collins grabbed them and looked. There the sub was, surfaced in calm waters.

"As carefree as a rubber ducky in a tub," McEnnerney said.

"Nothing on the news channels. I checked. Any communication with it?"

"None, other than the emergency locator signal pinging 'here I am.' Rather insistently."

"Nobody answers your attempts to hail her?"

"Precisely."

"Where is it?"

"The Puerto Rico Trench, the boundary between the Caribbean and the Atlantic. Happens to be the deepest spot in the Atlantic."

"It's been hiding in those depths?"

"With its stealth capabilities, it could have been hiding about anywhere." McEnnerney checked his large Blancpain Le Brassus watch, the internal workings of the mechanism visible through the rest of the open face. "SEALS should be there by helicopter in about an hour, with a whole lot of help coming by sea not vastly far behind."

"Maybe whoever took it wanted us to believe it's been hiding in those depths. You think anyone's alive on board?"

"Don't know. But they could easily have sunk it, had they wanted to."

Collins sat, was silent for a long time, then tapped out a musical rhythm on the shiny desk with one hand, Elliot Smith's "Miss Misery," to help focus his rambling thoughts. "I don't think they could have done this, whoever *they* are, without American help."

"Stands to reason, perfectly logical. Except everywhere I've looked says we're not involved. I've gone through all the cupboards and peered not only under all the beds, but under the floorboards. If some hands were dirty, I'd know." He'd sat atop the agency's Middle East desk for two decades before being elevated to deputy director and little got past him.

"How? This is almost as impossible as knocking down both World Trade Towers."

"Your point is well taken. Almost. We tracked a Severodvinsk Yasen-class nuclear attack sub. We think it's the K-329 out of Novosibirsk. About a week ago she was submerged far enough off our coast for it to be normal, but due to current considerations maybe far too close."

Collins stopped strumming.

McEnnerney said, "I don't trust anybody, and that includes the Israelis. What's your new bosom buddy, Eli, think?"

"That the Palestinians are involved, likely with the Russians. They go way back to when the Soviets were arming anyone who could stand up against Israel."

McEnnerney nodded. "I have thoughts that meander that way myself. This Ramzy Awwad suddenly surfaces, someone of his stature after all these years, who had faded into the wallpaper. Would almost have to be something big to get him to come out again. I imagine he'd have stage fright. Or maybe the opposite, could give a fuck who gets hurt. So who does our Ramzy know? Once upon a time about everybody. And how badly, we don't need to ask ourselves, do the Russians want their hands on this sub's technology."

"How many of our people on board?"

"Six. They were on just for the ride. Once they docked our boys were supposed to step off and we turn the whole kit and caboodle over to the Israelis to run her home."

"Any Jews?" Collins asked. "Of the six?"

"None. I checked. Not where you typically find American Jews, underwater. Though they don't seem to have any trouble with skyscrapers."

Collins laughed.

"And maybe Gutman's no longer disappeared. Maybe everybody's dead in there. Or maybe their communications were ripped out and they're doing the hora waiting for us."

"What do you think?"

McEnnerney sank back in his chair and glanced at his watch. "Why don't you bring us some mocha macchiatos, non-fat, two Splendas in mine if you will. While you're out, I'll give the Israelis a buzz. Leave them out in the cold too long and they start reminding you of Auschwitz."

Shlomo Avni sat in the office of Commanders for Israel's Security (CIS) in Tel Aviv. He knew several of the men but was emotional and honored to be invited to sit with this group. Six men filled the long rectangular table, seven including him. At the head sat Amnon Reshef, the retired IDF major general and former commander of the Israeli armored corps. At seventy-eight, bald and clean-shaven, he looked great, wore light wire-rimmed glasses and a long sleeve, blue, button-down shirt open at the collar. Out of a real concern over the country's direction, in 2014 Reshef had founded CIS, which now numbered over 250 former high-ranking commanders of Israel. Shlomo ran his eyes to former IDF Chief of Staff Dan Halutz, former Police Chief Assaf Hefetz, former Chief of the Mossad Shabtai Shavit, and once head of the internal Shin Bet security service Ami Ayalon. All in their seventies except for Halutz, who would be there soon.

"This will appear tomorrow in *Yediot Ahronot* and *Haaretz*," Reshef said, pushing the proof of the full-page ad in front of Shlomo beside him. Interesting choice, Shlomo thought. The country's largest daily and their oldest newspaper, the intellectual and left-leaning *Haaretz*, scourge of the Right. "Then it will go up on billboards everywhere, along with online videos that will ask whether the billboards bother you."

Ayalon said, "The videos say that the billboards will soon disappear but the two-and-a-half million Palestinians won't."

Shlomo looked at the ad, a little bit shocked but impressed with its audacity. It pictured a crowd of cheering Arabs, many with the V for victory sign, others waving Palestinian flags, and in English in the upper left corner in large letters: One State for Two People—PALESTINE. On the lower half of the page a big red blotch over a green background with white Arabic script: Soon We Will Be The Majority. Best research Shlomo had read, with the high Arab birth rate, put the tipping point around 2025, when between the Mediterranean and the Jordan River Jews would become a minority in the land they had fought so hard to reclaim and build.

"We want immediate separation from the Palestinians," Dan Halutz said. "We change the rules of the game by putting Israel's security first through peace, not war. We keep an IDF presence in the West Bank until a permanent agreement is reached. Doesn't matter if it takes a few lifetimes."

"The Palestinians won't like that," Shlomo said.

"They'll like annexation a lot less," Ayalon said. "They have some forward thinkers there, especially in the younger generation. Our current leadership is sunk in incremental tyranny. The Barbur Art Gallery is under threat of closure for hosting a Breaking the Silence event. Incremental tyranny is the process where you live in a democracy and suddenly you understand it's not a democracy anymore."

Shavit pushed a coffee mug away. "The religious Zionists and too many others care more about territory than people. People don't hold an intrinsic value for them. Their core value is to occupy land at any political price. It will turn into a disaster. It is a disaster."

Amnon then read the Hebrew text on the facing page.

Two-and-a-half million Palestinians in the West Bank want to be the majority—and this is who you want to annex? If we don't separate from the Palestinians Israel will be less Jewish and less secure. We need to separate from the Palestinians now.

More and more of the world was dropping in line with a different one-state solution than the Israeli right proposed—that one called for one man one vote, which would dismantle the Jewish state.

Reshef continued. "We're calling on Israel to preserve conditions for negotiations with the Palestinians by freezing settlement construction, accepting the Saudi Arab Peace Initiative as a basis for talks, and recognize that East Jerusalem will be part of a future Palestinian state."

Shlomo breathed out loudly. "The American Jewish organizations would consider this anti-Semitic if it was coming from anyone but this group."

"They're a vocal minority of America's Jews and don't speak for the average Jew," Shavit said. "What do the Americans in Congress know about Israel. They show up and our leaders take them to Holocaust memorials and high-tech parks. Do they send their kids to patrol Jenin or Nablus? To man checkpoints where children stab at them?"

Reshef added, "Passing laws to imprison kids who throw stones makes us strong?" Reshef almost spat out the last words.

"The timing of this because of Gutman's disappearance?" Shlomo asked.

"No, it's been long scheduled for tomorrow to coincide with the opening of the Paris peace talks," Reshef said. "You're here because of Gutman's disappearance. If he's gone or dead, it provides a new opening. We need someone younger, not immediately identified with this group, but who has a military mind and some real common sense to run in the post-Gutman vacuum."

Excitement was building inside Shlomo, like a runner out of the starting blocks and gaining speed. "Who took Gutman?"

"That's the question," Shavit said. "Nobody knows. A lot of us think it's his wife. She already talks about her son as the next prime minister. She's known to be impatient."

"How could she pull this off?" Shlomo said.

"How does anything happen?" Halutz suggested. "People have friends in the most unusual places. Look how the Russians helped elect Trump. The most impossible things always happen. It's a law of the universe, the frequency which they do."

Shlomo said, "If anybody could pull this off, it would be this group."

"Absolutely correct, but we're not behind it. But now that it's happened... Have you thought about running? You're the poster boy for prime minister: kibbutz, army, high-tech security that's saved countless lives, respected across the globe."

"The thought occurred to me recently. I'd like to see a reinvigorated Labor Party. They're stupidly afraid to take on the Right. I'm surprised Ben-Gurion hasn't risen from the grave and come after them."

Reshef smiled. "Good."

"However, it's a big step, and what it will do to my kids to be in the spotlight..."

"Something to hide?" Reshef asked.

"Yes and no. My wife's the sweetest woman on the planet, a quiet kibbutznik. She had been the only woman I was with. I strayed once, an army lieutenant, fifteen years ago. She was everything my wife wasn't, tough. It was everywhere, on desktops, in closets at work. My wife knows. My kids do not."

"You could survive that coming out," Shavit said. "Your children too. They'd hardly be the only kids to make such a discovery. If it even came out. One woman, fifteen years ago, and you told your wife, would actually work in your favor."

"It's impossible that he's just disappeared. We'll find him." Shlomo said.

Reshef stood and paced uneasily towards the window. "If he's found, I'm afraid he'll try to turn whatever happened into some kind of heroic escapade and will scare the population that there are even greater dangers out there."

"For which we need him," Shlomo finished Reshef's thought. "So I'd have to turn it into a symbol of his weakness and the weakness of his whole approach. And the danger of relying on one man."

There was a lot of nodding.

"You want to think about it?" Reshef asked.

"Yes," Shlomo said. "It has less to do with whether you find Gutman. I love a good challenge. If I decide I'm in, I go whether Gutman is rescued or not."

Captain Eric Johnston, the SEAL Team 2 leader, sat in the rear of the first of the two Black Hawk helicopters that had lifted off from their base in Little Creek, Virginia. He glanced at the fourteen men in his chopper, then stood and looked out the large widow at the dark submarine in the water, he estimated a hundred yards from them. He listened as the rotors made the familiar deep chop chop sound. He'd have given anything to be on the Black Hawks carrying SEAL Team 6 to Osama bin Laden's compound. Those birds had been modified, an extra two blades set into the standard four blades to slow the rotor speed to mask the identifying sound.

He peered down as the Black Hawks descended a good distance from each other but on the same side of the sub, the sea below each parting in outgoing small circular waves. He lifted binoculars from around his neck and looked through them. The sub bridge was deserted. He swept from right to left and saw no other ships as the USS *Bainbridge,* their nearest destroyer, was a little more than two hours out.

He felt the Black Hawk hover just above the water.

"Let's go," Johnston said.

Silently, the men moved and the door was opened, the rotors even louder now. Four rubber amphibious boats laden with submachine guns quickly shot down into the sea. Johnston jumped and hit the cold water. He scissor kicked, and as his head broke the surface he heard the SEALs from both choppers splashing in. He looked up and saw the two men cradling machine guns who remained inside the open door in the event they were fired on from the submarine or elsewhere. The frigid open ocean was a perfect operating theater. The Black Hawk that had embarrassingly gone down inside bin Laden's compound had been caught in a vortex of hot air due to high temperatures that night and the lack of airflow inside the compound walls. Hovering over the yard, it lost its lift power.

Johnston hauled himself into the rubber boat, followed by his men. He waved to his second-in-command in the nearest dinghy. He had trained them not to wait for verbal commands and immediately they paddled in unison. As the two Black Hawks lifted higher, the rocking of the dinghy calmed. Johnston often thought of this rowing as symphonic, the absolute unison of each boat's strokes, as if each of the four dinghies was a separate section of an orchestra playing its own rhythm, but together a harmonic whole.

He saw no movement as they reached the sub first. The sides of the sub above water were beveled to slice more efficiently through the sea, and above that rounding was the flat length to the bridge. Johnston looked to see if anyone was secreted behind the bridge but there was nobody in his partial view. He shimmied up on his belly and then stood. Soon four of his mates joined him, as one remained in the amphibious. He waited until all twenty men were standing and then led them aft.

The hatch opened without resistance and Johnston was first down the metal ladder into the belly of the boat. He'd been briefed that like all other American submarines this one was divided into three compartments. He came down in Operations. The compartment was empty. Johnston listened but heard no sounds anywhere. He moved through the Control Room, Sonar Room and Radio Room, followed in single file by his men. No equipment seemed damaged, there was simply nobody manning the stations. Odd. He entered the Torpedo Room, glad the submarine had not been loaded with ordinance for the show run so there was no risk of a nuclear missile theft by any one of a long list of crazies who might covet that prize. He wondered if it was a mistake, as missiles might have helped thwart the attack. And then as he entered the Berthing Area, he understood.

He clicked the radio transmitter on his shoulder and there was a cackle, then he spoke. "Report that the men are here. They're alive."

The crew slept in the main berthing compartment. Three rows of racks were stacked on each side of the tight passageway, narrow aluminum berths with a mattress, a long, narrow store drawer below the mattress, and a three-foot-high storage locker to the side for the seaman's dress uniform. Each berth had a curtain for a modicum of privacy but all the curtains were open. About every third berth contained a sailor who seemed asleep. Small breathing sounds escaped them.

Johnston turned to his second-in-command immediately behind him. "Make sure they're all alive. Then check for the prime minister."

Johnston continued to the Officers' Staterooms. There would be four, each with the same stacked bunks, but only three officers per compartment. Johnston walked into the first; the two fold-down desks and fold-down sink had not been released. The bunks were empty. He tried the second stateroom and saw the same. In the third he found the Israeli commanding officer and chief petty officer snoring soundly. He had been shown photos of Israeli epaulettes. He had not seen the Israeli prime minister. The count he'd made in his head, now with these two added, indicated nobody missing. All the Israelis and Americans who had left were on board, or at least the same number of people were.

He left them and continued to the last officers' quarters, a small fear in him that the prime minister was there dead. The worst news was usually at the end.

He opened the door and walked in. It was not large enough for the three officers bunked here to stand at the same time even with the desks and sink retracted, which was not a problem as this stateroom too was empty.

Fifty-eight left port. With the prime minister, fifty-nine. He headed back into the main berth area and approached his second-in-command. "What's the count?"

"Fifty-eight."

"Searched everywhere?"

"Everywhere, sir."

Johnston nodded, did not trouble himself with what had happened or what had been used to drug the crew. His mission was to secure the sub and report.

One of the SEALs came jogging up towards them as fast as he could in the tight quarters. "Captain, we found this." He held a pistol in a shirt he'd likely grabbed from a locker so as not to smudge any fingerprints.

Johnston took it and spoke matter-of-factly. "Serdyukov SPS." The Russian Special Forces eighteen magazine, semi-automatic pistol. It had a range of only fifty meters, but Johnston had seen video of its steel-core bullets racing through thirty layers of

Kevlar or a car door like it was butter. "Where'd you find it?" he asked.

"Near the hatch. Landed in the corner on rags used to dry the ladder. Someone must have dropped it when climbing up and it hit there."

The second-in-command returned. "Sir, the computer system's been hacked, somebody who knew what he was doing. And there's a sizeable section of the hull cut away beyond the bridge."

Johnston nodded and reached for his transmitter. Exactly what he would be ordered to do if they had control of a Soviet stealth sub.

Eli walked alone through the Old Town Wurzburg walk street. Four-story buildings lined both sides, each painted a different pastel—pink, yellow, a light green. The efficient Germans had somehow managed to make the old street wide enough for the tracks of the blue electric trolleys to operate in both directions. Well-dressed Germans milled everywhere in and out of beautiful shops on both sides of the street.

Eli waited with a crowd of patient Germans as a trolley blocked their way and then moved. It was amazing how with the Right rising globally, Germany was both modern, intellectual and fabulously liberal. More than any perpetrator of the Holocaust, and his father owned a number of books on the subject, the Germans had refused to deny their past, the way the Polish and French collaborators still did. Germany had confronted genocide with new laws, a Jewish Museum in Berlin, a huge outdoor Holocaust Memorial, a museum of SS atrocities, and forthright school curriculum. Eli had several times walked through Berlin and read the ten by ten centimeter brass plaques with the names, birth and death dates, and the address of Jewish victims everywhere in sidewalks in front of their former homes.

The young Germans were a lot like him, to the degree he could convince himself he was hip. He liked art house movies, jazz, and had a collection of vinyl records. These Germans had lived their lives in the shadow of the Holocaust, ashamed of their elders, and now had responded with this incredible warm reception of refugees. Eli was impressed by what had emerged here. At the same time, he felt the incongruity. How was it possible that this country of learning, of science, of great philosophers, with a passion for culture, produced the gas chambers? Maybe with just the right ingredients brought together evil could arise anywhere.

An hour earlier he had received word, not yet public, that the submarine was found without the prime minister. Oddly calm at the news, Eli walked. Gutman was being moved somewhere, for some reason, and Ramzy Awwad had his fingerprints around his neck. With the submarine released, the search narrowed. They could have left Gutman dead aboard. He felt confident now that the prime minister was still alive and that he could find him. The answers lay with Awwad, and Eli was glad he was the one on Ramzy's trail.

Up at four a.m., Mordecai Gilboa drove north through the darkness. The Bible Marathon started at 5:30 a.m. from Rosh Ha'Ayin just inside the old border, near where Israel had been only fifteen-kilometers wide before the Six-Day War, a nine-mile narrow waist he hammered home when speaking to visiting American groups.

He had risen against the talk about canceling the second-annual run and passionately argued to keep the schedule despite the prime minister's disappearance. The marathon had spiritual meaning more important than even a great prime minister, who God could replace. Their history was everywhere. The Book of Samuel described the catastrophic defeat by the Philistines right here. Thirty thousand Israelites had been killed, including the two sons of Eli, the High Priest of Shiloh, and the Philistines seized the Ark of the

Covenant—the gold-covered, wooden chest that held the stone tables of the Ten Commandments. A man from the tribe of Benjamin ran the entire way to Shiloh to tell Eli, who had trained the Prophet Samuel in the ways of God. The distance was exactly forty-two kilometers (twenty-six miles), the world's first marathon.

Gilboa arrived at the outskirts of Rosh Ha'Ayin and was excited to see what he guessed was over two thousand runners, mostly settlers, but other religious men he knew were joining them. The race would climb through the hills of Samaria to Ariel and end at Shiloh, where the Ark of the Covenant was kept before taken to the battlefield.

The Palestinians needed to accept that this land had been theirs and was theirs again. Since the marathon ran east across Samaria, the military had closed the main Palestinian north-south road for seven hours. The Palestinians had been notified well in advance so they could make alternative plans or stay home.

Mordecai parked, and in the dark walked towards the starting line. Immediately people approached him, excited, shook his hand, wanted to run with him. Some out of friendship, others he knew currying favor. They could ask anything, he'd do what he wanted. Mordecai shook hands, embraced friends, but said that he was running alone. He would commune with the ancient route as it climbed these hills.

Mordecai ran with a group on the newly paved four-lane Route 5 Highway. The tall poles down the center concrete divider sprouted twin lights that protected the settlers' way, and were still on as dawn broke ahead of them. Mordecai felt exhilarated. The checkpoint was massive, a long, elevated concrete slab on concrete poles spanning the entire highway. Mostly the soldiers were silent as he passed, though several raised rifles in solidarity. Soon the hills became rockier, with some Arab buildings or homes on both sides. Mordecai panted lightly. He ran for pleasure and to check the security around Kiryat Arba, and for months had hit the hills in nearby Jerusalem to train.

His breathing was hard as Highway 5 dipped and rose with the terrain, the scrub brush brittle and sometimes brown from the lack of rain. Then the highway climbed a mountain. Mordecai watched some runners fall back and he pounded the granite harder, sweat running down from beneath the front of his cap. He didn't wipe it, kept going. Finally, at the peak, before the Arab city of Biddya, long tables were set up, manned by religious women protected by soldiers. Breathing hard, Mordecai stopped, took a plastic bottle, poured some on his hot face and then drank. As he did, he had a panoramic view of Tel Aviv at the coast in the distant dawn and his heart almost exploded from joy—or, he laughed to himself, it might be the exertion. Two men neared and slapped him on the back. He recognized but could not place them, so he smiled. He estimated he had covered about half the twenty-five kilometers to Ariel.

A pounding half hour later, he saw the low, rectangular, yellow buildings behind the chain-link and barbed wire fence of the Barkan Industrial Park. They had built it in the 1980s to strengthen the Jewish presence here. Now there were 120 businesses and factories, much of it built on so-called confiscated Palestinian land, but there was no such thing. Deeds meant nothing; it was all Biblical land. At Barkan, they manufactured textiles, food products, air-conditioning units, and gave the Palestinians jobs, much of these materials exported to Europe. The Europeans refused to see that BDS, the racist Boycott, Divestment and Sanctions movement—a global campaign against goods produced in Judea and Samaria in an attempt to pressure Israel to relinquish this land—robbed these Palestinians of jobs. He could not believe that the great Israeli international company SodaStream had been forced to close its factory because it was in a settlement and relocate to the Negev

Desert, laying off six hundred Palestinian workers. The Palestinian leaders who had fomented BDS didn't care about their own people. Half the Barkan workforce of 20,000 were local Palestinians. Well, it didn't matter, the settlers were here to stay, had won. At the thought, Mordecai quickened his long stride. Past the huge industrial area the hills became barren again and would remain that way until he reached the miracle of Ariel.

He felt ethereal, had passed that hard place where he wanted to stop, and now he was flying across the highway near the head of the pack. There was nothing he could not accomplish—help build a hundred Ariels, become prime minister. He passed the Arab town of Haras just off the highway, all small white structures with a minaret on a hill. At Ariel's western outskirts a long length of stone arches of a hotel stood below thick electrical wires. He kept going and then suddenly Samaria came alive. Leafy trees rose ahead of him, a field of pink flowers, a lush corn field, rows of tomato vines, and beyond an endless sea of two-story, red terra-cotta roofed settler homes, the streets lined with palm trees.

He was surprised how fast he approached Ariel. Built in 1978, Ariel now had eighteen thousand residents, plus a fully accredited university with twelve thousand Jewish and Arab students, studying together as it should be in Greater Israel, and the Ariel Center for the Performing Arts. Some Israeli actors and singers, maybe a hundred lefties, originally boycotted the Performing Arts Center, but once they saw we wouldn't be intimidated, the performers withdrew the boycott letter. Mordecai looked back and emotion rose in him. Runners stretched out for as far as he could see and reminded him of their wandering in the desert when they had left Egypt to return home.

Ramzy paced through the large German army base. This Bible Marathon exasperated him. These small daily indignities—the long lines at an Israeli checkpoint at a standstill while the soldiers ate lunch, trucks delayed for hours before being searched when they moved goods from one Palestinian city to another, some villagers separated from their fields by that concrete barrier having to queue at a checkpoint to get to them— near paralyzed Ramzy with rage. He found he had become angrier with the years rather than softer, less patient. Though the soldiers had no right, he could understand their entering the camps in the middle of the night to search for weapons and explosives. This was war and that's how war was fought. But at any time the Israelis could order a curfew, close the road to a village, or shut down the main commercial and passenger highway for half a day so the settlers could run past their villages without even seeing them.

Just last week the Israeli army confiscated 104 dunams—the old Ottoman unit of area equal to what a team of oxen could plough in a day—to build a settler road to bypass the Palestinian village of Nabi Ilyas. The land belonged collectively to three Arab villages. This was what the Israeli occupation was, a slow chomping away at their land, so the world and maybe their own people would not notice. He truly could not understand how these people, who had wept so many tears throughout history, couldn't care less as Palestinian mothers cried at the deaths of their children. During a hunger strike at Ofer Military Prison near Ramallah, settlers grilled chicken and meat outside to taunt the prisoners, soldiers joining them to eat. How could the Americans ignore all this?

Three weeks ago, the Palestinians had run their own marathon, but the planners could not find a single forty-two kilometer route anywhere in the West Bank that did not cross an Israeli checkpoint. Gazan runners wanted to join them but were initially prevented by the Israelis, who relented under international pressure and forty-six runners from Gaza joined the three thousand Palestinians and foreign supporters. They had to follow two laps of the same course near Bethlehem to complete a full marathon.

Ramzy stopped along a white wooden fence and gripped it tight with both hands to calm himself. He virtually never raised his voice. In the Lebanese refugee camp, after all hope of return was gone, his father launched into violent tirades, accused his wife of adultery with the bus driver and the man who sold ice cream, and when Ramzy had intervened his father slapped him. So Ramzy had learned to turn inward and say little. When his father started shouting, he and his sister clasped hands and ran. Ramzy wished now that he'd had the insight to stay and hug his father, but he had been nine and too frightened. When he had time he would begin a short story called "Two Marathons." But he did not have that time now.

He continued to a small grass area near the refugee quarters and from a short distance watched Dalal sitting on an army blanket surrounded by bundled children, their parents standing a distance away. These kids were his children and his grandchildren and his mood lifted. She was telling them the tale of "The Bewitched Camel." He had heard her tell it many times to the children in Damascus, about a camel who laid golden eggs until he spied a princess, fell in love and stopped laying golden eggs. In the end, he became a man and married her. Ramzy turned back and continued to walk, both saddened to separate again from Dalal but buoyed that he would soon be leaving here to face the Israeli prime minister.

Eli walked in the thick forest just beyond the army base, sensing something was about to happen. Gutman had been taken off the submarine, which made him easier to locate. He had not bought a new jacket and wore only a long sleeve shirt. In the cold, Eli lit a cigarette. He'd not smoked since the army and was not sure why he was starting again. The forest was deserted and he sat on the ground and inhaled, the cigarette like an old friend he didn't trust. He smoked the cigarette to the stub with a sense that this could be his last mission, and he felt a small fear of the unknown. He wondered now if he had the courage to find a completely new path in life and wondered where it might lead?

Eli stuck with things, one woman, one career, and found people who made vast changes brave. Israel too was a mess and he wondered if the country had the courage to change. With nobody around he had the desire to scream to release the tension inside him, but of course he didn't. Instead, he struck a match, lit another cigarette and drew in the hot smoke to warm himself.

With Arik beside him, Shai entered the Walter Reed National Military Medical Center in Bethesda. He knew it had been named after the US Army physician Walter Reed, who during the building of the Panama Canal discovered that mosquitoes transmitted yellow fever. Shai found it typically American that no one knew who Walter Reed was. They were a people with short memories.

"Shai Shaham and Arik Navon," he said to the front desk, using their real names. No reason to bamboozle the Americans, this time anyway, and they were handed laminated passes on lanyards. As Shai walked into the room first, Yohanan sat up higher in bed. Shai took his measure of him—square jaw, stubble of a dark beard, black hair parted down the middle swept back on both sides. More the look of an American movie star than beach volleyball-playing Israeli, or say a Russian military officer.

"When can I get out of here?" Yohanan said.

"We could make a dash for a Starbucks," Shai said. "But I think the Americans might wrestle you to the floor before we got out the front door. Seems everybody wants answers."

"So do I. We were out maybe three-quarters of an hour. I was in the reactor compartment monitoring the dials, making sure everything was right. I felt a little sleepy. The next thing I know I'm being woken in a sleeping berth."

Arik was excited being here, did not think he'd be let off the leash so soon, and glanced at Shai, who he knew would muzzle him if he barked too loudly. "You hear anything?" Arik asked. "Voices? In what language? Russian?" As soon as he'd finished he felt himself shrinking in his body, had been overeager. He'd been trained to reach out with seed in his upturned palm and let the quarry come nibble.

"Sure," Yohanan said testily. "Russian, Hebrew, English, Esperanto. I heard it all."

"So you heard nothing," Shai said.

"Precisely."

Arik considered how to redeem himself. "How was the prime minister? Anything unusual in his behavior?"

Good, Shai thought, important, brief. Let the target talk, unless of course you were drowning him with verbiage to encourage him to spill in order to breathe.

"He was gracious. He came through and spoke to all of us. If anything, he seemed"—and here he switched to English—"ebullient. He kept saying it was a great day. I took it that the sub was his baby and he expected the new administration would allow him free reign at home to fire at whoever he felt like--if only metaphorically."

"You never know," Shai said. "This new Right here might force a deal on us. Everybody before them was too afraid of who might yell at them. These folk just yell louder. May be a blessing in disguise."

For a long moment nobody spoke.

"How about the crew?" Arik asked, wondering if Shai was trying to get Yohanan to reveal a political persuasion. "Anybody seem unhappy the prime minister was using this very serious instrument of warfare for a joy ride?"

Shai noted that Arik's colloquial English was quite good. The boy had worked hard all along his journey to get here.

Yohanan sank back in his pillow. "People are unhappy when they're surprised. Nobody was surprised."

Shai asked, "Any scent of gas before you went under?"

Yohanan thought for a hard moment. "Maybe. I hadn't thought about it till now. Maybe there was a kind of sweet scent in the air shortly before I passed out."

"How were the security precautions?" Shai asked.

"On our side, we all knew each other. US Naval Intelligence vouched for their sailors."

"Metal detectors?" Arik asked. "Body searches?"

"No. They feel safe here."

"When you entered the naval base?"

"They checked IDs. We came in together with armed naval escort. They met us at the hotel and drove us in minivans."

"If there were American submariners onboard, why did they need you to replace the injured crewman?"

Yohanan eyed Arik with unbridled disdain. "They didn't. But once Gutman and the Americans were back ashore, you think they were going to sail to Haifa without a nuclear reactor officer?"

Arik had been feeling smarter, but that was stupidly obvious. He had to stop trying to impress Shai.

"What happens now?" Yohanan asked. "We take the sub to Haifa or wait here?"

"Why don't you rest a bit more," Shai said. "Come, Arik, I could use that good cup of coffee. You think such a thing exists on this base? The Americans seem to be sticking espresso machines everywhere. Though not quite as dangerous as amping up their soldiers in the field with amphetamines. Mostly."

Arik followed Shai as he headed towards the door. Shai turned back to Yohanan and said, "Since you're fine, I think we'll have all you boys flown home. Wipe the decks clean so to speak.

Bring in a new crew to take the sub to Haifa. You wouldn't mind if we chatted a bit more in Jerusalem, would you?"

"Why would I fucking mind?"

"Met your father," Shai said. "Great chess enthusiast. I see where your English comes from. By the way, curious why he didn't head to America."

"In America everybody's so polite you never know what they really think. Never would feel like you're standing on solid ground there, he says. He likes Israel—no formality, lots of intimacy, people are rude and mean it. I like the French, who show little but never fake it."

Shai said, "I prefer Italians. They speak loudly, take up all the space around them, draw their words in the air with their hands, and eating comes before anything else. Paradise." He headed towards the door. "Yohanan, since you're on lockdown, Arik here will call your father and let him know you're fine."

"Thank you."

Shai turned to Arik. "I certainly know what it's like to worry about my son. When I text him too much all his answers are 'Great,' 'Cool,' to get rid of me, even thinks I don't know he is. Yet if I trip, he's full speed to make sure I'm okay. Why don't you call right away, so both Yohanan and Mikhail can rest easy."

CHAPTER 9

Meir Bardin walked down the Via Delarosa with Tzipi Ben-Ami watching a group of Palestinian schoolboys playing in the wide, sunny, stone lane, backpacks on. One boy crouched behind an outdoor café table, hiding, as his friends down the way were puzzled, unable to find him. They could be Israelis.

Meir said, "I'm more often in America than the Old City. Maybe it's a mistake. Thanks for asking me to join you."

He loved telling stories and jokes, and laughing at the punch lines, but wanted to tell her a different story.

"In 1960," Meir said, "Miriam and I were in Paris waiting in this long line to see the movie *Exodus*. It was exciting to have Paul Newman star in a film about Israel. I don't remember how, but the theater owner found out two Israelis were there. He came out, brought us to the front of the line, wouldn't let us pay and led us to fantastic seats."

Tzipi thought about how different their history would be if Rabin had lived. Some kind of peace would have been achieved by the man who engineered the Six-Day War triumph and turned peace statesman. The Jews might still be beloved as the plucky people who had made the desert bloom and brought innovation everywhere they went.

Meir sighed. "Today it wouldn't be completely safe for us to stand in that same line."

"Some of it's our fault. When challenged we immediately attack and defend ourselves. We're never wrong, but of course everybody's wrong, a whole lot of the time."

These East Jerusalem stone streets might someday be part of a Palestinian entity, Tzipi thought, but she agreed with Gutman that the city would never be physically divided again. She was not so far from Gutman's philosophy, but could not stand his dictatorship. Only a coalition partner threatening to bolt could effect change, and what they wanted was rarely what the people did.

She saw the arched entranceway of the Abu Shukri Restaurant in the continuous stone façade, the shop before it with hand-embroidered dresses hanging outside; she might have a look. The restaurant's turquoise metal doors had been folded to the side and would be pushed across when closed. It was all open air here, with delightful pedestrian lanes and some broader squares, occasionally with a fountain.

Abu Shukri had built a small restaurant here in 1948, Tzipi knew. Right on the way to the Holy Sepulcher and Al-Aqsa Mosque. With all the tourists after sixty-seven, he enlarged. Meir took off his kippah as he walked inside. He ate vegetarian in a non-kosher restaurant, but was mindful of *marit ayin* (appearance to the eye) and so removed his kippah so no Jew passing would see it and believe the restaurant served kosher food.

He was surprised how large it was inside. A dozen wood tables crowded with men and women, some traditionally dressed, others in western clothes, and everywhere plates piled with pita, falafel, eggplant salad, and on every table a plate of thick hummus. The songbirds trilling in cages dropped from the centers of stone arches were operatic.

A jovial Palestinian, fortyish, his stomach testament that he enjoyed his own fare, came over and he and Tzipi kissed on both cheeks.

"Meir, this is Fadi Taha, the original owner's grandson. Fadi, Meir Bardin."

"Welcome, welcome." Fadi reached out his hand, shook Meir's and led them to a table against the wall, about the only place available Meir saw. "What can I bring you to drink? Orange juice? Freshly squeezed lemon juice? Coca-Cola?"

"Lemon juice," Meir said.

Tzipi nodded that she'd have one too. "Fadi, first tell him the secret of your hummus."

The Arab smiled. "In fact, there are two secrets. First, my grandfather would enter the shop at two a.m. to boil the chickpeas and drain them in the traditional way with a cloth. His helper then ground them by hand, every morning, so everything would be fresh. Fresh is also the second secret. Fresh parsley, and most of all freshly squeezed lemon juice despite the extra cost, not the bottled kind. Fresh olive oil from our fields, garlic cloves bought in the market that morning. He was doing this before anybody else. And maybe there is a third secret. We do not measure ingredients. We mix and taste. It is passed down from father to son to know the exact taste."

"So bring us some hummus and pita already," Meir said with jovial loudness.

"May I choose the rest of the lunch for you?" He had seen Meir pocket his kippah. "We serve no meat."

"Perfect," Tzipi said.

Meir looked around. A group of German tourists queued noisily and impatiently outside. It was a wonderful place. Living together like this should be the definition of Greater Israel.

Fadi returned quickly balancing hummus, two extra plates,

silverware and two glasses of lemon juice with lemons dancing on top.

Meir broke off some of the soft warm pita, scooped it into the hummus and then took a large bite. His eyes enlarged. "This is terrific!"

"*Shukran*," Fadi said, Arabic for thank you. "We have a restaurant in Beit Hanina my brother runs. Our cousins are in both places. We would like to open branches all over—Ramallah, Nablus, even Tel Aviv and Haifa. We had an investor from the Emirates who wanted me to come and open restaurants there."

"But you wouldn't," Meir said.

Beit Hanina was a beautiful neighborhood of East Jerusalem, sprawling over the hills on the road to Ramallah—but with the high concrete barrier wall running beside and splitting off part of it.

Fadi smiled. "We are like the Jews. Who can leave Jerusalem?"

As plates of steaming falafel and rice, cold vegetables and salads filled the table, Meir spooned food onto his plate, overflowing with ideas.

"They could partner with some reputable Israelis. Expand throughout the country. With all these cousins they could safeguard the homemade flavor."

"I wasn't thinking that when I suggested we come. But it sounds perfect."

"What were you thinking?"

"I'm not sure exactly," Tzipi said. "I'm looking for optimism. I feel it here. I don't know exactly why." She sipped some of her lemon juice, which surprisingly was both unsweetened and sweet, and then she brought her eyes to meet his. "We must find Gutman. It will embolden our enemies and all the crazies out there if we don't. But if we do, no, when we do, I don't want to give up this sense of a hope for change I've been feeling."

She was tough and he liked her directness. "I think I know what you're feeling. Mordecai Gilboa has been making some noise about running, if Gutman is gone," Meir said. "He'd be a renewal of the disappointment. We need a revival of the dream."

"I no longer believe in Likud but can't bring myself to join Labor. I'm looking to start my own party. Secular, capitalistic." She smiled. "Not the crass kind. Inclusive. I like the way you thought of this place expanding all over Israel. But I don't think I can carry the country."

Then suddenly Meir saw it. Why she had come to him in the first place. "You're offering me the top spot?"

"Yes, but not as a figurehead. Not even as a joint ticket. The stakes are too high now. I'd run as number two on the list. It would be our party, but in any disagreement your decision. I honestly believe we're a nation of people who, with a few exceptions, care more about the country than their own role in it. That's the revival of the dream I see. I think you're the best person to bridge all the factions."

"Except the settlers."

"I think you can," she said. "We can. You have religious commonality with them. I breathe Betar." Her right-wing youth organization still brought passion to the Right. "Anybody can find something wrong with one of us. Everybody can find something to like between us. They won't agree with all we'll propose but we have the language to talk to them."

"You think he'll be found?"

She had not eaten much and spooned spicy red eggplant over some rice. Tzipi looked up. "I think we have that conversation then. But my instinct is, enough screwing with the nation already."

Meir sat unmoving for a long time. When he arrived in the 1950s, hostile Arab states seethed at their border and focus on survival was required. They had more than survived and it was time to settle how they would live. Even if Gutman reappeared, they could run and still effect change, maybe even substantial change, and maybe even win.

He looked at Tzipi, amazed at what she had conceived. She had spent her life physically safeguarding the state, while he had lived to influence its character and goodness.

"We're also going to have to find you a husband," he said. "Enough of this being alone."

She chuckled. "I may be getting to the point where I'll let you do that. But let me be clear, I said maybe."

He was both nervous and excited. "Thank you for entrusting me with this."

Sami Abadi sat in his small room in the Wurzburg Camp talking to a family who had fled Aleppo right before the Soviets and Assad dropped so many bombs the debris fell on almost everybody there.

"ISIS fines you for smoking," the Syrian said, his hand shaking as he lit a cigarette. "Nobody came to help us. We believed America would. Instead, they ban us." He lifted his skinny arm, veins protruding, scars on both hands. "Do I look like a terrorist?"

"The Germans are doing more than anyone could have imagined," Sami said. "Usually the world surprises for the worst. The Germans once did that to themselves."

A boy of sixteen came running in. His left arm was in a cast and a freshly healed bomb fragment scar ran across his cheek. Cigarette burns dotted his neck and face. He'd told Sami that in Homs he provided cell phone videos to the news outlets. Caught, he had been imprisoned for three months. From Homs he took a bus to Aleppo, where he stole a phone off a dead soldier's body and began shooting videos again. Since the civil war started, Sami had seen so many unknown heroes in Syria.

"He has a backpack on and he's heading across the camp,"

the youth said.

"Towards the front gate?" Sami asked.

The boy nodded rapidly.

Eli was pacing in the white apartment when the phone rang. He listened to Sami's report. Eli was content enough with the mixed team of watchers he'd assembled, some agents, some Berlin Embassy personnel, but every Israeli was ex-military. Eli headed outside to his rented BMW 220d coupe, with all-wheel drive in the event the pursuit ran off road, glad Ramzy was finally on the move. Soon his cell rang, the sound hugely amplified by the car's speakers. Eli pressed the answer button on the steering wheel.

"He's headed south on Autobahn 7. It runs to the Austrian border, Salzburg. Mercedes GLE 400, dark blue." He gave the license number, which Eli remembered easily. "Someone's driving him. Man, maybe fifty."

"Okay," Eli said and rang off.

He dialed the advance team to the south and directed them to the Munich Airport, a little over a hundred kilometers before Salzburg. They had plenty of personnel to follow him by car into Austria, if that's where Ramzy was headed. If he boarded a plane, they needed someone on it with him, or if not possible, at the very least who saw the destination so a team could meet the flight.

He dialed Orit, was lucky she had been on the Continent. Born Karine Ganem, the dark, Tunisian Jewess with glistening, waist-length black hair and matching eyes waited with the advance team. A young-looking thirty-eight, Orit very usefully attracted men of all ages. Eli knew, however, that Ramzy would not slip into a honey trap, and any attempt would reveal her as an Israeli agent. Dalal was Ramzy Awwad's anchor. To cut it, no matter how alone, would set him adrift on raging seas.

When she answered he said, "I won't be able to say goodbye

at the airport. Stay close but don't flirt, don't talk to him. If he talks to you, tell him your life story, don't ask much."

"Of course," she said.

Eli hung up. She knew how to handle herself. He was the one who needed handling with all these excessive instructions. He pushed the accelerator deeper. There was little traffic ahead as the autobahn rose over the Holzbach River. Finally on the move, to Eli's surprise he felt uneasy.

Knowing he was breaking protocol, he dialed the country code for Israel and the number. If the Germans were listening he didn't care. He felt certain they were headed out of Germany, and anyway, there was little lost if the BND knew Israelis were operating on their turf. They were all allies these days, for this fragment in time, against Islamic terror.

It was late in Israel and his son would both be sleeping and not recognize the +49 coming up on his cell phone screen.

"Dad?" Yigal said, half-asleep.

Eli laughed. "How'd you know?"

"I told Grandpa not to tell you. How long was that going to last."

"I spoke to your mother."

"She didn't tell me. Dad, I'm okay. It only hurts all the time."

Eli laughed, and for a moment was surprised at the silent tears rolling down his cheeks. Then he was not surprised at all.

"It's no problem," Yigal said. "Nobody was killed. I'm already better. Mom even yelled at me, so you know I must be okay."

"She never yells. She must have been worried."

"Less worried then," Yigal said. "That's my point. How are you, Dad?"

"Fine," Eli said reflexively, then added, "I miss you. I wish I was there."

"I'd be glad if you were here but I don't need you."

Eli sped around a large truck, the BMW's engine not even straining. "How do you feel, being in an attack?"

"At first I was furious. I was in the middle of editing this great footage my friend shot. I was in that world and then I'm lying on the floor, my head bleeding and everything unbelievable pain. Now, after our planes bombed them silly, I wonder who on the other side was hurt like me. Or can't feel anything at all. And I'm starting to feel guilty if I want to leave the country for film. What's film compared to living here?"

"Film's a lot," Eli said. "It's what you do. It's everything. That and love. It's all about who you love and loving what you do." At that moment, Eli admitted to himself he still loved what he did. Eli's phone buzzed with an incoming call. "Son, I have to go."

"Love you, Dad."

"I love you too."

Feeling whole, Eli pushed the button on his steering wheel.

The voice said, "They're off the autobahn in Munich. Probably the airport."

In the thunder and rain, Mordecai Gilboa's sons, Gideon and Rafi, sat in the back row of the bus heading from the settlement of Ariel to Jerusalem.

"They were so great," Rafi said.

The religious didn't need anybody else, Gideon thought, they had their own world. He too had loved the rock concert performed by religious trio The Solomon Brothers, the three youngest of seven siblings with the exciting Sruli on mandolin. He wished the rain had waited a few hours to start. Traveling on settler roads, the bus would make a stop at Ma'ale Adumim just outside Jerusalem, the largest Jewish city in Judea and Samaria. Their father would pick them up there. Gideon listened as the bus driver turned the sound up on the news report.

"I'm making pancakes tomorrow," Rafi said. He placed his forehead against the cold window and looked into the dark. "With strawberries from the garden in them. Like you said, the strawberries go in later. I don't want you to watch."

"Fine," Gideon said. "You're actually getting okay at it."

Rafi noticed a white plated Palestinian truck just ahead of them slowing in the rain to climb the rise, and he felt the bus grind down a gear to not hit it.

"I see lots of times there aren't soldiers at the entrance checkpoints, so the Arabs are coming on our roads," Rafi said. "Not just when it's raining."

The rain noisily pounded the roof of the bus and slashed at the windows, streaking them. "Mom says it's okay," Gideon said. "That the soldiers are trying to make their lives easier when they can."

"Then it's good."

The Palestinian truck slowed further. They were near the small settlement of Ma'ale Levona, which housed one hundred twenty families. Rafi knew because their father made them know every settlement *and* its history. Rafi liked to figure things out but hated memorizing, but he had to so he did. He knew Ma'ale Levona overlooked the mountain pass of Wadi Haramia, where the Maccabees battled the Seleucids in 167 BCE. Rafi looked out the window again. The hills were terraced with Palestinian olive groves, low stone walls at the base of each terrace, and atop the highest hill the triangular red tile roofs of settlement homes.

"I'd be a little scared to live in such a small settlement," Rafi said to his older brother, but then added hurriedly, "Don't tell Dad."

Gideon punched his arm. "Of course not, scaredy-cat."

"Don't. That hurts."

Rafi decided to listen to the news, which explained a Palestinian girl, exactly Gideon's age, with another girl, exactly his age, had stabbed a seventy-year-old Palestinian man in Jerusalem the year before, thinking he was a Jew.

"How stupid," Rafi said.

Gideon shrugged. "Until they talk, sometimes I can't tell the difference either."

The announcer continued that the older girl had stabbed two people with scissors, only slightly injuring a sixteen-year-old boy. A police bomb disposal officer had shot and killed the fourteen-year-old and gravely wounded the older girl. The three-judge panel had now sentenced her to thirteen and a half years, as according to the defendant the two girls had decided to stab Jews because they were Jews. The judges noted that the attack was initiated for nationalistic and radical ideological reasons. The announcer quoted the judges: "It appears the offense was committed against a backdrop of murderous ideology that is widely spread, like poison, in different forms of wild incitement."

"They sound like politicians not judges," Gideon said. "But we have to give them long sentences, even if they're kids, to stop this."

"Does it work?" Rafi asked. "It seems like this stuff keeps happening. Maybe if we sentenced them to jail for forever it could stop?"

Most of the way up the hill on the two-lane roadway, the truck ahead of them stalled. The bus driver swore loudly. He wiped at the fogged windscreen to clear it. There was hardly anybody on the road at this hour, and though he could not see far for oncoming traffic, he made this run six days a week and knew nobody would be heading at them.

He pulled the bus out to the left to pass, brought his head forward and squinted through the windscreen, his vision blurred both by the old wipers and the heavy rain. He was right, no traffic coming towards him. Suddenly, he felt his wheels at the edge of the cliff. He had driven out too far on this road bordered only by small bushes. Both front and back tires on the left side skidded over the bushes. He braked hard, turned the wheel to the right.

Kids screamed as the bus teetered on the edge of the small bluff. The driver tugged at the wheel fiercely, but caught in the mud the tires didn't respond. Then the bus was over the edge, sliding down as the driver frantically tried to steer. They plowed into a boulder and tipped over. The driver pitched forward, his head crashing into the windscreen. On its side, the bus skidded down the muddy, wet hill. Kids bounced against the roof, the seats, everywhere. Then Rafi felt them stop. There was screaming and crying and blood, and his arm was in such pain he bit his tongue so hard he tasted blood in his mouth.

A loud crash outside woke Izzat Nazzal, and beside him he saw his wife Nadjla was also up. He pushed the covers aside and went to the window of their house in the outskirts of the village of Al-Lubban ash-Sharqiya. In the rain, he saw an Israeli bus had gone off the road and was resting on its side. He told Nadjla, who ran to get their children, and in their pajamas they all hurried into the rain to help.

As he trudged through the mud, Izzat called Israeli emergency services and gave them the bus's location. For an instant, he recalled almost thirty years ago when an old friend had been shot in the village while riding on his donkey and a woman killed by her front door, and then the Israeli car sped towards the settlement of Eli. Settlers had stuck in retaliation for the assassination in New York of the Israeli rabbi Meir Kahane. Israeli police arrested three people but released them, they said, for lack of evidence. A small fire erupted from the engine of the bus and he shook his head to push the memory away.

As Izzat reached the bus, which lay on its side, he saw that luckily the door had swung open on top. He put one and then his second foot on a tire and hoisted himself onto the top of the slippery bus. He told his wife and two older children to reach for him from the tire, and one by one he pulled Nadjla, his eldest daughter, and her younger brother up. Nadjla slipped on the smooth side of the bus and kicked her muddy slippers over the side. Izzat ordered the three to drop down into the bus and lift people to him while he kneeled to pull them out.

He looked at the flames licking the engine and said, "Hurry."

Izzat lowered Nadjla first, followed by their seventeen-year-old daughter, Leila, and then he wiped the rain from his face with his soaked pajama sleeve. He was hesitant about his ten-year-old son, wishing his fifteen-year-old son were here, but he had slept at a friend's.

"I want to," Daoud said, as he started to lower himself headfirst. The three younger children remained in the rain beside the vehicle. Lightning cracked the dark, followed by deep thunder. Izzat held both his son's legs as the boy went arms first into the crying and screaming Jewish children.

Once Daoud was standing, he saw that though the bus rested at an angle, he could walk down the main aisle by holding on to the seats on both sides. He found a girl who seemed scared but not hurt, and though he didn't know if it was okay to touch her, she threw both arms around him.

"Mama," Daoud called.

His mother came, took the girl from him, who muttered, "Thank you, thank you." And then in Arabic, "*Shukran.*"

Deep in the bus, Rafi was dazed, and sitting somehow. With his good hand, he wiped at the blood dripping from his nose where it had slammed against the metal seatback of the row ahead of him. His glasses were gone and his left arm hung lifelessly from his shoulder in terrible pain, which he tried to ignore. He had to find his older brother.

He looked up and saw a Palestinian woman, scarf over her head, and two Palestinian kids, an older girl and small boy, all in pajamas, lifting kids up through the top of the bus. For a second, he thought he was dreaming, that they all had died and that God was really not the Almighty but a trickster and this was what heaven looked like.

"Gideon!" he cried out.

There was no answer. Rafi got up and saw his brother unconscious in the row behind him. He tried to pull him up with both hands and felt so much pain in his left arm he screamed and fell over. I can do it, Rafi told himself.

Leila made her way to him using both hands to glide along the seats.

"My brother, my arm," he said to her in Hebrew.

"No problem," she said in the same language, weirdly to him exactly what an Israeli would say.

She bent, and facing Gideon, reached both forearms under his armpits and lifted him. Rafi could see her erect nipples against her wet pajamas. He was so embarrassed, in so many ways, that he was looking there now that he closed his eyes and told himself, lucky Gideon's a skinny kid, never eating and always playing soccer. He watched the girl backpedaling, dragging Gideon.

Most of the kids in the front of the bus were up and out now and she turned her head back and spoke to her mother, who was standing on a seat lifting a boy to her husband.

"Oosh, Mom, he's heavy."

"Together," her mother said as she jumped down and hurried towards her.

Just then, Gideon woke and said to the girl, "I think I'm okay. Rafi," he called out weakly. Then Gideon felt like he was going to throw up.

"I'm here," Rafi said, touched Gideon's shoulder from

behind. As he spoke, his bad arm swung against something hard and a wave of pain rolled through Rafi that was so strong water dripped from his eyes. The rain began pounding even noisier against the bus.

When Leila and her mother, hauling Gideon, reached the front, these two boys were the last passengers inside. Leila climbed up on the narrow edge of a seat and her mother lifted Gideon to her. When Gideon was standing somewhat steadily on the side of the seat, Izzat looked in and asked in Hebrew, "How are your arms?"

"Okay," Gideon said. He reached up, then he rose and his feet dangled in the air as the man pulled him to the safety of the pouring rain.

"This one's arm is broken," Leila said to her father.

Izzat lowered himself feet first into the bus. His leather sandals were wet. "Go up top," he said to his daughter and gave a loving look at his wife.

With both hands on Leila's waist, he lifted. The girl then put her arms on the outside of the bus and drew herself up.

"This will hurt," Izzat said to Rafi in Hebrew, "but I will be quick."

He grabbed Rafi exactly as he had his daughter and Rafi was in such pain he thought he was flying by himself. Then his face was in the rain and he felt the girl's arms around his waist. He was up, seated on the side of the bus, legs crossed. Leila turned him around to where men from Ma'ale Levona were running and sliding down the hill.

"Be careful, his arm," Rafi heard her say, and then passed out.

Rafi drifted in and out of consciousness. Sirens rose, and then after what seemed a long time he felt like he was being lifted onto something flat and hard and then brought up the hill through the rain and mud. There a large explosion and somehow he knew it was the bus. The people carrying him slipped climbing up the incline, the stretcher pitched, but they didn't drop him. Rafi opened his eyes and saw two helicopters dropping onto the highway. Must be Unit 669, Combat Search and Rescue Unit, Rafi thought, as he knew the names of a lot of the IDF units. This is almost exciting, he thought, and then he was unconscious again.

Three hours later, Mordecai Gilboa ran into Beilinson Hospital at the Rabin Medical Center in Petah Tikva. An army captain had phoned and explained that a local Palestinian had called emergency services and that the family had rescued everyone on the bus. The injured had been flown or driven to three different hospitals, and both his sons were at the Rabin Center, injured but not gravely. Miraculously, there had been no fatalities.

Mordecai ran into Rafi's room. He saw his son lying in bed, his arm and shoulder in a cast, eyes closed.

"Rafalah," Mordecai said quietly so as not to wake him, less frightened now.

Rafi's eyes opened. He was drifting on pain medication and for a moment thought he was still being carried up the hill, and then he saw his father.

"I wanted to make pancakes with strawberries. I'm hungry. Can Mom do it?"

Mordecai laughed with joy that his son could speak. "Of course, but you're getting almost as good as her."

"Where's Gideon? He looked bad. I couldn't help him."

"Here too. He has a concussion but they told me he's fine. I found you first."

Rafi smiled, which made his nose hurt. "Dad, I'm in love with a Palestinian girl. Is that okay?"

She had to be part of the family that rescued his boys. "I think that's wonderful," he said. And a little to his surprise, realized he meant it.

"I've switched from Cubans in the new rah-rah America," McEnnerney said to Shai and Arik, stubbing a cigar into his desk ashtray. "Though I understand your missing prime minister has a fondness for Cuban Cohibas."

"Not quite sure I understand the connection between people in power and expensive cigars," Shai said. "I prefer the taste of pastries filled with poppy seeds and apples."

McEnnerney laughed. "Next time you come in, I'll have some waiting." McEnnerney opened a cigar box on his desk. "Offer you fellas?"

Shai smiled and shook his head no.

Arik said, "Sure, love to try one."

"Gran Habano Corojo, vintage. Until the embargo in 1960, Cuba was the ticket for top-flight cigars. Had it all—rich soil and the know-how. After the Bay of Pigs, some of the cigar masters hightailed it to Honduras and the Dominican Republic, where there's damn good soil too. These fellas come from a leaf cultivated in 2002 but hand-rolled right in the good old USA, namely Miami." McEnnerney tossed a box of matches to Arik, who caught them with one hand. "Qualify as made in America."

Arik lit and then pulled on the cigar. "It's not too strong."

"I'm supposed to cut back to none," McEnnerney said. "But who knows how long anything's going to last these days, including me. So what the hell." He took a fresh cigar for himself. "I used to smoke La Gloria Cubanas, but only so people could see the wrapper and know I could. How stupid is that?"

"Completely stupid," Shai said. He had known McEnnerney for almost three decades, had kidded him each time they met about not being married. Shai had expected McEnnerney would age into chasing young women, who with enough expensive effort he could bed. One of his happier miscalculations.

McEnnerney ran a hand through his gratefully still red hair.

"What we got from our people aboard the sub is more or less what you got from yours, diddly squat."

"We're putting them on the night flight tonight, then some of our finest will have another go at them in the warm hearth of home," Shai said.

"What about the SPS?" Arik asked.

McEnnerney sank back on his chair and lifted his large shoes to the only clear area of his desk, the right corner, where they often rested. Arik noticed the scuffmarks there.

"We find a Russian pistol hiding in plain sight. The rest of the sub is as clean as a baby's bottom. So, do I think it was human error or was it planted to point us to Moscow, where we naturally like to look?"

Shai said, "I hate ascribing anything to human error. A trained special services man losing his weapon seems unlikely. At the same time, making mistakes is the beginning of the human condition."

McEnnerney abruptly brought his feet down, paced to the window and looked out at the sun beginning to set behind the bare trees of Virginia. He turned back. "So it's either a screw up and a flashing beacon, or a road to nowhere. And Ramzy Awwad?"

"We have a team following him as we speak," Shai said. "He's on the move. It's late in Germany, obviously."

"Headed to?"

"In the short term, Munch Airport. It's where he goes from there I'd like to know."

"Why'd he go back to Germany?" Arik asked.

"Maybe to throw us off, or simply to spend some time with his wife before he disappeared again," Shai said. "Maybe he's worried we'll leave him dead in an alley for this and he wanted to say goodbye. He's spent a great deal of his life away from her. It's hard, not sure it's something you understand yet, Arik."

McEnnerney approached, leaned both hands on his desk and turned to Arik. "What I'm hearing in the suburbs is stuff like men want their wives to wait before they watch shows they're streaming. The wives are complaining. They're bored at home but the men want them to hold off."

"I don't understand," Arik said.

Shai picked up the thread. "He's saying that behind the bravado, men need women. Women need men too, but they're better at being alone. If Ramzy had time to kill, he would want to spend it with Dalal, even at a risk. He's done it before."

"How long since you've spoken to him?" McEnnerney asked. "You two being buddies and all."

"I talked to him in Los Angeles recently to arrange for Eli to see him. As for friendship, it didn't survive our settlement policy. He's become darker. I don't think I'd actually spoken to him in almost fifteen years. There's a lot of people I don't see anymore." Shai looked wistful. "I suppose it's age. Everything shrinks."

"Well, I feel fortunate to still be in your circle. Can you find some time to stop over tonight for dinner, or at least a drink? You're on the late flight to Tel Aviv?"

"Yes," Arik said.

McEnnerney sat. "I'm sure your young colleague can find something more enjoyable to do. Anne Marie says without your harassment I'd never have gotten married. If I don't drag you over, she'll have my head and nothing else of me."

"Completely untrue," Shai smiled. "You were smart even when you were a stupid kid. I'll see if I can find a little bit of time, but only for her, this is truly more than enough of you for one day."

"Shall we say six p.m.?" McEnnerney said.

"I'll try."

"Do more than that. And for fuck's sake don't bring anything." McEnnerney looked at Arik. "Take care of him."

"I think it's the other way around. I'm lucky to have this opportunity to learn."

"Bright boy," McEnnerney said. "Let me make a call and see if I can find someone smart to show you the sites. Pretty all right?"

Orit pulled the scarf tighter over her head as she ran down the jetway easily in four-inch heels, lucky she got the last seat on the flight to Paris. She hurried in and the flight attendant shut the door behind her. The plane had two rows of seats on each side. She was in 10B. She walked down the narrow passage in her short skirt and heavy coat with a fur-lined collar. The plane was completely full, and as she approached her seat she allowed no reaction that Ramzy Awwad was in 10A. Maybe it's fate, she thought. As she dropped into the seat she was all long legs, then she bent forward gracefully and eased her Yves Saint Laurent quilted, black leather shoulder bag in the space in front of her.

"I hate these small planes," she said in French with an almost indistinguishable Arabic accent, both languages absorbed from her Tunisian-born parents. She had decided on an unappealing role to blunt any suspicion that she was watching him. "I hope I don't have a panic attack."

"Fortunately it's a short flight," Ramzy said.

"Not short enough. I need a Scotch."

"You coming from a special evening?"

She laughed with a tinge of weariness. "It seemed like it was going to be." She stood, took off her jacket, and as she sat again lay it over her lap, as for now the cabin was warm. "My tastes are quite simple; I'm easily satisfied with the best."

"Winston Churchill," Ramzy said.

She laughed without embarrassment at getting caught. "I also borrow from the best."

"What do you gain from living as you do?" he asked,

switching to Arabic.

Orit felt her legs were her best feature, and she turned flat chested into an asset with low-cut blouses she wore braless. During downtimes, she often took photos of herself in the bathroom and practiced adding curves. Photoshopping is a skill that might come in handy, she once said to herself in the mirror.

"My parents were born in Tunis," she answered in Arabic. "We ended up in Marseilles with about every other immigrant. Ugly drug smuggling hub. Everywhere kids smoked hash from North Africa. The drug dealers walked around openly with AK-47s. The police wouldn't come into half the neighborhoods, so Muslims set up their own checkpoints. My brother drove a truck for a food bank that brought free food to people in the Air-Bel quarter. One night he came across this unofficial roadblock—sandbags, concrete blocks. The *jeunes* searched his truck to see if the *flics* were hiding there. When they found no police they let him pass. He came home so scared he threw up." She crossed a long, bare leg over the other. "I had to get away. These were my ticket out. Once I saw how the best feels, I liked it a lot better."

It was a legend Eli had created with her from the truth that her family had fled from Tunis to Marseilles to Israel.

He asked with true curiosity, "What does living the good life lead to?"

Her face dropped. Orit had inhabited this cover for so long, with so little time at home, she sometimes had to remind herself that the woman with makeup and stilettos was not her. She had been self-conscious about her height in Israel and always wore sandals.

"If you're lucky," she said, "you find an older gentleman, and in exchange he's not brutal but actually kind. You open your heart to that kindness, even though he falls asleep at eight o'clock watching television, and while he helps your loved ones, you truly love him." She knew her cover and real life converged here, as she had nothing to fall back on when she aged beyond the use of her allure and at some point she would need to find someone.

"And if you don't find such kindness?" Ramzy asked.

"Then you provide for those you love any way you can, and try and tell yourself that your suffering is worth it. That you've gotten them out of the Air-Bel. What do you do?" she asked.

"I'm a translator in a Syrian refugee camp in Wurzburg with my wife. She teaches the children."

Orit smiled. "Very romantic, working together that way. I'm not joking."

"I did not think you were. We're not always together, so now we've lucky."

"Is it hard at your age? You don't mind... I meant the difficult living conditions?"

"No."

"There's so much news in Paris about the refugees. The television footage upsets me, but truthfully I forget about it quickly. Does that make me terrible?"

"No. It makes you like most people, trying to make it through your own week. Do you know about the Calais Jungle Camp?"

Though she did, she shook her head no, as her cover would not focus on such matters.

"Several months ago the French dismantled it. Bulldozed it to the ground."

"*Quelle horreur*. Were people killed?"

"Not then, but it was a mess. Ramshackle wood shacks and tents for over six thousand people. A thousand children alone without family. People were trying to smuggle themselves into England on lorries going through the Chunnel. Refugees from everywhere—Africa, Afghanistan, Syria, Iran, Eritrea, Pakistan. They bussed them to reception centers all over France. Abandoned hospitals, barracks, hotels, anywhere there were empty buildings. A lot of the villages are unhappy about their new guests. One town protested the government's desire to settle them in an abandoned wing of their psychiatric hospital."

"Maybe the villagers should take up residence in it. It's all terrible," Orit said. "Especially the photos of those bleeding children in Syria."

Ramzy closed his eyes for a long moment and then opened them slowly. "Most of the refugees don't speak French. They can apply for asylum. The Afghans will be bussed back to that war zone. The Africans will be deported. The Syrians and the Iraqis have the best chance to stay. They've allowed the children to stay in Calais in converted shipping containers. They need helping searching for any family that's still alive. With your Arabic and French, you could be of enormous help. That is, if you have the time?"

She laughed. "I'm not going to tell you what happened with my gentleman friend in Munich, other than you saw me run on the plane. Let's say, I have nothing but time now."

"It's a different kind of good life," he said.

If she was flirting, she would have rested her hand on his lightly now and her instinct was to do so, that all men liked the touch of a beautiful woman, but she was mindful of Eli's explicit instructions and then she saw that Ramzy would recoil. *Merde*, she thought to herself. He was making her actually want to go to Calais and help.

She smiled. "Maybe it would be a welcome vacation."

Ramzy laughed. He found people were often willing to help, if they knew how.

"Are you going there?" she asked.

"Not quite yet. I have a somewhat long journey to take first. But I have friends there. I can put you in touch with them."

"That would be great." She bent, being careful to keep her

short skirt from rising, reached for her bag, pulled open the magnetic snap flap and removed her cell phone. "Can I give you my number? I'm Michelle Beaulieu." She reached out her perfectly manicured hand, red nails in winter, creamed colored in spring and summer.

He shook it and said, "Ramzy Awwad." He removed his cell phone, which was off for the flight, and turned it on to take her number. She gave it to him. "I'm leaving Paris tomorrow but I will have someone call and give you instructions on who to see in Calais."

When he had her number, she asked, "May I have your number? When I meet one of those fabulously poor but goodhearted Doctors Without Borders there, I'll need to thank you."

"You'll meet one of those doctors the first day. What you'll let happen is less certain." He took her mobile from her and typed in the number of the phone he used to call Dalal. "I can't always answer," Ramzy said, "but I will call you back."

She was excited to have gotten his number for Eli, but was thinking too weirdly that when this was over, she might go to Calais, help and meet one of those doctors.

Eli sat in the passenger seat of the BMW coupe, their Berlin Embassy trade attaché behind the wheel.

"Should be eight and a half hours to Paris," the attaché said. "I can make it in a little over seven."

"Anything will be fine."

Eli wore the warm jacket foisted on him by the trade envoy, and with the window down he smoked, a habit he wondered if he could easily relinquish. His watchers at Orly Airport would follow Ramzy, who hopefully would bed down for the night and not move until morning, allowing Eli time to reach Paris. He felt that they were in the last act now with the climax near. He stubbed the cigarette in the ashtray, closed his eyes and began to drift. As he slept, he dreamed he was on a bicycle pedaling in a lake, and as the bicycle sank he hit the bottom, still riding, and pedaled fiercely along the bottom trying to get out. He woke, sweat at his hairline, wondering what was bothering him.

An hour and a half later, Orit stepped into the jetway clutching her French passport but there were no armed soldiers there, not yet she thought. At French airports, machine gun clutching guards waited in the jetways to meet all flights from Muslim countries. She had been careful, after saying goodbye to Ramzy, to deplane first and not look back. As soon as she was in the arrivals terminal, fairly crowded at this hour since businessmen hopped around Europe on these night flights, she phoned Eli, surprised when he answered that she'd woken him.

"I ended up next to him on the flight." She paused, hesitant to say it. "I liked him."

"And," Eli said impatiently.

"He gave me his cell number."

Eli sat up in the racing BMW, startled by what she'd accomplished. They could track the GPS in the phone, but maybe more importantly they could listen to his phone calls, common technology used by legions of hackers.

"I liked him too," Eli said quietly. "He draws people to him. Makes him doubly dangerous."

The driver pulled off his earphones, which he'd used to take calls while Eli was asleep.

An hour later, Eli said, "Find out where Awwad is now."

The sun was just beginning to brighten the horizon behind them as they passed the champagne vineyards of Reims northeast of Paris. "Small hotel near the Arc de Triomphe. The Elysees Ceramic. No doorman."

"How long until we're there?"

"If we beat the morning traffic, an hour and a half."

"The number Orit got?"

"He spoke to his wife briefly after he checked in. We don't think there was any code in the talk but they're going to run it through the software in Herzliya."

So the number's good, Eli thought, suspecting it would be. Though he often used Orit on seductions, easy for any stunning agent to pull off, she had a bigger heart than most, which he had hoped might draw in Awwad.

"If he's not moving, find someplace for coffee with a bathroom," Eli said. "And I wouldn't mind something hot just out of a French baker's oven."

"A bathroom will be harder to find. The French prefer to piss in the street. They're trying these new *pissoirs* outside the Gare de Lyon. Hay on the bottom flowers on top. The nitrogen from urine combines with the carbon from the straw, kills the smell and feeds the flowers."

"Ingenious." Eli laughed, louder than warranted. He was feeling the tension.

Early in the morning, before his kids went to school, Shlomo sat in a towel at the kitchen table, wet beneath it from a long swim. The rest of the large house slept. He looked again at his son's midterm report card on the table. The one failing grade had convinced him to run for prime minister.

His son Dov's second-lowest grade was a 91 in Arabic. Math and Science were both 100s, English 98 and Art 92. His fourteen-year-old's most impressive mark was a 50, a fail, in The Culture of the Jewish People. Posters of the Israeli actress Gal Gadot from her starring roles in *Wonder Woman* and other American blockbusters were tacked to the ceiling in Dov's room. When the smug Naftali Bennett, who Shlomo knew from Bennett's high-tech days as a software entrepreneur, became Minister of Education two years ago, he introduced this category of The Culture of the Jewish people into the curriculum.

Dov had been inspired by his adoration of Gal Gadot, who was as Godlike as anything he had ever imagined, Dov had explained with great earnestness. His class had been assigned to compose new prayers. Dov had decided to write three prayers: for the protection of the country from missiles shot from Gaza in the south, from Hezbollah in the north, and from Iran in the east. To complete the map, he added a prayer to protect from sea monsters from the west, and explained to his father that he really did not believe in sea monsters but it was the only danger he could think of from that direction.

Shlomo decided not to tell him that he had been his son's age when Palestinians of Abu Jihad's flavor of the PLO boarded an Egyptian merchant ship in Lebanon and when sixty miles off the Tel Aviv coast were lowered into small boats. Luckily, when they came ashore they were spotted by police on beach patrol. One boat, the one with most of their weapons aboard, exploded in the firefight. The attackers got into the Savoy Hotel. Their elite counterterrorism unit, Sayeret Matkal, stormed the building. They killed seven of the bastards and captured one. Five guests and two soldiers died, including the Sayeret Matkal commander at the head of the charge, where Israeli commanders always positioned themselves. This was the greatness of their army, not the politicians' bullshit that they were the most ethical army in the world. Facing an opposing army, they did what was necessary.

Shlomo encouraged his son to think outside the box and stretch norms, as the country's best routinely did. So Dov, with Gal Gadot in mind, had written the prayers with God as a woman. "May she, who art in heaven, use her care and concern as a mother and the strength she knows from protecting the family to..." Dov explained in the section after the three prayers, which were similar except the prayer for the protection against sea monsters, where the she-God wore the Royal Tiara and wielded the Lasso of Truth. He did not include in the text, but had told his father, that the she-God who was all-powerful did not need an invisible plane, as she could just appear wherever she chose.

The teacher had claimed the prayers were disrespectful, all of them. She said she had hardly been able to read them. Dov had then asked her, "So what's the fifty percent for?"

"Effort," he reported she said.

"So why don't you make the effort to give me the right grade. A ninety, at least."

When he told his dad the story last night, Dov added, "I wasn't actually trying to be sent home, but it would have been good. She gave me the option to rewrite them."

"You refused?"

"Of course. I did the assignment. Finished."

Shlomo pushed the report card away with a smile, which soon faded. This ultranationalist view trickled down from the Minister of Education and his right-wing cohorts until it became a rushing river flooding over the breadth of Jewish culture. God as a woman now was blasphemous in an Israeli public school.

He threw the towel off, and cold, walked naked upstairs to slip beside his wife's warm body. But first he stood just inside Dov's room and watched him sleep. He walked in and kissed the back of his head. He could not fathom where the country would be when Dov was a father if it continued to close doors rather than barge through them.

In his youth, Shlomo had daydreamed about becoming a warrior and participating in vast battlefield victories. He was not exactly sure when he first realized battle lacked glory, that the point of strength was deterrence. He thought it was even before his first friends had bled to death.

He headed back to his wife. The real glory was to walk at dawn along the sands of their own country.

CHAPTER 10

Shai walked with Tzipi along Train Track Park near his home, mindful that his wife would be happy he was getting exercise. Israel was great at these innovations. The train tracks had been removed beginning at the old Khan Station, the historic terminus of the Tel Aviv to Jerusalem line, which ceased operation a few years before high-speed rail construction began in 2001. To connect Jerusalem neighborhoods with a ring of parks, engineers had fastened concrete imitations of wood planks to the rails to create a pedestrian path. Grass and gardens ran alongside the walkway. Old bus shelters had been converted into open-air bookshelves, the volumes borrowed and returned on the honor system. The grass widened at intersections into squares with benches and playgrounds. The station itself was reborn as shops, restaurants and a vegetable and flower market.

"This old Ottoman track was the first rail line in the Middle East," Shai said. "Started in 1890, took two years to build."

"Wonderful. Jewish *sechel*," Tzipi said, referring to the concept of spiritual ability to think, weigh and resolve. "But if we're so smart, why can't we find our own prime minister? So what's with

Orlov, the elder?"

"We saw a case of a sleeper who recruited his son in America five years ago. The parents got caught, were deported. They weren't highly placed; father was head of a futurist think tank. The twenty-two-year-old son was rising in the military, computer intelligence, born in the good old USA. Disappeared, presumably back to Russia. Recruiting their kids is what they're really after with these sleepers."

"I know, I know," she said impatiently. "These kids growing up in the West have the language, the culture. They pass background checks."

They needed these native speakers. Presently their Russian-speaking air force officers were coordinating over Syria to avoid misinterpretation as Putin's SU-34s dropped satellite-guided missiles while Israel was increasing bomb runs into Syria. She had the classified reports locked in her desk. A few weeks ago, Israeli F-15s had taken out missile caches the Syrian Fourth Army was ferrying to Hezbollah, one on the Beirut-Damascus Highway and another at As'saboura, midway between Damascus and the Golan Heights. Like President Assad, the Iran-backed Hezbollah were Shiite, Hezbollah emerging as one of the few victors in the disintegration of Syria.

Shai picked up his pace. "The father goes to the Russian Embassy. The son's next up to replace the nuclear reactor operator, who Ramzy has taken out. Highly specialized training and the son knew he would be next up. They do us a favor and don't kill anybody because there's no need to. The Russians get the technology and the Palestinians get Gutman."

"Could the Palestinians have launched this to affect our political landscape, give a less hardline candidate an opening?"

"It's a stretch," Shai said. "Seems unlikely with al-Nusra at the party. They'd want to kill Gutman sooner or later and video it, show us none of us are safe. After a lifetime of disappointment, I think Ramzy's gone in that direction."

"We cannot let that happen, obviously."

Shai moved towards a bench beside the smooth bike path. "I've had the son arrested and held incommunicado. Let him stew. I want to use threats against him to break the father. We'll pick Mikhail Sergeiovich up after he hears his son's been taken."

Shai's legs hurt. He sat and Tzipi followed.

Shai said, "Paul McEnnerney wouldn't tell me how they stole the stealth technology from St. Petersburg, but obviously the Russians need to know exactly how the Americans tinkered with it. Slap in the face to rifle the sub's secrets then leave it in the Americans' backyard."

"This way they're not caught with the submarine and push the planet to the doorstep of World War III, given who's in charge in Washington now. Eventually, US satellites or some new technology would have found it."

"Yes, in fact those were exactly Paul's thoughts, shared with me over what he said was a fifty-year-old Madeira. Terrible, tasted like rotten fruit." Shai laughed. He approvingly watched a mother with a toddler in the rear of her bike and a baby in the front basket pedaling fast on the path. He lacked physical daring, so appreciated it all the more in others.

"McEnnerney look at the Americans on board?" Tzipi asked. "Any Palestinian sympathizers?"

"He's at that as we speak."

Tzipi put a hand on Shai's knee. "Maybe you should talk to Ramzy yourself?"

"I'm considering it. I don't know. Eli's on him in France. At the moment, I want to break Orlov and leave Ramzy to Eli. And I don't want to tip Ramzy that we know where he is."

"I've seen Meir Bardin twice now. I told him the two of us should form a new party and I'd take the second spot."

Shai looked away and did not respond, which he knew everyone who knew him experienced often with great frustration.

"You surprised I wouldn't ask for the top spot?" she said in the silence.

He stood. "Let's go back and see where Orlov the son is." They stared to walk. "You deserve to be at the top. Nobody would be better. But this way might be more appealing."

"My thoughts too."

"I thought you might come to that."

Tzipi punched him in the arm. "I don't like being played. You should have said so."

"Sorry. Should have, absolutely." He looked down to make sure he didn't trip. "Force of habit, the not explaining."

Eli sat with Orit in a parked Peugeot in the port city of Fos-sur-Mer on the Mediterranean coast. Ramzy had boarded the train to Marseilles, unbeknownst to him accompanied by three Israeli agents, while they had driven the seven hours to the South of France. After two hours of Orit behind the wheel at ridiculous speeds even for Eli, though unable to believe his life would end in a crash, he had driven the rest of the way. Eli gazed out at the port aware he was atypically silent. Fos-sur-Mer specialized in a methane gas terminal and container shipping to nearby North Africa, and to the east Turkey, Lebanon, Syria, Israel and Egypt.

"You think Gutman could be in one of those ships or in a container?" Orit asked.

Eli heard her as if she was far away, as his thoughts were elsewhere. He had been sleeping poorly with vivid dreams, neither of which was like him. Last night he had dreamed his bicycle was locked to a tree in the West Bank. He knew the combination but could not remember the order of the digits, and was in danger if he could not ride away on it. He thought about the bicycle he had bought for Yigal when he was a teenager. The merchant insisted he would not outgrow it, as the seat could be raised. Yigal outgrew it in a year. With the seat raised to its long height, the bike was unstable and Yigal had fallen and bloodied his knee and arm. He could not see any connection or figure out what was actually eating at him. Eli was not a fan of psychology and therapy where people talked endlessly and nothing seemed to change. He had chosen to drive the rest of the way to stop dreaming.

"I don't know," Eli said. "Maybe."

"Or maybe Ramzy's headed to where the prime minister is?"

"Yes."

"Shall I call Ramzy with some question about Calais, or to thank him?"

Like many beautiful women, waiting was not Orit's strength, as she was accustomed to easily obtaining what she wanted. Eli had flown in a similar looking Tunisian secretary from Herzliya to head to the Calais Jungle wreckage to solidify Orit's cover, in the event Ramzy checked.

"No."

Eli's cell phone rang and he listened to the report. "He's heading to the port. On foot."

Orit and Eli were parked a few blocks from the sea, at the edge of L'Etang de l'Estomac, a large stomach-shaped pond. In front of him, swans skimmed the surface like those in Africa. He suddenly wondered if he'd enjoy traveling with his wife to see places like Africa and watch swans rise off a lake. He knew immediately that he'd be painfully bored.

Eli opened the car door. The smell of salt hung heavily in the air. "Let's walk." They were in a large nature reserve with pines covering stone outcrops, reminiscent of Jerusalem. The weather was warm. As they strode in silence, on the far hill an old medieval walled city rose from the heights, a church at the crest and tall bell tower on a cliff promontory.

"How old do you think it is?" Orit asked.

"Maybe twelve hundred. Same period as the Crusader Castle at Atlit where I met my wife. Those are Aleppo pines up there. Grow in thin soil on steep slopes. We call them Jerusalem pines."

"What were you doing in Aleppo?"

"Liaison with Sunni militias. They found an underground chemical weapons storage facility south of Homs. Assad had been building it for seven years. It was fully operational for two weeks in 2013 before we took it out from the air. The tunnels were vast. In exchange, we provide aerial surveillance photographs to the militias. They track arms shipments to Hezbollah for us. Longer range missiles and chemical weapons top of our list."

The pines were tall with thin, bare trunks, almost all the thick greenery at the top. Eli's phone rang. He listened. "Okay," he said and turned to Orit. "He's walked up the gangplank of a freighter. SS *Baalbek*. Flying the Lebanese flag. Seems like all the containers are loaded."

"Any sign of the prime minister?"

"No."

The wide dirt path along the pond was empty, save for three bikers up ahead on mountain bikes with thick tires. Very small waves broke on the pebbles at the shore. A flock of pink swans covered a large swath of water near them, many preening themselves.

"How are there swans here?" Orit asked, excitedly moving towards them.

To Eli, suddenly she seemed like a young girl at the beach. "Don't know. They must winter here from the north. I've seen a lot in the Netherlands in the summer."

At the sound of Orit's approach, the entire flock rose noisily on incredibly thin legs, which made their long necks seem short in comparison, and they marched deeper into the pond. Eli felt like running in and chasing them and squeezed his eyes. He began to walk faster, which Orit matched with her naturally long strides.

A half hour later, Eli's phone sounded again and he listened, bit his lower lip, but it was the news he expected.

"What?" Orit asked.

"The freighter's pulling out. Awwad's still aboard."

"Any chance they can still bring the prime minister aboard en route?"

"Possibly," Eli said. "We have a submarine nearby watching for exactly that. I called for it as soon as Ramzy headed towards the southern ports. It was already on this side of the Mediterranean if needed."

"More likely the prime minister's already there," Orit said.

Eli did not answer immediately, looked at the port crowded with freighters and a single cruise ship. "That's how I'd do it. Not bring him ashore unless I had to. And I see no reason why they would here."

"Will we board the freighter?"

"Fortunately for me, the higher-ups will make that decision."

She understood what he was saying. If they did and Gutman was not aboard, they'd blow their chance to follow Ramzy Awwad. She was sure Eli didn't like deferring to politicians. Without question, he would wait and follow Awwad when the freighter docked.

"I don't care if I'm not well enough," Rafi Gilboa told his parents. "I want us to go and thank them. Now."

He was sitting up in his bed. Gideon was still in the hospital, but he'd be released soon.

"What can we bring that's not grown in the settlements?" Tali Gilboa said. Their two younger children could stay with friends after school.

"I think they'd see money as an insult," Mordecai said.

"I agree."

"Bring flowers from our garden," Rafi said. "Then Dad can look around once we're there and see what they need."

Mordecai looked at his son, thinking he was little like him, was somehow freer, probably his mother's influence. "That's perfect."

"Good." Rafi climbed out of bed and winced. "Mom, help me get dressed and then let's go."

Tali looked out the window as they sped north on the settler highway. "Is it safe to drive into their village?"

"Yes. I talked to the regional military commander. They called the village elder and relayed our request to thank the family in person. They're expecting us."

"I know what I'm going to say to her," Rafi announced. "I discussed it with my friends. Well, one friend, Itai."

His nonreligious cousin in Tel Aviv, his mother thought. "What did you decide?"

"I'm not telling. You'll see." Rafi looked at a terraced hill of very old Arab olive trees. He could tell the age by the thickness of the trunks. "So we were here before the Palestinians?"

"By thousands of years," his father said. "You know that."

"So if some space people, like aliens, but nice aliens, landed and they showed us by digging up some stuff in a cave, in lots of caves, that they were here before us, would it then be their land?"

"That's not going to happen."

"The Palestinians didn't think we were going to happen either, I bet. You never know what can happen. Like the bus falling down the hill and the way they saved Gideon and me."

Mordecai thought about what his son had said. He was surprised how much the selflessness of this Palestinian family had affected him. There were Palestinian workers in Kiryat Arba he really liked, especially Akram, who could fix electrical, plumbing, basically whatever went wrong. But he had thought of Akram and some others as different than the angry masses in Hebron, and it occurred to him now, maybe in the same way anti-Semites thought of their Jewish friends as not part of "the Jews," for him Akram was not part of "the Palestinians."

Deep in thought, Mordecai remained mostly silent during the drive. As he turned onto the older, unlined paved road into the village of al-Lubban ash-Sharqiya, Arab houses covered the flank of the hill to his right crowned by a water tower. Ahead to their left, right at the foot of the road, was a small mosque with a gold dome and a stone minaret. Another minaret rose halfway up the hill to their right.

"It looks a lot different than a settlement," Rafi said. "And those electrical wires look kind of crappy wound all around the top of that pole. Couldn't they blow up?"

"Yes," Mordecai said. He had often responded to this frequent observation by Palestinian sympathizers that the wiring was no different than everywhere in India, though he admitted now that was deflection and there were no such hazardous poles in Israel or the settlements.

Just south of here, Mordecai knew, was the restored caravansary of Khan al-Lubban, which he'd never seen. Originally built in the Mamluk or early Ottoman period in the 14th or 15th century, the inn was near underground springs where travelers on the caravan routes would stop. Khan al-Lubban, a main respite on the Damascus-Jerusalem road, had the typical caravansary huge courtyard surrounded by stone walls with vaulted arches. It struck him for the first time, ridiculous as it now seemed, that the Arabs had history in this land too, though it obviously did not stretch as far back, and God had not promised the land to them.

At the entrance to the village, a boy stopped them with a wild waving of both arms. They were easy to recognize even without their yellow license plate. "Welcome, welcome," he said in English. "Follow me. Welcome."

"This is fun," Rafi said. "I'm only a little scared."

Tali wondered with a suppressed smile if he meant scared of being in the village or talking to the girl. Tali was happy to be here, beyond grateful to the family, but essentially not surprised at what they had done. Israel had been treating wounded Syrian civilians and rebel fighters at the Ziv Medical Center in Safed and other northern hospitals, and especially since the battle of Aleppo, had donated clothes, tents and staples through UNICEF. There was no possibility other than living together in this land.

The boy motioned with an outstretched hand for the car to follow him and then he ran down the road in his sandals, kicking up dirt.

Soon, they walked into the small, stone Nazzal family home, Izzat standing just inside the door to welcome them. In a long embroidered dress, Nadjla did not speak Hebrew and requested through her husband that they sit in the diwan, the central room, with couches and chairs around the table.

Rafi's eyes searched for the daughter, who finally entered from the kitchen, also wearing a long embroidered dress and carrying small plates of olives and pine nuts. He was really excited. Because he was a child, after she set the plates down she approached him. For modesty, she would not have spoken first to a foreign man.

"You are not hurt badly?" she asked in Hebrew.

Unable to speak, he shook his head no.

Izzat said to Mordecai, "The chicken is halal. Will that be okay?"

"Yes, thank you," Mordecai said. The Muslim ritual halal slaughter of meat was near identical to the laws of kosher slaughter, and he had eaten halal meat before.

Tali approached Nadjla and handed her the bouquet of colorful cyclamens and anemones. Nadjla wore a headscarf but no veil and her dark skin deepened as she blushed and hurried into the kitchen to find a vase.

"Don't forget to look around," Rafi whispered to his father.

"Okay," Mordecai said, feeling a little disoriented.

He could smell the food in the kitchen. This was all backwards; he had come to thank them but they were entertaining him. They sat around the table with Izzat and his son Daoud, while Leila and the smaller children stood against a whitewashed wall. Then Leila hurried to help her mother, Rafi watching her every step. A still fan hung from the white ceiling.

Nadjla entered with the flowers in a colorful ceramic vase and her daughter brought plates of *maftoul* on a large, hand-pounded steel platter. The traditional Palestinian dish of couscous in a fragrant broth of garlic and lemon had skinned chicken quarters on top. Nadjla and Leila ladled the food onto plates. Mordecai had eaten *maftoul* at Palestinian council meetings served on one huge platter with the men eating directly from it with spoons and surrounded by newspapers to absorb the drippings. He suspected they ate that way and were serving the food in individual portions in the event they had any sensitivity eating off one communal plate with them.

"Thank you, this is wonderful," Mordecai said. "But it is not necessary. We should be serving you. We came to thank you for what you did for us and for all the others."

Izzat smiled and Mordecai saw he had teeth missing on both sides. He wondered if he should offer to pay for some dental care, as he could get a good deal from a childhood friend in Jerusalem.

"*Inshallah*, the bus fell into our laps and not in a field far from anyone."

Inshallah. If God wills. Mordecai thought and wondered how many times he had said *Baruch Hashem*, blessed is God, at good news. Not the same, but not different either.

"You did not have to help. For a Palestinian bus, I would have called emergency services and then stood aside."

Tali said, "I'm not so sure. I think you would have jumped in. What you do is often more than what you say. Most people are the opposite."

Mordecai touched her hand affectionately.

"Allah commands us about what we must do for the stranger. So there was no question among any of my family but to help."

Rafi, who had been silent and had not touched the food in front of him, stood up and approached the girl against the wall. He was glad that he could not see what he had seen before beneath her wet nightshirt, as that would be too much and he was nervous enough. She was even more beautiful with her long, thick, black hair dry and dropping below her shoulders. Abruptly he said, "I'm Rafi. What you did is *sababa*," the common Hebrew use of the Arabic slang "perfect, amazing."

She laughed, embarrassed. "I'm Leila. It was actually an adventure, fun. Made me feel like I was better even than the boys my age, or at least as good. You are most welcome."

Rafi winced at her mentioning boys her age, but it didn't matter. He had come to say what he had practiced with his cousin. "Can we move over there?" he asked, nodding across the room.

"Sure." She led him to the door to the bedrooms and they stood in the entranceway.

"Promise me you won't laugh," he said.

She laughed, then put both hands over her mouth. "Sorry. Of course."

She was so beautiful and tall he could hardly bear it, but he knew eventually he would be taller than her. "Okay, here it is. I want you to know that I love you, but that I know I am just a boy and you are, well, almost an adult. So I am asking if we can be friends." He reached in his pocket and pulled out the crumpled paper with his cell phone number on it. He thrust it at her. "My number. Here."

She took it from him. "I am glad we met. It will be nice to have a new friend."

"You can text me anytime, even in the middle of the night." He exhaled heavily. "I want to think that maybe when I'm older... but that's probably impossible. But being friends is not."

"*Ala kefak*" she said, more Arabic slang Israelis used to mean "that's great." Hebrew had ossified in biblical verses for centuries as the Jews spoke Yiddish. Lacking vocabulary, modern Hebrew borrowed liberally from the mellifluous Arabic everywhere among them and a lot of technical words from English.

Tali had worried Rafi would be heartbroken, could not hear their exchange, but both kids were smiling and laughing.

After the meal and sweet tea with nana, Izaat asked Mordecai, "You are our guests. What more can I get you?"

Mordecai was not sure he would ask, but then said, "I'd love to see the Khan al-Lubban."

"Do you know what the name means?"

"No."

"The caravansary of frankincense. It was a resting place along the incense route." He called to Daoud to join them. "Your boy is still injured and I think he will be fine here." Izaat smiled, seeing the Israeli boy would prefer to stay. "We will walk, it's not far. Your wife is most welcome too."

"I'd love to see it," Tali said.

Mordecai looked around one more time to see what he might buy to thank them. He started to go into the kitchen to see if they had a dishwasher but then stopped. He was being paternalistic. He decided as soon as Gideon was better, he would invite them all for dinner at his home, wondered if they would come into a settlement as lots of Palestinians would not. He bet they would. He'd invite some friends from the Kiryat Arba Council and Ahmed's family. He was happy, and Tali and Rafi would be thrilled.

Mordecai thought of the Lord's words at Mount Sinai. You shall not oppress a stranger, for you know the feelings of this stranger, having yourselves been strangers in the land of Egypt.

He would get those shops in Hebron opened.

CHAPTER 11

In the passenger seat, Shai looked up as Arik parked in the small square packed with police vehicles in the Russian compound. The old prison's stucco walls gave way to stone halfway up its height, and above that towered a chain-link fence topped by triple bales of barbed wire. Just outside the Old City, Russia had begun construction on the walled compound in 1860, built an Orthodox Cathedral, men's and women's hotels, their consulate and a hospital. The Ottomans expelled the Russians. After World War I, the League of Nations carved up the defunct Ottoman Empire, handed Lebanon and Syria to the French, and the Mandate for Palestine to the Brits. Shai thought it was fabulous how many rulers had come and gone, each for far shorter than they'd imagined. The Brits, in their inimitable empire building, turned the fabulous walled area into their headquarters with administrative offices, and built a new police station and prison where they incarcerated members of the Jewish underground. His practical people returned the cathedral to the Russian Orthodox Church, leased the former Russian Consulate back to them, threw open the entrances to the public, and more recently used the prison for West Bank recalcitrants, whose wives, in long colorful dresses, were often seen queuing outside with food in plastic carrying bags and were welcomed in.

The Holy Trinity Cathedral, with its huge, white, stone facades crowned by eight massive steeples topped with crosses, attracted busloads of Russian tourists, many of whom flew up for the day from the inexpensive Egyptian luxury hotels on the Sinai beach at Sharm El Sheik, the peace stable enough to permit direct flights. From there, the tour buses zipped to the Old City, where enterprising Palestinian shopkeepers featured walls of gold leaf Russian icons the visitors bought with crisp American hundred and fifty dollar bills of unclear origin.

Shai entered the interrogation room, leaving Arik to peer through the two-way mirror and listen through headphones.

Orlov was whistling to *Prince Igor*. As Shai walked in, he glanced up and continued whistling. Shai waited.

Orlov gazed at a window he couldn't see through and spoke to it. "Thank you for letting me know my son was found," he said to Arik.

Not sure of himself but emboldened, Arik tapped twice on the glass, intending it a thank you.

Orlov smiled, then the smile was gone and he looked at Shai, who in the interim had taken a wood chair and sat across the table from him. He looked tired.

Orlov said, "Where's my son?"

"Ayalon Prison in Ramla."

Where they kept Arabs. Orlov shrugged. "Far better than the bottom of the ocean."

"Mostly nobody would disagree there," Shai said. He returned to silence, and after a long pause said, "I gather you knew some important people in Moscow?"

"I was useful. For a time. In the new capitalist planet, no need to translate into English, easier to buy the rights," Orlov said.

"If you're going to keep me for an extended period, I'd appreciate pen and paper. Maybe I'll accidentally write out what you want to know. Or make up something. I could try my hand at fiction."

"Sure. I'll arrange it."

"You think my son, or maybe I had something to do with kidnapping the prime minister?"

"Maybe you don't detest the Motherland as much as you'd like us to think? There'd be a big reward down the road for helping them get their hands on that submarine."

Orlov sneered. "What's Russia? A new czardom fueled by a revived Orthodox Church and age-old popular nationalism. They murder masses of people in Syria just like in the Gulag then toast each other with champagne. Russia will never change. It's in the blood."

"How long have you been collecting stamps?" Shai asked.

"Since I was a boy. My father wrote letters to famous people all over the world. Bragged about who he corresponded with. Vain and insecure man, always worried about what other people thought. In a restaurant, if I got angry at his lecturing me, what bothered him was people seeing me raise my voice, not what hurt me. Some good in it, taught me to become a better father. These famous men had underlings and secretaries who answered. He gave me the stamps. I immediately loved them more than I loved him."

"The Russian ambassador, what kind of stamps does he collect?"

"Who sends letters with stamps anymore? I told you, he has no collection. Still, it was a pleasant diversion for the afternoon. He's not an altogether stupid man. Reasonable taste in music. More than reasonably good vodka."

Shai abruptly stood. "I'll remember to have writing implements sent in." He left the room and went out into the hall.

Arik rushed up, the headphones still dangling around his

neck.

"I don't know if father and son are in on it or not," Shai said. "If they are, Mikhail Sergeiovich will not break easily. Let's put him in a cell and let him sit."

"Are you going to get him writing gear?"

"Of course. Find him a nice notebook, a fountain pen and ink. Nobody talks when outraged. "

Shai knocked on the door, and then without waiting for an answer, entered Ami Nir's office. The Mossad chief sat behind his desk in a perfectly pressed Savile Row suit, starched white shirt and blue silk tie, his jacket on, gold cufflinks peeking out, full head of black hair perfectly swept back. Shai still could not accustom himself to a Mossad chief who was a media darling and religious, though he did not wear a kippah. All his predecessors had preferred shirtsleeves and the shadows, and few people even knew the real name of their once legendary leader, known even by his closest friends as The Colonel, who was unkempt, round, and brewed sun tea as a hobby. What The Colonel and Nir had in common, Shai reminded himself as he sat opposite Nir, was inventive minds, though The Colonel's scent was sweat and worry, while Nir's was designer aftershave and swagger.

"How'd it go with Orlov?" Nir asked. "The father. I have the useless reports on the son's interrogation."

"Sticking to his stamp story. I think he'd be okay spending the rest of his days in prison as long as his son did not."

"What's your instinct?"

Shai was silent for a long moment. "I think even if he was part of it, neither of them would know where the prime minister is now."

"So he's a dead end?"

"Not for certain, but I think that's the long trail and it

probably ends at a cliff. What I too think, is the rumblings about vaulting Gutman's son to the top of the Likud list are growing louder. Emotional appeal to the electorate. About this you know more than me."

Nir allowed a small smile. He had spent two years as head of the National Security Command and the prime minister's national security adviser, and was close to Likud ministers. Since stepping into stewardship of the Mossad, he had focused greatly on Iran. He had deepened relationships with Arab governments and intelligence services, all Sunnis, who felt almost as much fear as Israel did from Iran's nuclear warheads.

"If I had an imaginative mind," Shai said, "I'd say the mother could somehow be behind it, got impatient about her son's future. I'm pretty sure that's some Shakespeare play."

"But your bet is elsewhere?" Nir asked.

"I follow breadcrumbs and leave policy to people smarter than myself."

Nir laughed. "You may leave policy to them, but it's not because they're smarter. Cesspool compared to the clarity of the field where you find the bad guys and shoot."

Shai smiled. They were not friends but Shai held a grudging respect forNir, had learned to overlook his style because there was substance beneath his abs. "What do you hear from our Arab brothers?"

"They're as puzzled as we are. If it's Ramzy, he's not working with any of their governments. But then he wouldn't be, would he. They've paid mostly lip service to the Palestinians. Though the Saudi Peace Initiative is the real deal, which is why Gutman's buried it."

Shai was surprised Nir spoke so forthrightly about Gutman's stonewalling the 2002 initiative, a ten-sentence proposal to end the Arab-Israeli conflict re-endorsed by the Arab League in 2007. It called for normalizing relations between the Arab countries and

Israel in exchange for a full withdrawal from the West Bank and East Jerusalem, and a just resolution of the Palestinian refugee problem. Depending on how one counted, there were 4-6 million Palestinian refugees in the world. In any math, far more than could be squeezed into the West Bank. Everybody knew there was considerable wiggle room in the Saudi plan.

"Are the Arabs hiding something about Ramzy?" Shai asked.

"They swear they aren't. I'm pushing. I'm inclined to believe them. With Iran rising, we're suddenly closer to allies with Riyadh and the Emirates than enemies."

Shai nodded. Before, their enemies were nation-states behind clear borders. Suddenly they shared the same adversaries: terrorist organizations and semi-nation states in varying sizes and ideologies, and the Imams they followed. Most of these groups, along with Hezbollah, spilled across nations' borders. Where once they worried only about Syrian troops, which they could easily contain, now the Yarmouk Martyrs Brigade, allied with ISIS, controlled a ten-mile swath along the lower stretches of the Golan. They were armed with heavy military equipment, including anti-tank missiles picked off the ground after Syrian army troops fled back towards Damascus. A stone's throw farther north was the Al-Nusra Front, the al-Qaeda affiliate in loose affiliation with ISIS. These local fighters had greater loyalty to their clans, so whether they would continue to battle the Syrians at ISIS's behest or turn and trek up the Golan Heights was fluid. These insurgents were everywhere, in the north Sinai desert to the Shiite Houthis rebels in Yemen who regularly attacked Saudi shipping in the Red Sea and might aim at theirs too.

"We can use all the friends we can get," Shai said.

"The freighter makes only the one stop in Thessaloniki?" Nir said.

"Yes, then straight to Beirut."

"I favor boarding her as soon as possible. Before she gets to Greece. Though I can't see them taking Gutman off there. Once they get to Beirut, Ramzy and his whoevers have the clear advantage." He tapped the desk impatiently, his cufflinks echoing a secondary sound. Nir made his own decisions, but longtime in the Mossad seas, before he did he sought higher ground to look around. He respected his people's views. "Your thoughts, Shai?"

"I'd like to try something first, before we throw all the dice and board her. Only one roll there. Too great a chance of snake eyes, and even if he's there, who's to say we can get him out alive."

"What?" Nir said impatiently.

"Get someone aboard in Thessaloniki, a fake customs inspector. The good news is it's easy to bribe the Greeks. The less good news is I have nobody here we can use. I've sent Eli there but I need to give him a little help as time is of the essence."

They had had little need to operate in Greece and had no presence in the country. However, there were Sephardic Jews, literally 'Jews of Spain,' in Thessaloniki, descendants of the expulsion of the Jews from Spain in 1492.

"Okay. Fine. But nobody can get into every container."

"Agree. I think what we're looking for more is armed guards, unusual crew members, a closed section of the ship, anything out of place. And of course, the unexpected."

"How the hell can an amateur determine that?" Nir's nostrils flared.

"Sometimes amateurs are more bold, curious, want to impress so they create less suspicion. If there's nothing, still leaves plenty of time to board her and nearer our waters."

"Which is the only reason you have the go ahead. Now tell me, what the hell does Ramzy want with Gutman? You know him."

"I knew him. Though I don't think people change much over time, disappointment can harden you. But if he wanted him dead, we'd have found the body already. He likely wants to make some point."

"Al-Nusra?"

"Maybe. Would shake our country deeply. But it could be to trade for something."

"What?"

"We need to stop it before we find out."

Nir pushed back angrily in his chair and rolled over to the window. Shai suspected the ministerial pressure to unearth the prime minister was intense, and he was glad not to have to sit in those meetings.

"Get out," Nir said. "Let me know the second you have someone on board."

"I have to go see the Sephardic Chief Rabbi to help find Eli a pretty girl to use. Given that it's an Arab freighter and all."

As Eli walked into the spectacularly restored Monastir Synagogue, he knew Orit's ability to distract or bribe Thessaloniki harbor officials to secure an entry badge would be the easiest part of the operation. Of the pre-World War II Thessaloniki Jewish community of fifty thousand, only two thousand had survived Nazi thoroughness. The Red Cross had saved the building with a ploy to commandeer it for storage. Recent grants from the Federal Republic of Germany had returned the synagogue to its former grandeur.

Eli looked at the row of stained glass windows circling the upstairs women's section. On a long chain, an amazing chandelier dropped over the central podium. Smaller chandeliers descended from the ceiling, and on the main floor stained glass windows of pink and yellow with blue translucent Stars of David brought light in from opposite sides.

It seemed to Eli it was easier to hold onto pain than release it, that pain in its familiarity became a replacement for the loss. It was certainly true in his case. You felt the pain, that person was still part of you. If you let go, then they were completely gone and what was left was emptiness. He did not care what all the gurus proclaimed about the serenity letting go brought. He had no time for serenity.

He wanted, in this southernmost tip of Europe so far from where the goose-stepping began, to take a moment to absorb this community's pain. Save for a handful, everyone died here, a world of families, fathers and sons, fathers and daughters, mothers and babies. Celebrations of marriage and childbirth never occurred, in their stead the shrieks of suffocation and dying. He imagined those lives filling these seats. He wanted to scream but his face betrayed nothing. Oddly, he was becoming comfortable with the urge to let it all out.

From a back office, Abraham Negren, the President of the Jewish Community, walked across the white and black stone floor squares accompanied by a woman in her early thirties, his daughter, Rachel Negren, a small exotically dark and attractive woman, her high heels clicking double-time ahead of her father. They exchanged introductions in English and remained standing rather than sit in the empty room.

"Whatever I may do for you will be an honor," Negren said. He had received a call from the Chief Sephardic Rabbi of Israel asking that he help the visitor and that he bring a young woman, preferably in her thirties, to the meeting. He had not been surprised by the request.

Eli came right to the point. "A cargo freighter will dock here tomorrow. It cannot go beyond the two of you, but it's possible the prime minister is aboard. We need someone to pose as a port inspector. A local woman, as Arab men are chauvinistic and less likely to see a small, very pretty woman as a threat." All men, actually, he might have added.

"Their mistake," Rachel said.

"You'll walk around, poke anywhere you like. If the prime minister's there he could be in a container, sedated. No port inspector could go through all the containers once loaded."

"So what am I looking for?" she asked.

"Armed men, guards, any unusual tension. Anything that seems off from what you would expect. Any place they don't want you to go. I'll want to know whatever strikes you, no matter how small."

"This is very dangerous," her father said.

Rachel said, "Why else would he be asking. I'll do it."

Negren's father, from Athens, had been deported to Auschwitz-Birkenau in 1943 and had been among the few Greek Jews who survived there. He had been given a job in the camp's "Canada," the large sorting area for the contents of suitcases and the clothes of the gassed, in an unpopulated area of the vast camp, so named for the similar open spaces and abundance of Canada. Negren's Thessaloniki mother had been hidden by the Greek Orthodox Church after Archbishop Damaskinos ordered the issuance of false baptismal certificates to the country's Jews. Abraham's father had died in his fifties, suffering from early dementia hastened by those continuous rifle butts to his head. His mother, at eighty-nine, played tavli, Greek backgammon, with other ladies five days a week.

"No," Negren said loudly and nervously, the sound echoing through the high room. And then, just above a whisper, "you can't."

Both his parents had lost all their siblings, their children, their parents to the ovens. His mother was a broad and greatly joyful woman, who had actually grown a marijuana plant on a balcony of their house. His father had been wildly affable with friends in the cafes, but at home he yelled. Negren had the expansiveness of his mother and had championed and contacted the German government to restore the synagogue, but his father's bullying when he was a child had made him timid.

Rachel approached her father. "Papa, I am doing this," she said in Greek. "This is my chance to be like those who helped mama."

"We can find someone else."

"No, we have found me."

She turned to Eli. "What do you need?"

"Someone who can alter a port entrance ID."

She turned back to her father. "Papa?"

He stared at her knowing he had lost, a deeper part of him happy that he had. He had consciously raised her to be strong.

Negren looked up. "Niko, who did the stain glass windows. He has such talents. Cameras. Documents." He turned to Eli. "What if something goes wrong?"

"We have a submarine nearby, with a land attack team on board. We'll have them ashore tonight and positioned nearby. She'll have a listening device on her. We hear something we don't like, we go in immediately and get her."

"See, Papa? Just like when I went out with boys in high school and you followed me. I won't be alone. I'll be safe."

He turned red, had not imagined that she knew. They had never discussed it. He was impressed with her powers of silence as well as her bravery. He could not have boarded the ship, even at her age.

"If anything, they'll be expecting a full-scale assault," Eli said. "They won't be looking for a pretty Greek with the proper credentials. This is not their port, so they have little connection to any authorities here." He turned to Rachel and said, "Thank you."

"I'm more scared than I act."

"We all are," Eli said, and though he would have said it to calm her, he meant it.

A laptop was open beside Eli on the hill where he sat. The dot on the screen, the GPS inside Ramzy Awwad's cell phone, indicated Ramzy Awwad had not left the ship since it had docked last night. Their assault team had come ashore from the INS *Rahav*, Hebrew for Neptune, the God of the Sea, and another example of Israeli bravado that produced results. Mostly.

The SS *Baalbek* carried a name with equally ancient roots. The Roman Temple of Baalbek still sat in Lebanon's Bekaa Valley, more known for its hashish fields than the well-preserved ruins with retaining wall stones of 300 tons. Through binoculars, Eli watched as Ellinki Viohihania Ohimaton, Greece's only surviving vehicle manufacturing company, based here in Thessaloniki, loaded trucks and small sedans into containers to be lifted onto the *Baalbek* by the enormous cranes permanently installed on her flat deck.

More interestingly, crates of tobacco were being loaded into containers to be raised on the *Baalbek*. Israeli agents operated freely in porous Lebanon and Eli knew the country well. Nearly two million refugees had crossed the border from Syria, and unable to find work, they spent their days in makeshift encampments smoking. Much of the Syrian tobacco industry had closed or had their factories blown to bits in the Civil War, leading to unprecedented demand for cigarettes from their Lebanese neighbors. Unable to grow enough tobacco to meet the demand, the government-owned Regie Libanaise des Tabacs was importing Greek cigarette tobacco. Eli moved his binoculars and scanned the huge port with tankers and cranes everywhere, on the docks and on the freighters, and between them now a number of cruise ships. The sea inside the port was a lovely flat blue.

In the nearer distance he watched Rachel, who looked impossibly small, her heels replaced with work boots, approach the outside gates of the port moving fast. He lifted the headphones from beside the laptop to listen to her. As she spoke Greek, he was reassured to hear no tremor in her speech.

Soon Rachel approached the ramp that led up to the deck. As she did, a crane operator on the dock, lifting a green container aboard the *Baalbek*, gears grinding, whistled at her though she was wearing khaki pants and a long sleeve khaki blouse. Her laminated port identification badge swinging on a chain around her neck, she did not look his way. No Greek woman would. In one hand she held a clipboard with a sheaf of papers, all in Greek which nobody on board could read.

As she started up the ramp, to her relief nobody approached to ask who she was. She enjoyed modern ways and had declined to marry young, always believing there was something more she might do with her life. Now, greatly surprised, even though she had been waiting, she had that opportunity.

As she stepped onto the deck, an Arab officer with bars on the epaulettes of his blue shirt approached. Containers of all different colors were stacked three and four high, two different sizes; the larger seemed twice as long as the shorter. They covered the entire flat front of the ship.

As Eli had instructed, she spoke in Greek and then repeated in English. "Standard security inspection." She handed her clipboard to him. The inspection notice alone on top was written in Greek and English, an authentic document from the office Eli had broken into last night. This was lackadaisical Greece; there weren't even guard dogs for him to drug behind the fences. Her father, she thought proudly, had gone with him on a ladder over the fence to help identify the proper papers.

The officer looked from her shoes to her head and then lingered at her breasts, which he could easily do without moving his head as she was so short. Orit had helped her buy a tight work shirt. "They're all we want him thinking about," Orit had said, a tad envious of her shape and unbuttoning another button on it after

Rachel came out of the dressing room.

"What do you want to see?" he asked in English. "We're on a busy schedule."

"The sleeping quarters first," she said. "Some of the freighters are being converted to smuggle in refugees for a high price."

"So, where should these people go? Come on."

She followed him up an outdoor steel stairwell. At the top, as she stepped into the ship, fear seized her and she reached for the blue pen in her shirt pocket for reassurance, as it contained her audio transmitter. Then she pushed it carefully back in her pocket afraid she'd break it.

"E deck," he said.

They climbed red steel stairs, ribbed to protect against slipping, and she felt better moving.

"On this ship, A deck is the offices, B the kitchen and mess, C has the gym and washing machines."

She climbed easily after his fast pace, saw nobody as the crew was elsewhere. If the prime minister was here, Eli said they could be keeping him sedated in a container but some of those watching him would be in the sleeping quarters. E deck was narrow with a high ceiling and railings along one wall in case of storms, the doors framed by fake, shiny wood laminate.

"The doors are open, no time for keys on board. They have compartments they can lock in each room. Nothing's been changed, no refugees."

"I do what I am asked to," she said.

She opened the first door and entered. The room was neither large nor small, with two twin beds and its own bathroom. As he came in after her and neared, fear caught in her throat that he might touch her, or worse. The room was empty.

She brushed past him back into the corridor with rooms on

both sides. "I need to go through them all," she said and tapped the clipboard.

He looked at his watch. "Go on, but hurry."

Room after room was vacant and none had weapons in view. They turned the corner to an identical corridor. She entered these rooms one at a time, all empty. At the end of this corridor she opened a door and an older man looked up from the desk where he was typing on a laptop. He spoke to the officer in Arabic, who answered. It was the man whose photo Eli had shown her. She assumed someone listening to her understood the Arabic. Suddenly she needed to pee.

"May I use your bathroom?" she asked.

He stood, elegant and courtly. "Of course."

She entered the bathroom and once she closed the door behind her, her entire body started to shake. She pulled her pants down and urinated, and then just sat there. Sweat beaded on her forehead. She closed her eyes, the shaking stopped and she went to the small sink, washed her hands and with a hand towel dried her brow. She replaced it on the rod.

She walked out swiftly, clipboard in hand, and headed immediately into the corridor. She continued through room after room, hurrying now, wanting to be off the ship. She saw nobody else. All hands must be at their stations.

As they headed down the red stairs, at C deck she saw a sign leading to the gym she had not seen on the way up, though the officer had mentioned it.

"I'd like to see the gym," she said.

"Why?"

She thrust the clipboard towards him. "I don't know why. It's on my list." She wondered if she had learned enough, spotting the older Arab typing, but felt she had not.

"Okay, then you get off."

"Please don't make me call my superiors," she said, almost enjoying this.

She strode down C deck, where the corridor was wider. She was not sure why she wanted to see the gym. Mostly she was stalling, hoping some men carrying machine guns would be climbing up the stairs in the opposite direction, the Prime Minister ahead of them.

She reached for the gym door, was not sure if she was making it up, but the officer seemed nervous. She knew they could hurt or kill her before any of Eli's men even reached the gangplank, but she believed in fate and this was hers whatever happened and if she went out this way better than not trying to help. She saw the empty green table tennis table first, then the man working out at the punching bag, two others lifting weights, the sound noisy, an empty exercise bicycle, and a fourth pulling himself up the horizontal wood rods of the tall climbing wall. As she entered, all four of them seemed to freeze silently where they were. The two with barbells lowered them. She wondered with more curiosity than fear whether they were going to move for the machine guns that were leaning against the far corner.

The officer again spoke in Arabic to these men, who did not at all seem like sailors to her.

"It's nice," she said. "I'm sure the crew spends lots of time here." She turned and headed back into corridor, certain someone was about to grab her and thinking that her father would not survive this.

"They're security. ISIS operates from ports they control in Libya," the officer said from behind her.

She turned and said the first thing that came into her mind. "Nowhere is safe anymore." Rachel headed back towards the stairwell. "I don't need to see the offices."

She hurried down the stairs, and when she emerged on deck the fresh sea air was intoxicating.

The officer approached her. "Do I have to sign?"

"No, only I do. I'm sorry for taking your time but we do not have the capacity to handle all the refugees that are coming here."

She looked at the colorful stacks of containers and reminded herself that she was Greek and they had no reason to suspect her. In the outdoors she felt better, but thought they could probably hear her heart beating fast through the pen in her pocket, and somehow she felt safer if they had.

She reached the ramp and hurried down it, trying to make herself move slowly so she would not seem suspicious. When she stepped onto the dock she looked back, but saw nobody at the ship's railing watching her. She wondered if she had learned anything that mattered.

"So we have four armed terrorists," Ami Nir said to Shai in Nir's office.

"That she happened across. There could be any number more."

"Obviously."Nir's jacket hung on a rack in the corner. He unknotted his tie, pulled it complete loose and tossed it on his desk. "Since ISIS pirates do operate out of Libya, there's the ridiculous chance he was telling the truth."

They kept a distant eye on all ISIS movement, and on occasion aided them against Iranian-backed Shiite militias in Syria, something Nir found to be a distasteful necessity but Iran was a mortal threat. Nir knew about five thousand ISIS fighters had pushed their way into a destabilized Libya and in early 2016 took the Eastern oil seaports of Es Sider, Ra's Lanuf, and the large port city of Sirte. By the summer, Libyan forces, their advance softened by Western air strikes, had freed Sirte in a bloody battle and much of the weakened ISIS troops decamped to the desert outside Tripoli. Still their pirates operated with speedboats, which did not require a port, and the tobacco aboard the *Baalbek* could be offloaded easily and then sold in Lebanon or across North Africa at huge profit.

"How long will it take to look through all those containers?" Nir asked.

"It's impossible. Too many and not enough space to move them even with the cranes on deck. They're stacked three and four high. We'd have to take the ship to Haifa."

"Or wait and try and follow your Ramzy after they dock in Beirut?" Nir took the tie, placed it around his neck and mock hung himself. "We're good in Beirut, but maybe not good enough."

"If we take the freighter it's all or nothing."

"How long until it's due in Beirut?"

"Three days," Shai said. "I prefer letting her dock. In three days, I can get a small army into Lebanon."

Nir stood up, walked towards his window. "We can board her and sail her back to Haifa without the world knowing. Subs escorting her underwater like a school of fish. Arabic speakers at their radio. Keep her headed straight to Beirut. I bet it's not a hundred nautical miles to Haifa."

"Eighty-one from the port itself," Shai said.

"Even if we took her off the coast of Greece and it got out, I doubt anyone would mess with our little fleet."

"It's risky, but with the prime minister missing the Italians and French would give us some latitude," Shai said. "NATO too. There's a Dutch Walrus-class sub tracking the Russian fleet off Syria. The US has a Virginia-class sub shadowing the Russians too."

Nir wondered what the Russians would do if they learned they had the *Baalbek*? The *Admiral Kuznetsov* aircraft carrier and *Pyotr Velikiy* (Peter the Great) nuclear missile cruiser were operating near a leased military installation in Tartus, Syria, the Russian Navy's sole repair and replenishment facility in the Mediterranean. The two floating piers there were too small to accommodate the large vessels, which had arrived through the Turkish straits. The Russians had just signed a new forty-nine year lease that allowed them to dredge and greatly expand Tartus. With the Israeli F-35s stealth air fighters just arrived from America overhead, he did not think the Russians would want an escalation at sea.

"Their 60R Romeos could pose a problem for our subs if they were so inclined," Shai said.

Nir sank into his seat. The Sikorsky MH-60R Romeo helicopters operated off frigates and destroyers as well as aircraft carriers. Equipped with infrared radar, dipping sonar and sonobuoy launchers that acoustically detected submarines, each helicopter boasted four weapons stations armed with homing torpedoes and anti-ship missiles.

"I'm inclined to take the freighter," Nir said.

Shai knew Nir liked grand plays, which had almost always worked for him. He was Gutman's boy Friday in a way virtually no Mossad head had been attached by the hip to their prime minister, and would almost certainly be replaced by a new government. If he rescued the prime minister he'd be a national hero and maybe enter politics himself.

"Your call," Shai said.

"We can pull it off," Nir said. "Nobody will care about a missing freighter, in the unlikely event anybody figures out it is."

"I'd say that's true, yes."

"If we take her, would you do it now, or off Beirut?"

Shai was silent and then said, "Someone could call from anywhere on the ship with a satellite phone while we're boarding. I doubt anything's going to change in the next two days. So while there's a case for getting him as soon as possible, I'd take her right before she entered Lebanese waters. Least international incident. Shortest time possible to Haifa."

"Prep it, both letting her dock and not," Nir said. "We have a little time to decide. I'm going to need ministerial approval to take the ship."

If it went terribly bad, he would blame the cabinet. Shai wouldn't have done it that way, would go without consulting them. Shai said, "Their machine guns should have been locked away while in port."

Nir stood again. "Yes, that's greatly why I'm leaning toward taking the freighter. ISIS pirates don't attack ships in port. So were they there to protect your Ramzy Awwad, or something grander?"

"Ramzy doesn't travel with armed guards. Never known him to."

"I know," Nir said loudly. "I've read your file on him. He kills us, he works with us, then he's... So, is the prime minister on board?"

Shai headed towards the door. "I'll prep both operations."

"Damn it, Shai, you know him. What's Awwad doing?"

Shai stopped abruptly and his legs hurt. He had to get back in that goddamn swimming pool and lose this weight again. "I don't know. But this is his last party. Whatever it is, he's been planning it for a very long time. We'll get drones with cameras ready to go from inside Beirut. I will not lose him. I won't. I'd rather not risk charging onto the freighter. We might get lucky and he'll hold on to that phone Orit got us."

"When have we ever gotten lucky?"

"Never." Shai's mouth curved into a small smile. "Well, maybe a time or two."

Heavy rain clouds moved in between late day swaths of sunlight as Eli drove the final ascent to Jerusalem. Limestone buildings in the small valley to his left were bathed in brightness, the hills around them dark. He felt emotional, crushed out his cigarette and phoned Shai.

"I'm just heading back into another meeting with Nir," Shai said. "Come in an hour."

As soon as Rachel had cleared the port fence, he'd sped to the airport. The quickest route was a flight to Turkey and then Pegasus Airlines, as there were thirteen direct flights a day from Istanbul to Tel Aviv. With the extra hour, rather than head home with Yigal still there and face those feelings, Eli called his father, who was out walking. Meir suggested they meet at the Pompidou Café. Though parking anywhere near the trendy Emek Refaim Boulevard was near impossible, Eli raced past a spot right before the café, shifted into reverse, and tires squealing angled back into it. This four-block stretch in the German Colony boasted fashionable cafes, restaurants, a sushi bar, a wine bar with a thousand bottles in the cellar, Italian sorbets, Max Brenner chocolates and a branch of Steimatzky books. On the side streets, spacious stone Ottoman mansions had been divided into apartments. Eli was happy to be home.

The café was wide with a slanted glass ceiling, large sliding glass doors and plate glass on all sides, a combination coffee and liquor bar in the center with red cushioned stools surrounding the counter. His father sat on the patio on a large, wood double seat with light red cushions before a low, black, stone-topped wood table. This was no longer his father's socialist Israel, Eli thought, loving the modernity. Two *café hafuch*, literally "upside down" coffee, sat on the table. The steamed milk goes in first, then the espresso shot, and then the milk froth is spooned on top. Israelis, a little too stubbornly, seem to want to do everything their own way. His father had found a spot where they could talk privately.

Eli sat. "Are you going to run for prime minister should we fail to bring him back alive?"

"I think so. Yes. But I'm inclined to, even if he is. I won't win but I could affect his platform for him to form a coalition."

Eli knew if he succeeded in rescuing Gutman the doors of tolerance and fraternity his father could open would be slammed shut with more fear orating. Though some real good could come in the next election from the various sides emboldened to think about possibilities in the vacuum of Gutman's disappearance. He did not however feel any conflict, the possibility he would end his father's chances of actually becoming prime minister, was at the heart of his recent unease. His job was to rescue Gutman regardless of the collateral cost. Dehydrated from the flights, Eli drained most of the lukewarm coffee in one long pull.

Meir told him about his meeting with Tzipi Ben-Ami. "Do you know her?" Meir asked.

"No," Eli said. "Way before my time. How'd you meet her?"

"A mutual friend, big supporter of my work and the Democratic Left in America. Not that the two should be confused with each other." Meir fit everywhere and gave workshops on identity at the yearly Right leaning American Israel Public Affairs Conference in Washington.

Eli smiled. Being with his father always centered him.

Meir continued. "I was surprised she gave up the top spot, but at the same time I wasn't. She's practical, another endangered trait in increasingly polarized times. Have you been home?"

"No. Soon. Eventually."

"What's on your mind, son?"

"How do you know something's on my mind?" Eli said.

Meir's smile was a twinkle. "You just got back and you're here."

"Something is bothering me. I can't get to the heart of it."

"Tell me."

"It's just that. I'm having weird dreams that seem to be yelling at me." Eli told him the dreams.

Meir was puzzled. "I don't know, maybe the locked bike and

216

Yigal falling off it has to do with your not being here for him when he was hurt in Sderot." Meir was not a believer in therapy but dreams seemed a signpost. "Eli, how can I help?"

"I don't know. I don't even know why I came to see you. Everything about this mission seems either impossible or too easy."

"Explain."

"It's just that. I go to Los Angeles and stumble across exactly who I'm looking for but then he gets away. Then immediately I have another lead again, right in front of me."

"Isn't that how it always is?"

"I don't know. Maybe."

They sat in a long but somehow comfortable silence. Eli did not share that he started smoking again, convinced it would be temporary.

Then Meir said, "I met one of your superiors, came to a lecture I gave in Hebron. Man a little younger than me, but not by much. Said he'd heard a lot about me from you, as well as people in the Mossad I lecture to."

"I know who it is. He's smart, been at it along time," Eli said. "We're close. What did he say?"

"I asked if he should be talking to me about you. He essentially said he's pretty much in a position to do what he wants. I took that to mean he can find other things to do if necessary."

"I don't think he's much afraid of anything except losing people in the field. He gets in the personal business of everybody he cares about. Exactly like you, so I'm not surprised he showed up."

"I think he came to hear me because of how much he likes you." Meir let loose his huge smile. "So how could I not like him."

Eli said nothing about what he was suddenly thinking. "How's Mom?"

"I think she'll retire soon. She doesn't want to but she's tired. She has enough with the grandchildren to keep her happy." His wife had longed worked in administration at Hadassah Hospital.

Eli rose. "Tell Mom I'll try to come back and see her, but I'm not sure I'll have time. Don't tell Yigal I'm here."

Meir stood, was taller than Eli and heavier. As they hugged, Eli gripped him longer than usual. He whispered into his father's ear. "Run, Dad. No matter what." He did not finish that he meant *no matter what happens to me.*

Meir kissed his son's cheek.

On the sidewalk, Eli stood across from his car but made no move to get in. What the combination lock in his dream was about might be coming clear, and he was more scared than he had ever been in his life. As night fell over the city dropping the mountain temperature, Eli drove towards the Knesset and the nearby government buildings that housed the Jerusalem branch of the Mossad. He parked and walked around a concrete walkway that led to the end building. Eli approached the nondescript brown night door in the middle of the tall stone façade and punched in a code on the pad set to the right in between the large stones. Everything seemed topsy-turvy and he almost expected the numbers not to work but the door lock clicked open.

Down a brightly lit impeccably white corridor, the security guard expected him and did not rise from his desk and the bank of screens in front of him with closed-circuit feed of the outside from a variety of angles. His Uzi submachine gun lay casually on the floor.

Shai's door was open. As Eli entered, Shai remained at the window with a view of the lit lower Hebrew University campus, built because they were cut off from the Mount Scopus branch in East Jerusalem after the 1948 War of Independence.

Shai turned. "Nir just got approval to take the *Baalbek* and bring her to Haifa. Shayetet 13 leaves at dawn. If you want, there's a spot for you. You need to be in Atlit by five a.m."

Eli had not been certain where he was headed next and was

surprised Shai had so bluntly come to the point. Shayetet 13, one of the most secret branches of the Israeli forces, specializing in counterterrorism, intelligence, sea-to-land and sea-to-sea rescue and boarding, operated from the quiet natural bay in Atlit, south of Haifa. Eli had met his wife at that campfire below the ruins of the Atlit Fortress on the peninsula that jutted into the sea, and since he was not sentimental they had actually never been back. Now he was emotional that he was going to see it again.

"Yes," was all Eli found himself saying. Neither man had sat. "You in favor of taking her?" Eli asked.

"Did I ever tell you this was my old mentor's office?" Shai said. "The Colonel." Shai sat heavily in a chair and he seemed to deflate with the movement. He opened a lower drawer and took out a single Dunhill Montecruz cigar in a cedar-lined aluminum tube. "He used to smoke these. The room stank of them. I think they were a diversion to keep whoever he was talking to a little off guard. I've had this one in this drawer since he died. 1995. The biggest people on the world's stage go and the planet moves on effortlessly without them, hardly noticing. There are lot of things I want to forget. The Colonel's not one of them."

This was not like Shai and Eli felt uneasy. "I saw my father. He says you were at one of his lectures."

With the cigar, Shai motioned Eli to sit across from him and he did. "I've wanted to meet him for years. You wouldn't be Eli if you'd grown up elsewhere. Anyway, wanted to shave a look at what the settlers were up to in Hebron. So killed two birds with the same stone, as the saying goes."

"Tzipi Ben-Ami approached him. You two are friends."

Shai nodded. "I adore her. She's the best of us. Tzipi has more balls than any man in government. I gather she and your father have a mutual friend. Lots of people call your father the honorary mayor of Jerusalem. He knows everybody everywhere. Would wear me out, talking to so many people. He thrives on it, seems to me and he's not even lonely at home."

"Though I don't want to be that way, I'm a little envious of it. You, on the other hand, seem to know all the right people. Ramzy Awwad, Tzipi, now my father."

"Yes, well that would be the way to do it, if you're not looking to fill an auditorium."

Eli rose abruptly. "Orders are to take Awwad alive?"

"I would prefer that, yes. Call it old age but I'd like to know the why of all this."

"If I rescue Gutman, then I end my father's chances of becoming prime minister."

"If I thought that would change how you are out there, I'd order you some much deserved leave. But I don't. You're my rock, Eli. Go see you son," Shai said. "I'm worried about what Nir's decided. You need to have Yigal off your mind."

CHAPTER 12

Clad in all black, Eli stood on the deck of the INS *Hanit* at the front of a contingent of Shayetet commandos, both worried about the risk in boarding the *Baalbek* and glad he would soon have some answers. At three a.m., in the star-filled, inky, moonless night, Israel's three Sa'ar 5 corvettes and three submerged submarines were converged on the *Baalbek* in the open sea, almost equidistant between Cairo and Antalya on the Turkish coast.

Service in Israel's Special Forces mirrored the three-year conscription of Israeli men, however Shayetet 13 volunteers served four-and-a-half years due to the specialized training. They had boarded dozens of ships, including the Iranian *Klos-C* in the Red Sea, laden with Syrian M302 rockets flown from Damascus Airport to Teheran and then trucked to the Persian Gulf and loaded on the civilian vessel bound for Port Sudan, from where the rockets would be smuggled through Egypt to Hamas in Gaza. From there both Tel Aviv and Jerusalem would be in range. While Eli had been in Latakia on the Syrian coast, his militia contacts had alerted him to the Liberian-flagged cargo vessel *Victoria*, which Shayetet 13 intercepted two days later en route to Port Said in Egypt loaded with an arsenal destined for Hamas. About a third of the containers on deck had weapons hidden under Syrian lentils, cotton, and wheat. Eli could fight such battles around the clock without fatigue.

The INS *Aliya*, a Sa'ar 4.5-class missile boat, rounded out the flotilla. The three corvettes, built by Northrop Grumman in the early 1990s to Israeli design, were the largest battle ships in Israel's fleet, each carrying a crew of seventy, torpedoes, missile launchers, sonar, gun mounts and electronic decoys. Atop the *Aliya* sat a helipad beside a helicopter inside a hanger; a crane rose from the rear. Four advanced Sa'ar 6s, under construction in Kiel, Germany, with the guilt-burdened German government contributing one-third of the $500 million dollar a piece cost under the 1953 Reparations Agreement, would begin to arrive in 2019. Among other updates, each would boast thirty-two vertical launch cells for Israeli Barak-8 surface-to-air missiles, developed jointly with the Indian Navy.

Eli looked out at their men who had been dispersed on all four Sa'ars, both so like him and not. He had loved his religious Hesder army unit, which combined shortened combat service with advanced Talmud study and agricultural assistance where needed. Like these warriors, those in his unit had much in common and forged deep bonds.

All lights everywhere had been extinguished and the motors cut. The near frigate size corvettes sat almost still in the quiet waters, just out of binocular view from the *Baalbek's* bridge. Eli climbed into a Nautic Zodiac with seven other men, all of them cradling a pair of oars, a compact Uzi submachine gun, and wearing a small backpack. The men had Glock 19 semi-automatic pistols loaded with rubber bullets, live ammunition clips in their jacket pockets. The Uzis were filled with lethal rounds. Men on each vessel began to lower two Zodiacs by rope from each Sa'ar. Black Tohatsu outboard motors protruded from the back of each for the return. In Atlit, Eli had loaded his Glock with live ammunition and did not take an Uzi.

"Sir, you can sit in the front, don't need you to row," the blonde, blue-eyed Shayetet captain said to Eli as their Zodiac touched and bobbed in the dark water and a cold wind rose.

"I'll row," he said. They calculated forty-five minutes to the *Baalbek*. Two subs would surface simultaneously with their arrival, one remaining submerged. The pilots, engineers, radio and engine crew to bring the *Baalbek* to Haifa remained on the Sa'ars.

Eli took a few uncoordinated strokes and then fell in unison with the silent men, their oars making almost no sound. The sky was so full of stars it was as they'd been tossed everywhere from some magical bucket. Seeing Yigal had been less upsetting than Eli had expected. He supposed it was either that his son was already healing and Eli had much else on his mind, or simply that anticipation was generally worse. He had slept a little on the plane from Istanbul to Tel Aviv, and had finally fallen asleep after joining with his wife in his own strange-feeling bed a few hours before the alarm went off, a navy car already outside. He had not dreamed. But as he felt Noa waking to say goodbye to him, he had hurried out of the bedroom not wanting her to see the agitation spilling through him at their separating again, worried it would frighten her.

The commandos would disable the crew and leave him to find Ramzy Awwad, who would likely be armed. The marvelous Rachel Negren had gotten Ramzy's stateroom number, E8. Atlit planners explained that a crew of twenty to twenty-five would operate a cargo vessel this size, not including Kalashnikov-toting guests. At this hour, they expected only one deck officer on the bridge on navigation watch. Nobody else aboard should be awake, other than the restless.

Their orders were to attack and quickly control the ship. The *Baalbek* had taken on cargo in Portsmouth in the south of England before she entered the Mediterranean. She might have detoured towards the mid-Atlantic or had the prime minister brought to her anywhere on the ocean.

A half hour later, Eli saw the illuminated bridge in the freighter's rear tower. A small light too seemed to wink from the front of the ship. His upper arms ached. As if sensing it, the commander reached over and with one hand over Eli's oar silenced his rowing. Eli was grateful.

He looked back at the seven men moving together. There seemed neither an air of dread nor anticipation on their faces. Shayetet trained until their responses were as reflexive as breathing. The GPS on Ramzy's phone, tracked through satellite communication on the Sa'ar, had shown Ramzy was aboard.

As the eight zodiacs reached the stern of the hulking freighter, at the bow two periscopes rose above the surface. There had been no boat lights anywhere in sight during the rowing in. Simultaneously, each man, except for Eli, removed a kind of pistol from his backpack with a silencer on the front and a star-shaped hook of prongs. Without waiting for a signal, each shot a whizzing line of rope high up over the hull of the boat to the ship's metal railings. Every one caught.

Up they went, hand over hand like human monkeys, as Eli waited in the Zodiac with a single crewman. As they split into teams to enter the ship, take the bridge and secure the crew, the commander threw a rope ladder and it shimmied silently down the hull right in front of Eli, who grabbed it. He climbed up, listening for the sound of shooting, but the night was silent save for the grinding of the freighter's huge motors.

The freighter's hull, above a shallow draft, rose twenty-five meters above the small chop of the waves as she plowed east. Eli moved up the ladder deliberately, no need to compare himself to these much younger men or do something stupid and end up hurting himself in a plummet and gasping for air in the water. Panting, soon he pulled himself up over the railing.

Two commandos stood on deck, Uzis ready should anyone emerge from outside the womb of the ship. Beyond that, there was silence as if they had not boarded. The quiet unnerved Eli. He climbed the dark steel stairwell into the ship's innards, his mouth dry. The Shayetet second-in-command stood outside the offices on A deck.

"Sir, the bridge is secured," he told Eli. "One officer. We have him tied. Nobody in the communications room." He motioned his head down A deck. "B deck empty too, kitchen and mess. They hadn't started breakfast yet. Gym and laundry rooms also empty and secured. No resistance thus far."

Eli nodded and climbed towards E deck. If they were not spotted boarding, they had hoped it would go this way. As he stepped into the high corridor he heard his first sounds, the commandos running on ribbed rubber soles, calling orders in Arabic and English, gathering the crew. Lights shone in the corridor and Eli followed the numbers and turned to the next corridor. Along the way men choked on cloth gags, arms bound behind them by plastic strap handcuffs, eyes frightened, hair mussed, in sleeping clothes.

The door was open to E8. Eli entered and found the Shayetet 13 commander checking the bathroom.

"Empty," he said to Eli.

Eli's heart sank as he looked around the room. Ramzy's bag and belongings were gone. In some unexpected way, he had been looking forward to interrogating Ramzy. The commander spoke over the waterproof communications device attached to his jacket. Voices squawked back over his intercom, a first, a second, then a third.

He turned to Eli. "No resistance so far. We're just checking the engine room now. No weapons found in the quarters. We'll start a thorough search once we have everybody on deck."

"Take the captain to the communications room."

"Right away. Should I bring our crew aboard?"

"Get them here and as soon as the vessel's secured bring them up."

Danger might burst from a container. Eli descended the stairwell almost too quickly and slipped, but grabbed onto the railing, listening, hoping for the sound of gunfire that would tell him enemies were protecting something of value. He heard only the clatter of the commandos driving their captives into the stairwell above him.

As Eli entered the communications room he turned on the lights, which flickered and then held. Eli was breathing hard, part exhaustion, part from a sense this mission was beginning to look like it had been in vain. He pushed aside any thoughts of what might have happened, for now—he had work to do. The worry tugged at him anyway.

The commander brought in the ship's captain, a bald Arab with a black moustache at the early stages of gray. He was barefoot in a white T-shirt and gray sweatpants, bound and gagged.

"Take off his gag," Eli said.

"*Kuss Ommak,*" he swore in Arabic, the most common of curses that Israelis also used—literally, "your mother's vagina," but more colloquially, "fuck you."

"Please sit," Eli said in Arabic, and pulled over a chair.

The captain sat awkwardly on the front of the metal seat, his arms still bound behind him.

"Ramzy Awwad, stateroom E8. Where is he?"

The captain laughed. "So much for the great Zionist intelligence services. He is gone."

"The men with Kalashnikovs?"

"Gone too. You are too late. In the lifeboats. Gone. Gone."

"When?"

"Last night."

"Where did they go?"

"They did not say."

"Did a ship come alongside?"

"No." The captain shrugged. "I know nothing. He said he was leaving. He apologized for taking one of our lifeboats. His friends had weapons. I did not ask questions. I hugged him."

"Did he say he was going to Beirut when he came aboard?"

"The soldiers boarded the day before. They said nothing, he said nothing. There was nothing I wished to know. When we fight, we are all brothers. Like the Jews around the world."

Eli approached, sat on the end of the table near the captain. "Where did you keep Prime Minister Gutman?"

The captain laughed again. "You think he was here? If he had stepped aboard this ship, I'd have killed him myself. War criminal. Pig."

"Was he in one of the containers? Is it specially marked?"

"Have you read the work of Ramzy Awwad? I am Lebanese Christian. Still it was an honor to have him on board, even for a short time."

Eli did not answer. "How was Ramzy contacted to arrange leaving on the lifeboat?"

"What do you mean? When he came aboard he told me he would be leaving that way. Are you Eli?"

Eli tried not to show his surprise, did not think he was successful. The back of his neck was damp.

"Ah, I see you are. Good. Ramzy left me a present for you. He thought I might see you but he was not certain."

Eli knew now that Gutman had not been on board, that Ramzy Awwad had been leading him by the nose. That's why it had been so easy to find him in Wurzburg.

Eli nodded weakly. The captain had trouble rising and Eli moved near and helped him up. Then he took a knife from his pocket and slit the plastic handcuffs. They climbed two flights of stairs to the bridge, Eli a step behind. An Israeli boat pilot was now at the helm, Israeli seamen in casual clothes were taking over the engine room, and Eli knew more were moving into the communications center.

The captain went to a long U-shaped bank of controls and screens in front of thick, rectangular, plate glass windows in wood frames that circled the bridge. Two large black office chairs bolted to the floor but on metal slides that allowed the chairs to move forward and back rested behind the controls. The captain reached for a drawer. The commando on guard there aimed his Uzi but Eli waved him off, knew this was not a trap of physical danger.

The captain took out a cell phone, obviously the source of their tracking Ramzy, with a paper note wrapped around it held by a rubber band. The captain handed it to Eli.

He pulled the note off and read in English script: Nice woman, your friend on the plane from Munich. There are a lot of good people on both sides.

Ramzy had made Orit. Eli's mouth went slack. Ramzy had led them here as a decoy, to focus all their energies while they secreted the prime minister elsewhere.

Eli headed down to the communications room, where he correctly guessed the Shayetet 13 commander was waiting.

"Give the freighter back to them and let's go. Ramzy Awwad left last night. Gutman was never here."

From her car in the heavy traffic leaving Jerusalem, on the right side of the road Tzipi saw a sherut (literally "service") taxi stand. The big black Mercedes-Benz with four doors on one side and rows of bench seats where you paid for your individual place was almost full. A young Palestinian, maybe mid-twenties, was walking slowly towards the sherut. He was thin and bald, she guessed from chemotherapy, and was walking half-dazed and unsteadily. He managed to get into the last row of seats and the lumbering taxi edged into heavy traffic right ahead of her car.

Movement stopped and suddenly the sick young man was out running across the highway towards the checkpoint across the road and the sherut station beyond it. Tzipi somehow sensed that the confused youth had stepped into a taxi heading in the wrong direction.

As the young man reached the opposite side of the road, weaving as he ran, the soldiers there, fearing a suicide bomber, pointed their weapons and shouted for him to stop.

Tzipi swerved into the left lane, made a sharp U-turn and immediately sped back towards the confrontation.

Soldiers continued to shout but the youth did not stop. He needed the taxi seat to get to the hospital. He was so weak. Three years ago, he had amazingly won a Green Card through the US Government Diversity Visa Program, one of fifty thousand Green Cards allotted by lottery each year to people from all over the world. Then the Hodgkin Lymphoma grew inside him, but he still hoped to achieve that dream of living in America. He had been treated twice a week in intravenous chemotherapy sessions and was actually starting to feel better and hopeful. He came from an illustrious family; his father was a renown driving instructor and his grandfather the first in their Arab-Israeli town in the Galilee to serve in the Israeli police.

Tzipi rolled down her passenger window. "I am Tzipi Ben-Ami," she shouted across her car seat, the sound disappearing in the traffic noise. "Do not shoot!"

She watched in horror as a young soldier fired twice, hitting the youth in the chest and stomach and he crumpled to the ground on the side of the road like a rag doll. Soldiers ran towards him rifles still pointed. Tzipi swung her car off the road between the bleeding youth and the trotting soldiers, got out and stood imposingly. She raised a hand.

"Stop!" she shouted. Immediately recognizing her, they did. Tzipi could see the young man moving. "Put him in the back of my car. Now!"

The soldier who had fired, shaking, ran towards the youth. A young officer approached Tzipi. "Please back away, Minister, we have to check him."

"He's not a bomber."

"Please, Minister," he said louder, putting up an arm to block her.

She shoved his arm away and ran to the bleeding youth, who was moaning. Tzipi pulled open his jacket and shirt to check for an explosive belt and exposed brown skin and blood. She lifted the thin youth with difficulty, blood soaking into her skirt. The shooter ran towards them and took him from her arms.

She hurried to her car and opened the back passenger door. When the youth was in the back seat and the door shut, she pushed the accelerator hard. Shaare Zedek was near. "I'm taking you to the hospital," she said to the young man. "What's your name?"

"Amir."

"In Hebrew, Amir means powerful."

"In Arabic—" The youth coughed blood. "Prince."

"Then, Prince Amir, keep your eyes open and tell me about your village."

She hammered her horn and raced around traffic roundabouts as he talked with pride about his family. Then he was silent. She glanced back and he did not appear to be alive.

When she arrived at the emergency entrance to the hospital, she called out orders. As Amir was gently lifted from the back seat, she saw that he was still breathing.

"We're all to blame for this," Tzipi whispered to Amir as they carried him into the hospital.

Eli sat next to the pilot in the Eurocopter Panther as the helicopter broke Israel's coastline. With a range of 370 miles, the Panther had just enough fuel to make it back from the debacle on the *Baalbek*. Eli looked out. Flying this low, the country was breathtaking: people on bikes and skates snaking along the strand in Tel Aviv, the ancient port of Jaffa to his right, the stone Mosque of the Sea at the water's edge. For centuries, the hill behind it allowed centuries of sovereigns to view the coastline in either direction for danger. It had rained the night before and soon they were over flat wet fields and the rotors grew louder.

Exhausted from the anticipation and then the hard letdown, Eli closed his eyes. Half-awake and equally asleep, he heard the thumping of the rotors like distant thunder as the helicopter lifted along the pine-filled rise to Jerusalem. Jews needed to understand what the city meant to Muslims. In the seventh century, Muhammad originally prayed towards Jerusalem not Mecca, the revered city intended to be the holiest place in Islam.

The touchdown atop the Ministry building next to the Knesset jolted Eli awake. He had been dreaming he was sleeping beside Noa, the alarm sounded but he did not stir. He was surprised he had slept so deeply, despite the heavy tiredness, and knew it was due to the increasing clarity he was feeling, and where logically he should have been more nervous, he was less.

An armed soldier had opened the roof entrance. Eli clamored down the stairs as the guard shut and secured the roof padlock. Eli headed to the snack room. He pulled out the Glock, set it on the long white Formica table then tossed his jacket beside it. He took an apple and orange from the refrigerator and poured a cup of coffee from the pot sitting on an old ring like in a Midwest American diner. He did not want to talk to anybody just now, yanked a chair back and devoured the food, but knew where he wanted to look next. He poured a second cup into the chipped porcelain mug and headed down the hallway to the research computer room, which was empty.

Eli sat before a computer and entered his security code. He looked up Ramzy Awwad and reread the files, mostly in case anyone later tracked his keystrokes, but also to be thorough. The coffee was bitter and Eli drank it anyway as he read, for the caffeine jolt. He took the cigarettes from his shirt pocket and tossed them on a counter, had no desire for them anymore. The mystery was the last decade, with almost no entries. Ramzy had been teaching children in the Yarmouk refugee camp in Damascus until April 2015 when ISIS overran the camp, and then he and Dalal had disappeared. He had published no stories during that long, presumably dark period. Shai's last notation of seeing him was fifteen years ago in London. They'd had coffee in the lobby of the Arab-owned Dorchester Hotel. Shai indicated they spoke about failures. They had chased the extremist Palestinian Abu Nidal, who was gunning down both Israelis and moderate Palestinian leaders in Europe, attacking airports and synagogues, killing over three hundred. Abu Nidal had been killed in his Baghdad apartment that year, 2002, by Saddam Hussein's secret service, the ultimate mercenary ironically accused of conspiring with the Americans against Iraq. They met shortly after Abu Nidal's death. Shai reported that Ramzy had retired and was somewhat morose, citing the failures of both the Camp David and Oslo Peace Accords.

So what catapulted him back into action?

Eli headed to the record room across the hall. Flights were booked by encrypted phones, but duplicate records were kept in the file room in the unlikely event their computers were hacked. He pulled out the physical file for the second half of 2016, the period immediately before the prime minister's disappearance. Rather than sit, he leaned against the wall and scrutinized each notation, looking for any link that might jump out at him. He knew, in the current darkness in his heart, what he was looking for, and then he found it.

Shai and Tami had travelled to Berkeley, California, in September 2016 before their son, Asher, started at UC Berkeley School of Law. They spent a few days in Washington, DC, on the way back, where Shai had meetings at Langley as he often did, and he had paid for Tami's ticket himself.

Eli slipped the file back and next went to see Arik, Shai's latest protégé, once Eli's role. As he walked down the hall to Shai's office, Eli relived their first meeting. Shai had appeared at the synagogue in the southern suburb of Gilo where Eli was studying Maimonides' twelfth century *Guide for the Perplexed* rather than pray. To this day, he was not clear how Shai had found him. He said only that he had heard Eli's unit had suffered devastating loss in Lebanon during a night ambush, and that though wounded himself in the arm and leg, he had carried out a close friend. He remembered exactly what Shai had said to him as they walked. "The elite universities everywhere can fill every freshman class with people with perfect grades, but what they really want is the standout in any field. Mossad is the same. We can pick from the elite military units. For case officers, I like philosophy majors, as they've been trained to think large. And scholars with big hearts who love details. You're a good deal of the latter. I give you until tomorrow at eight a.m. to decide, after that I withdraw the offer." He had handed Eli a card with nothing but a phone number on it. Eli was still keeping Shabbat then, though the mutual carnage in Lebanon had begun to erode his belief, and he waited stubbornly for a half hour after it was out, to show he was not desperate, and then called.

So though Eli had a younger sister and a younger brother, Shai had become the big brother he longed for to share the things you didn't want to tell your parents even though they meant everything to you. Eli felt now, that for the first time in his life, he was truly his own man and beholden to no one. It felt both empowering and empty.

So, in September Shai was in Berkeley and Ramzy was teaching at UCLA in Los Angeles. And then Shai had gone to see associates at Langley. A roundtrip flight to Los Angeles would not appear in these records, nor would Ramzy's from Los Angeles to northern California. In one place or the other, they had met.

Eli walked down the corridor to Shai's office. These corridors were unexpectedly quiet, but the Mossad's nerve center was in the coastal headquarters. Shai's door was shut. Suddenly everything fit together. Somehow, he had suspected it for a while now, though he kept pushing away facing it.

He knocked on Shai's door. When there was no answer, he turned the knob and entered. Shai wasn't here. Though Shai could be anywhere in the building, Eli thought, of course. He headed to find his lapdog.

Arik was behind his desk, eyes intent on his computer screen, his pupils dilated, either from strain or whatever he had used to stay up all night and monitor the operation on the *Baalbek*. He looked up as Eli entered and removed hanging white earbuds and Eli could hear Ivri Lider's "This Love of Ours." He suspected despite his good looks that Arik often suffered heartache.

"What the hell happened out there?" Arik asked. "They're going crazy in Herzliya."

"What did you get from the Russian submariner and his father?"

"Zero. And why the hell would he walk right into the Russian Embassy in Tel Aviv? Of all the places they could meet? Even the West Bank cell leaders are smart enough to meet in crowded Tel Aviv cafes where they're not noticed."

"Maybe someone wanted us to see him there?"

Arik rubbed his eyes with one wrist. "Huh? What's going on?"

"Where's Shai?"

"A driver took him to the guesthouse at Kfar Giladi. After last night, he wants to sleep for a few hours. I haven't been home at all. He's going into Lebanon tonight. Has a lead, a Maronite general sent for him. Wouldn't let me come. At his fucking age, he's going into Lebanon alone."

Shai had longstanding contacts with the Lebanese Maronite Christian army officers. Kibbutz Kfar Giladi sat in the land promontory of Northern Israel that jutted into Lebanon. They regularly used their guesthouse before slipping across that border.

"He'll be okay, does this all the time," Eli said. "Arik, do me a favor. There's a Panther on the roof. Can you get the pilot to refuel it and come back?"

"Of course. Should I tell Shai you're coming?"

"It's not necessary. I'll call him myself," Eli lied.

Ramzy Awwad sat alone in the back of the Syrian Navy, Soviet-manufactured Mi-14, a shore-based amphibious helicopter. Was it luck, fate, or a divine hand, he wondered, that an amphibious helicopter had fallen into al-Nusra's lap? In March 2015, heavily leaking oil, this one had set down in a field near Jabal al-Zawiya in northwest Syria. Al-Nusra captured four of the crew. The fifth fled to Jab al al-Zawiya, where he was executed. The al-Nusra Sunnis viciously attacked Assad's army, intending to establish an Islamic emirate governed by sharia law—God's divine law derived from the Koran and the Hadith, the accounts and teachings of Muhammad, as differentiated from *fiqh*, man's scholarly interpretations. However, unlike their Sunni rival, ISIS, al-Nusra did not impose sharia law on conquered territories who resisted it, so they had greater staying power in overrun areas. They were the most successful arm of the rebel forces.

Anti-regime mechanics from the nearby Aleppo Airport had

repaired the Mi-14 for al-Nusra and two Aleppo pilots had eagerly defected to fight Assad. However, six months later, the Russians invaded. From the Latakia airbase on the coast just south of al-Nusra territory, they seized the skies so the chopper had been camouflaged in a grove of trees.

The negotiations had been held with enjoyable Arab embellishment. For the famous Sunni writer and guerilla who had fought the Zionists before the al-Nusra leadership had sucked at their mothers' teats, they were more than willing to lend the helicopter and a pilot—for a generous fee, payable in cash, gold, or heroin from the east Lebanon poppy fields of the Bekaa Valley. No matter which, no questions asked about where he was going, as long as there was an additional considerable deposit in the terrible event the helicopter was downed—to take care of the pilot's grieving widow, as well as al-Nusra's great loss. Petrol, they had in jerricans in a cave, rows piled high; knowing that Aleppo would eventually fall to the Russian roar, they prepared. Because we are brothers and we have so much, for the petrol no extra charge.

The men had rowed Ramzy towards the faraway rendezvous coordinates, where a yacht took him towards southern Turkey. Off the coast at Antalya, the helicopter sat silently waiting in the dark sea like some bobbing prehistoric bird.

Ramzy looked out the window as the squat helicopter neared the Lebanese coast. To avoid detection the pilot dropped low and skimmed above the water. The Lebanese Armed Forces were hopelessly outdated and it was unlikely they would be spotted coming in across the coast.

Atop the ministry building Eli climbed into the helicopter under clearing skies.

As the rotors began to turn slowly, the pilot asked, "Where to?"

"Kfar Giladi. Set down near the guesthouse."

He nodded and punched in coordinates on his navigation screen though he didn't need them. He was from the north, Kibbutz Ashdot Yaakov, a five-minute drive from the Sea of Galilee. The exterior of Ashdot Yaakov's guest lodge units were painted colorful yellow, orange or turquoise and built between olive and date palm trees, part of the old socialist kibbutz's adjustment to capitalism.

"Did you hear?" the pilot said. "It was just on the radio. ISIS announced we killed five of them in the Suez yesterday, drone strike. A car in the north Sinai. We're taking it to them for the prime minister."

Eli said nothing as the rotors beat loudly and the Panther lifted off. Shai's father had loved to walk through the wadis in the Sinai Desert, had spent a lifetime snorkeling in the blue and turquoise seas at Dahab under British, then Egyptian, then Israeli, then again Egyptian rule. But no longer. The Sinai Province, the most active insurgent group in Egypt who pledged allegiance to the Islamic state in late 2014, had arced four rockets at Israeli's southern port city of Eilat two weeks ago. Israel would never acknowledge an attack on sovereign Egyptian soil, so ISIS played to potential recruits trumpeting Zionist aggression. Terrorism had turned the world upside down, the enemy bragging about battlefield losses. Israel had to eliminate these insurgents by their border, but would his grandchildren need to do the same? A recent poll showed one-third of secular Israeli Jews would leave the country if they could. Feeling melancholy, he touched the Glock in his jacket pocket, did not know what he was going to do or even say when he reached his mentor. A Beretta sat snug in his boot.

Two hours later, as the Panther descended towards Kfar Giladi, Eli looked down at the apple and cotton fields, both surrounded by tall cypresses, a bulwark against the winds. He brought his gaze higher, saw the border town of Metula, completely evacuated during the month-long 2006 Second Lebanon War when Hezbollah rockets dropped like rain. Israel now had a contingency plan, Operation Safe Distance, to evacuate an unprecedented 250,000 from the north and south borders if a conflagration with Hezbollah and Hamas broke out on two fronts.

To the west was Lebanon, the Golan Heights in the opposite direction, and beyond those snowcapped peaks that blocked the sea's moisture, the Syrian desert. Kfar Giladi was an old kibbutz founded in 1916. From 1945-1948, his Mossad predecessors had smuggled twelve hundred Jewish children out of Syria and hid them from the ruling British authorities in the barns and chicken houses there as the remarkably stubborn Brits prevented immigration.

The helicopter gently set down in an open space before the huge sculpture of a roaring lion on a stone plaza. In the valley below, with its checkered green fields, the sun glistened off an enormous fishpond. Israel had achieved so much but at a staggering price. During the Second Lebanon War—begun when Hezbollah crossed the border, killed three soldiers and carried two back to Lebanon—rockets killed twelve reservists at the cemetery here who were paying respects to fallen friends. Two years later, Hezbollah exchanged the bodies of the two they captured for a handful of Hezbollah prisoners, one who, years before, had crossed into Israel, killed a father and then repeatedly smashed his four-year-old daughter's skull with his rifle butt.

The stone lion, crouched atop tall stone blocks, bellowed down the mountain. In pain, in defiance? Eli wondered. The lion memorialized Joseph Trumpeldor, killed in 1920 defending the settlement of Tel-Hai, famous for his words, "It is sweet and honorable to die for one's country." Was it still, a hundred years later? Eli thought not.

"Shall I wait?" the pilot asked.

"No, go back to Atlit."

Eli hopped out and walked, enjoying the movement. The guesthouses were old two-story, black stone structures with dark, triangular, shingle roofs. Outside, wood steps varnished deep brown led to the doors on the second floor. Similar wood balconies protruded from the upper units. An old kibbutznik wearing a blue cloth hat was sitting on a power mower and cutting the grass. Eli approached and inquired about an older Israeli, overweight, who had recently arrived alone. The kibbutznik pointed to a lower unit.

Eli calmly tried the knob, which was locked, then knocked. Soon he heard heavy footsteps and the door swung open. Shai wore a long sleeve heavy shirt, khakis and was in socks.

"Ah, Eli, come in," he said, as if he was expecting him. "Give me a moment to put on some shoes and we'll have a stroll. Fabulous up here, the clean air, the views." Tradecraft demanded sensitive talk outdoors. Shai wrestled with getting on his shoes. "How's your son?"

"A few nightmares but otherwise fine."

"We have to have nightmares, don't we? Otherwise how'd we appreciate better times?"

Outside, they walked towards the kibbutz perimeter. "Heard the helicopter," Shai said. "Couldn't imagine who it could be. Should have known, but I'm not quite as quick as I once was."

"I doubt that. You went to see my father in Hebron because you had him in mind as a candidate for prime minister. You sent Tzipi Ben-Ami to him."

"Yes, well, I did think they might hit it off. Different backgrounds, totally different lives, but together rather like cogs."

They neared the old wire fence, the upper portions bent inwards at an angle. The wire was snapped and unrepaired in lots of places, Israel's casual confidence. An old abandoned watchtower on stilts sat atop a nearby hill, from a time when eyes not drones peered over the border. Below it, a two-lane ribbon of fresh granite lined with cypresses on both sides wound up the brown hills towards the

Golan.

"The Russians never had anything to do with this?" Eli asked evenly, despite anger rising through him. He was not sure if he felt more betrayed by Shai or stunned by the enormity of what he'd conceived and then accomplished.

"Yes, as it happens, that is the case. They destroyed Aleppo without a care in the world, just to mention their latest peacemaking effort. Not hard to get people to gobble up bread crumbs heading in that direction."

"The Armani suit in Los Angeles, the Russian culture officer?"

"Friend of Ramzy's from Moscow. Big fan of the film of his novel. Ramzy called me from some chicken restaurant in Los Angeles, said that Popov would do his bit. By the way, your Orit is the best. Ramzy never would have made her without help. Don't think there's actually a way to let her know, but maybe..."

Eli's voice was hard. "Orlov, father and son, had nothing to do with anything."

Shai shrugged to indicate their innocence. Marina, the Russian émigré who managed the Jerusalem Pool, had called Orlov posing as the ambassador's secretary and invited him to the embassy. Lovely girl, needed to find maybe a solid slightly older American immigrant for her. Near the communal dining room, they walked past a fabulous four-lane indoor swimming pool behind glass walls, as it was often cold here. "I have talked to Ramzy from time to time. Preferred it not in the reports. No real reason other than I don't like answering questions that are meant as attacks."

Eli was not certain what Shai intended in Lebanon and remained silent.

Shai said, "Orlov is what he seems, a true socialist, detests both Communist and American excess, though not quite sure what he makes of all our aping the West. Everybody copies America and thinks their result is superior."

"So the entire accident in Georgetown was to bring a Russian replacement to the submarine. You knew he was the only available nuclear reactor officer. Lot of car accidents, both in Georgetown and Los Angeles, with nobody killed since you were behind the wheel. The cop in Georgetown was a plant too, to explain why Fahmy didn't finish the job, and to leave his fingerprints for me to follow."

"Friend of Paul McEnnerney, yes."

Then Eli saw a piece he had missed. "You planted the autographed book in Khaled Fahmy's home in Al-Am'ari."

"Alas, yes to that too. Ramzy had it assigned for his class so there were copies in the UCLA bookstore. I had it slipped in while the family was out, in the event you asked them about it. Slim volume, didn't think they'd notice, or know if they had. Wish I could say I'm sorry, Eli."

"You wanted the service chasing the wrong lead."

"Not actually the wrong lead, but rather one long step behind. It's how I sold it to the Americans. They didn't want it traceable to them, wanted the Mossad busy in a solid direction so we wouldn't go looking under the other two cups for the ball. I insisted the sub be found. We can really use it, and then there's the cost."

Not knowing what he would do, the tension tightening in him, Eli said loudly, "Why?" Though the answer was obvious. His father and Tzipi, and even Shlomo Avni, who had declared his candidacy, could change the future before it was too late.

"Shall I tell you the exact moment it came to me? Last February, secret summit in Aqaba. John Kerry hammered it together. King Abdullah, el-Sisi and Gutman, the big-three. Kerry is a persistent bugger and pragmatic. Insisted on recognition of Israel by everyone in the region, had Saudi and the rest in line. Return to serious negotiations with the Palestinians in exchange for a pullback from their insistence on the total right of return of all refugees.

Kerry lined up the whole package, everything Gutman always said he wanted, recognition as a precondition, a regional peace process. Jordan and Egypt are there, from the sidelines Saudi Arabia and the Gulf States agree, all ducks in a row."

"How do we know they would have gone along with it in the end?" Eli said, but not sure what of the many possibilities he was angry at.

"We don't, of course, but it was in absolutely everybody's interest, especially now with all these terrorists hijacking countries not airplanes. We'll never know. Gutman balked at any significant pullback on the settlements and turned over the table. Said he couldn't sell it to his cabinet. Has been lying ever since that he's ready to make peace but there's nobody to talk to. I felt something I rarely do, pure rage. And I thought about the *Altalena*."

In an instant, it all became clear to Eli. In June of 1948, a month into Israel's War of Independence, Menachem Begin's paramilitary Irgun agreed to merge into David Ben-Gurion's Israel Defense Forces. The *Altalena* sailed from France loaded with arms donated by the French government. Ben-Gurion and Begin clashed about how the weapons would be divided, risking civil war. When the ship docked up the coast, the IDF moved to confiscate the weaponry. Begin ordered the *Altalena* to sail to Tel Aviv, an Irgun stronghold. When the ship neared that port, Ben-Gurion ordered the large guns on the Tel Aviv coastline to fire. The ship returned the volley, though some on both sides refused to shoot at fellow Jews. A fire erupted on deck, spread rapidly, and the captain ordered the sinking vessel abandoned. Sixteen Irgun members and three IDF soldiers died. Ben-Gurion had not been afraid to kill Jews for the greater good of an undivided nation.

Eli wondered if Shai's only child having left Israel had either accentuated his frustration or left him less to lose if discovered. Eli stopped walking. Before him, an entire hill outside the periphery fence bloomed with a carpet of wild pink cyclamens. He pressed his face through the large wire bars. Their beauty seemed out of place in the present moment, and simultaneously a reminder of the beauty in this country.

Without turning back Eli said, "Where's the prime minister?"

"Across the border. In the Bekaa Valley, I believe."

"Still alive?"

"Last I heard, yes."

Eli turned. "I'm coming with you."

"Of course. Why else would you be here given that you came alone."

"You armed, Shai?"

Shai smiled. "You know I don't like them." He didn't think Eli knew exactly why he had come. Did he hope to rescue Gutman? Could he kill the man who had brought him into the service and became his teacher and friend? "Shall we get something to eat in the kibbutz dining room? Alas, I'm back to eating everything and it's going to be a long night."

At ten p.m., a kibbutznik Shai had known for three decades drove them toward Israel's eighty-kilometer border with Lebanon. During the 1976 Christian-Muslim Civil War, not surprisingly Israel sided with the southern Maronite Christians. The barrier was christened The Good Fence and Maronites flooded into Israel and back, exported goods through Haifa port and sought medical treatment at the Western Galilee Hospital. The Maronites traced back to the adherents of Saint Maron, a monastic fourth-century hermit who had spent his life on a mountain near Antioch, the ancient Greco-Roman city now in Turkey. After his death, his followers migrated to the environs of Mount Lebanon.

Just west of Metula, they turned off onto a short paved road that ran to a long, low metal gate that otherwise blocked the road but had been left open for them. A green placard with white lettering in Hebrew, Arabic and English warned: NO ENTRY CLOSED MILITARY AREA!!! Once beyond it, Shai had the driver turn left onto a dirt road that ran along a high chain-link fence with electronic sensors and minefields on the Israeli side. A low mountain rose beyond it, where the predominantly Christian Lebanon Army maintained an edgy alliance with the Shiite Hezbollah Party militia born from Israel's overreach. During the 1982 First Lebanon War, local Shi'a clerics, roused and funded by Iran, created Hezbollah in South Lebanon to snipe at the invading Israeli troops. Now, Hezbollah won seats in the Lebanese Parliament, operated sophisticated television and radio stations, and deployed troops outside Lebanon, primarily in Syria. They had morphed into a small army.

They passed Fatima Gate, a double-high fence with an Israeli military outpost, where Maronites had crossed, sealed off when Israel finally withdrew from Lebanon in 2000.

"Your phone please, Eli."

Eli reached in his pocket and handed it to Shai. Shai removed the SIM card from both Eli's and his own phone and then tossed it all out the window into the low brush.

"I trust there's no tracking on you. Not something I'm afraid I could satisfactorily explain to our hosts."

"No."

Several miles down the road, Eli saw three soldiers waiting, weapons raised. Shai indicated the kibbutznik should park and Shai and Eli got out. As crickets chirped, nobody spoke. One solider walked to a makeshift opening they would have just cut and pulled the wire away. On the other side, the sound of a car engine coming alive rose in the quiet. Once Shai and Eli were through, the soldier closed the gap with several padlocks.

As Shai and Eli remained still, a Lebanese Army jeep sped

near. The Lebanese President, Michel Aoun, a Maronite, had been elected by the Lebanese Parliament in October 2016. The Maronite general in the passenger seat, Jean Lahoud, had worked with Shai on multiple operations in the early years against the PLO massing in southern Lebanon. More recently, Lahoud had passed to Shai the locations of Hezbollah missile caches hidden in caves.

The jeep stopped, Lahoud climbed out and he and Shai hugged. Lahoud turned to Eli and stretched out his hand. "Welcome to my country," he said in English. "But then surely you've been here before."

Eli shook his hand, the memory of his army service here tight in his chest. "Too many of us have."

"*Mais oui*, easy to see now. Though you should have known it then." He gave orders to his driver to change clothes with Eli. "Your uniform is in the back seat," he told Shai, and added playfully, "though one large enough to fit you was a challenge."

Shai smiled. "I often ask the impossible. You never disappoint."

"Indeed, I am marvelous."

Shai lifted the uniform from the rear of the jeep, heard the car start on their side of the fence, and without headlights, drove away. Shai turned back to Lahoud. "I see I'm a colonel."

Lahoud chuckled. "Too many prominent families so too many generals already."

"Then a general would be better cover."

Lahoud laughed. "Shall I give you my uniform?"

Shai said nothing and he and Eli changed.

They drove north and then turned up a mountain. The beautiful tree-lined Litani River snaked ahead of them. A late partial moon had risen and the walls and ruins of the crusader Beaufort Castle on the highest peak shone in the natural light. Beginning in 1976, the PLO held Beaufort with its vast view of northern Israel.

"The old railway station at Rayak," Shai said in Arabic.

"*Sacre bleu*," Lahoud swore. "That will take half the night. I will hear from my poor, suffering wife about being away again. In the early years she did not mind, but now..."

"My apologies," Shai said. "Truly."

"We have been married a long time. She understands," Lahoud said, and then he switched to English, which his driver did not speak. Lahoud had sharpened his English at the US Army War College in Carlisle, Pennsylvania. "Grand day today in the Middle East. Everybody's claiming the other side has cancer. First the Israeli chief of staff, your General Moshe Ya'alon, thought he was making a private speech to a group of your regular crazy rabbis. But we are in the world where you push a button and, poof, everyone hears. Told them that Palestinian cancer like terror has to be fought to the bitter end. Or some such thing."

"Complete lack of imagination," Shai said.

Lahoud laughed. "At virtually the same time, Iran's supreme leader called Israel a cancerous tumor and called for a holy intifada. So it seems there's a lot of cancer in the air. I hope it is not contagious."

"I haven't heard that stupidity is," Shai said.

"Really? Around here, it seems to be. What else can explain this morass?"

Eli remained silent, felt grudging admiration for Shai's relationship with the Christian general. Eli was in front with the driver, while Shai and Lahoud filled the back.

After the next bend, Eli's whole body tightened as they approached a checkpoint flying a yellow flag with a green logo, Party of Allah. From the A, a hand reached high to clutch an assault rifle, and below the rifle, all in green, a globe, a sword and a book, much like Iran's Revolutionary Guards flag—Hezbollah. Piles of old tires in the road forced the cars to slow and wind between them.

Eli reached and placed a hand in his jacket pocket around the Glock. He had an extra clip in his rear pocket. He felt a hand on his shoulder, turned, and it was Lahoud.

"Be still," Lahoud said in Arabic to Eli. A sleepy fighter in a red keffiyeh stepped into the center of the road clutching a rifle, cigarette dropping from his mouth.

"Move out of the way," Lahoud ordered. "Do not make me slow. It's General Jean Lahoud."

The young soldier darted to the side. Lahoud released his grip on Eli's shoulder as the jeep wove through the checkpoint and sped ahead. Eli took his hand out of his pocket and leaned back in the seat. They continued up the eastern flank of Lebanon in the shadow of the high, snowcapped anti-Lebanon mountains that formed the border with Syria. It grew colder as the jeep climbed.

"I'm glad you're here," Shai said to Eli in English.

"Why?"

"Lot to carry by myself."

"You're not exactly doing me a favor," Eli said.

"Maybe I am. How often do you get to find out who you really are?"

Eli said nothing. He did not fully know who he was; as a young man he had always been certain, but was less at this age. He wondered what he was going to do. Attempt to kill Ramzy and whoever else was there, immobilize or even kill Shai and call in Sayeret Matkal for hostage rescue? Twenty years ago he would have done exactly that. Yet, if he succeeded he would almost certainly end his father's chances to become prime minister. But who was he to determine the nation's leader? Could this be so big he would be determining Israel's fate? His father had told him to follow his sworn duty and not consider him. He turned around and looked at Shai, who smiled in the dark, seemed content, as if this was the culmination of his life—to be able to alter the future for the better.

Eli was suddenly furious Shai was so calm. Eli turned back and watched the road ahead, did not think Shai would want to be captured and endure a trial, nor did he think he was afraid to die.

Two hours later at three thousand feet in the heart of the Bekaa, they approached Zahle, a city of 150,000 mostly Greek Catholics. Vineyards filled the hills, the vines growing on wood lattices and dripping clusters of pinkish grapes. Ahead of them, the Berdouni River ran down the center of the valley. Red terra cotta roofs filled the valley and climbed the hills. On the way down, they passed restaurant signs in Greek and Arabic, with large leafy trees between cafes along the river, and everywhere churches. It was so idyllic, for a moment Eli forgot why they were here. In the dark, Eli spotted a tall tower, maybe fifty meters high, its façade marble and atop it a huge bronze statue of the Virgin Mary at that moment entirely surrounded by the glowing slice of moon. Eli loved the Middle East, with its intermingled disparate peoples. They were one large family, quarreling and self-righteous, seeking acceptance and affirmation, and confronted to accommodate differences. He wondered what an Israel at greater peace with its neighbors and the world would be like.

In the back seat, Shai snored. It angered Eli, who thought, he thinks maybe he doesn't have a goddamn problem in the world.

Past Zahle, they climbed again and soon reached the outskirts of Rayak. There were no cars anywhere and their head beams on high illuminated the curves in the two-lane roadway. From the mountains here, Eli could see the illuminated jewel of Beirut at the bottom of winding roads forty kilometers due west at the sea. It was cold in the center of the night, just a few degrees above freezing, and Eli's breath fogged in front of him. Rayak lay in the valley ahead. Eli could see the familiar lights of the airstrip of the Rayak Air Base there, as well as T railway tracks where the Beirut-Damascus line met the local fork that ran north to Baalbek, and then Aleppo.

Lahoud pointed at the wide, lit plaza beside the runway of the air base in the valley. "Only helicopters here now." Lahoud touched Shai's shoulder to wake him and Shai bolted up like a startled bear. "Rayak," Lahoud said.

It would be easy for Israeli choppers to set down there, Eli thought. The Lebanese on duty would prove little resistance.

Shai followed Eli's gaze. "You thinking our boys could land there?"

"Exactly."

"Maybe I'll give you a phone and let you make that choice."

Eli turned and looked straight ahead. Shai was capable of doing exactly that, but what about Ramzy?

They descended on the curved lane. Lahoud gave the driver instructions and soon, near the base of the hill, he turned into the abandoned Rayak Railway Station. In the early 1900s, Rayak had been a bustling hub on the rail link between Europe and Asia. The line no longer ran anywhere, and the dilapidated ruins looked like an amusement park. A beautiful brown locomotive sat on tracks in the grass, rusted yet still majestic. Wood buildings were crumbling, roofs only a few beams in the air, their facades better preserved. Grass and weeds grew between the tracks. A yellow train car sat on some overgrown rails, the glass in its windows gone. For the first time ever, Eli wondered if Israel could disappear again into history.

Lahoud had the driver pull off into the grass by the rusted passenger car. He shut off the ignition. Shai stepped out and Eli followed. Lahoud hopped down and walked with them a distance from the jeep.

"Do I want to know why you're here?" Lahoud asked.

"Anybody ever answer yes to that question?"

Lahoud smiled. "Generally the answer is clear, as I believe it is now."

"Thanks, Jean."

Lahoud kissed Shai on both cheeks. "In the end what we have is those we love and old friends. *A bientot, mon ami.*"

"I'm happy to call you a friend, Jean."

The jeep drove away.

From around the shell of the passenger car stepped Ramzy Awwad.

"Hello, Eli," Ramzy said. "Wasn't expecting you but good to see you."

Eli sensed but did not reach for the Glock in his jacket pocket. He felt it was good to see Ramzy, which is how messed up everything was.

"He has too much innate talent," Shai said. "Well, you can never plan for everything."

"How did you get the prime minister here?" Eli asked Ramzy, his voice hard.

Instead, Shai answered. "The CIA has maybe twenty black site prison ships in strategic areas. One's not far off our coast for interesting arrests in Iraq and Afghanistan. About the last place anybody might look was my notion. Hooded, in isolation, few people knew he was there. Ramzy has use of an Al-Nusra Mi-14. Not much problem to have it land in the water near enough to the prison ship. Our people look the other way at whatever goes on at that site. Few older CIA upper brass warmed to the audacity. Rather arrogant to think hostility towards them doesn't come at a cost."

Ramzy approached Eli. "Your weapon."

Eli could kill him, but he knew Ramzy would not be alone and he and Shai would be riddled with bullets. If Eli was going to, he would have to wait for an opportune moment. He reached in his pocket, slowly removed the Glock and handed it to Ramzy. He heard a single pair of footsteps behind him, turned and saw a man with a rifle aimed at his head. He left the Beretta in his boot.

"Let's get out of the cold," Ramzy said.

They followed Ramzy through the damp grass to a burgundy Peugeot behind the train car. Two more armed Palestinians caught up with them from behind.

"Who else knows it's Shai?" Ramzy asked.

"Nobody," Eli said.

Ramzy looked at Shai, who said, "I believe him. He's like a younger brother to me. I think he showed up to find out for certain." He turned to Eli and then back to Ramzy. "After that I don't know, so do keep both eyes on him." Shai approached his protégé. "I'm not going to try and talk you into anything. I would though prefer if we both saw our sons again."

"We've been watching you since Zahle," Ramzy said. "Nobody's following you. We need to be fast now, in case Eli's lying and we're about to have guests."

Ramzy searched Eli, found no transmission devices. "Shoes off please."

"I'm about to hand you a Beretta," Eli said.

"Gently please."

Eli reached down with thumb and forefinger and lifted the Beretta out. One of the armed men approached and took it. Standing on one foot at a time, Eli removed his boots. Another man tossed them in the train car, where they made two thuds.

"In the back please, Eli," Ramzy said.

The two armed men sandwiched him as Shai climbed into the front. Eli wondered if he would leave here alive, and which side would kill him. If Shai could take the prime minister, he could kill him the way Ben-Gurion had sunk the *Altalena*. It would devastate him, as it had Ben-Gurion. Though he was in mortal danger, Eli felt glad he was here. He was not sure why. To spare Shai a trial and the rest of his life in prison, with his health not that great anyway, Eli could kill him and then hide the body so nobody knew.

"What are you going to do with the prime minister?" Eli

asked the two older men, who had been fighting this war for so long.

Neither answered.

The sun peeked above the snow-covered mountains in the east. The Peugeot headed into the hills on a dirt road with vineyards on one side and bare-branched apple trees on the other. Near the crest, Ramzy turned into a narrow dirt lane apparently not traversed much as grass covered it, torn in places by limited car tracks. Through a grove of tall cypresses, the car pulled up to a two-room stone cabin, drapes covering the front windows. They stopped. The five men got out.

Eli approached Ramzy. "You could keep him here indefinitely."

"It's up to Shai. But nothing is indefinite. When eventually he's discovered, it will all come out." Ramzy knocked on the door twice and then once more. "If we leave him here, I'd have to kill you. For him? And for what? To have him return in a year, five years, a decade, to a hero's welcome? Then what happens? Do you really think he will not make everything worse then?"

Eli was silent.

"Why did you come, Eli? What do you want?"

"Hope."

"If the prime minister's dead and I let you live, can you keep it to yourself?"

"I don't know," Eli said truthfully.

"I want to know whether you love truth more than you love your friend. Can you live such a huge lie for the rest of your life, for Shai?"

"Not easily."

Ramzy entered the cabin followed by Shai and Eli. The two armed Palestinians disappeared between the cypresses. The cabin was cold, the crossed wood in the stone fireplace unlit lest smoke betray them. Two men rose from armchairs, each carrying a semi-automatic pistol. The door to the back bedroom was closed.

"You're quiet," Eli said to Shai.

"It would be a lie to say I did this with a heavy heart. In fact, when the idea came to me at Aqaba, I felt real certainty. The only thing stopping me was that I was not sure it could be done."

"I've always wanted to protect you, whatever the infighting," Eli said to Shai.

"He brings that out in me too," Ramzy said. "The desire to watch over him."

"Not intended, I assure you, but I appreciate the sentiment."

Shai opened the bedroom door and entered. The Israeli prime minister was lying faceup on the narrow bed, both wrists shacked to the metal frame. He was gagged, duct tape running around his head at the cheeks, his hair mussed. But it was his eyes that Shai noticed, wild somehow, maybe both with indignation and fear. Shai had met him on two occasions and could not tell if the prime minister recognized him or not. Shai did not remove the gag, not that he was troubled by what their leader might say or that he would feel anything. It was simply past time for more talk. Far too many words in circles that never landed had been spoken by him. Ramzy and Eli entered. Two guards took up positions just outside the open door to the bedroom.

Ramzy stood next to Shai, held a pistol in his hands. Shai reached over and took it from him. "My responsibility."

Eli calculated whether he could shove Shai, wrest the pistol from his weak grip, shoot the two guards and then an off balance Ramzy, before being killed. He had a chance.

Shai turned to Eli. "Ramzy will take us to a lake near here. We'll call in. A chopper can set down on the water. When we're home, you will do whatever is in your heart. You can tell them we followed a false lead or the truth. Ramzy will take the body and bury it far away. I had expected the prime minister would disappear without anyone ever knowing what happened."

From the corner of his eye, Eli saw the prime minister pull against the restraints and scream into the gag, which trapped the sound into a muffle. Eli looked at him. His eyes bulged. Sweat beaded on his brow. Eli knew now what he was going to do and was frightened.

Shai aimed.

Eli shoved Shai hard into Ramzy, yanked the gun from Shai's rising right hand. Eli hit the ground, arm extended, and squeezed off three rapid shots.

The first two hit the prime minister in the chest, the third struck directly between his eyes.

Author's Note

Enas Fares Ghannam, my mentee, lives in Gaza and is the author of 'Always on the Inside Looking Out' written for the We Are Not Numbers program. The writings of the fictional Ramzy Awwad are loosely based on the work of the Palestinian novelist and short story writer, Ghassan Kanafani. In 1972, the Mossad killed Kanafani in a Beirut car bomb in retaliation for the Lod Airport (now Ben Gurion Airport) Massacre five weeks earlier. Kanafani had been spokesman for the Popular Front for the Liberation of Palestine which took responsibility for the attack that killed twenty-six and injured eighty.

21916617R00146

Made in the USA
San Bernardino, CA
06 January 2019